# Taste of Passion

## DK MARIE

Cover design by: Avery Kingston

Library of Congress Control Number: 2018675309

Printed in the United States of America

This book is dedicated to my sister.

Not only because you encouraged (okay, demanded) me to tell Will's story but because you are one of the strongest women I know.  Your heart, courage, and strength are an inspiration.

Opposite Attract series

1. Fairy Tale Lies

2. Love Songs

3. Taste of Passion

4. Colors of the Heart

There is a loose timeline, but this series does not have to be read in order. Each book is a standalone.

# Contents

# Author Note

This story is a contemporary romance where love and hope prevails, but there are topics that might be troubling to some readers, such as the mention of the death/illness of a parent, overdosing, and drug addiction. Readers who may be sensitive to these topics, please take note.

# Chapter One

Cindy Meier took a sharp right, peeling into the restaurant's parking lot. Her tires squealed as she braked hard in front of the building, making the valet jump back, eyes wide.

Her rush wasn't because she was almost an hour late meeting her sister, Greta. Nope, her speed was for the thrill of it. Why have an Audi TT if she can't have some fun with it, right?

Putting the car in first gear, she set the parking brake then grabbed her calfskin jacket from the passenger seat. The sun was shining bright and beautiful, but April in Michigan still had Old Man Winter playing hide-and-seek with Spring.

A valet close to her age came around to open her door. She got out, offering him her brightest smile. His appreciative gaze ran over her. She had to admit, admiration never grew old.

Nevertheless, when he reached her face, she quirked a brow. He hastily looked away. It was undoubtedly against the rules for the help to ogle the clientele.

She breezed past him, opening the glass and iron doors of Rising. Pushing her sunglasses to the top of her head, she scanned the restaurant trying to find Greta. She spotted her sister's fiancé, Jacob Grimm first. Mixed with a starched, formal crowd, his shock of messy black hair made him impossible to miss.

*Huh, I didn't know he was joining us. We're just talking about wedding plans.*

Whatever. Jacob did seem heavily involved in the planning.

Making her way toward her sister's table, Cindy smiled. For some reason, it delighted her knowing his involvement probably drove Mother crazy. She had no idea how to handle Jacob. Plus, his presence made it more difficult for her to take over the wedding.

Halfway across the dining room, she found her sister and waved. That was when she noticed the third person.

A guy.

A hot guy.

Light brown hair, closely cropped on the sides, short and neat on the top. Large, almond-shaped eyes that might be brown. He also had a strong jawline, high cheekbones. The combination was sensual and masculine. She wanted to nibble along the sharp ridges.

The three of them stood when she reached the table. She hugged Greta, then Jacob.

Releasing him, she teased, "How are you, Thug? I'm surprised the concierge let you in."

As always, he played along with good humor. Chuckling, he joked, "They made me dump my forty before entering, and I had to promise to use silverware. Stupid rules." He shrugged, tipping his head in the direction of the handsome stranger. "This is my brother, Will. He's the Best Man. We figured he should meet the Maid of Honor."

Facing him fully, she offered her hand while trying to remember to breathe. He was even better looking up-close. Yup, brown eyes like melted, tasty chocolate.

She blinked, surprised by her strong reaction to him. As a model, she was around attractive men all the time. She was supposed to be immune to a pretty face.

Plus, he had some sort of shady background. That alone should be enough to cool any desire. Jacob and Greta were strangely protective of Will, but a few tidbits had made it to her.

He was the family screw up. The one Jacob had supported, taken care of for years.

That man before wasn't a mess, quite the opposite. He was polished and neat, a man who'd fit in at her father's investment company.

Her gaze fell to her favorite part on a man, his mouth. She gasped. He might have the beautiful, full lips that she loved. It was hard to tell. They were pressed in a tight line.

She returned to his eyes, noticing the color of them were beautiful but didn't radiate an ounce of warmth. He appeared pissed.

After a beat too long, he took her proffered hand. "Nice of you to finally arrive." His voice was smooth as silk, the words sharp as a dagger.

She smoothed her features, hiding her shock. *This* man wasn't going to talk down to her. "Is there a problem?"

"Yes." Will glanced at his watch, a thick silver one that complemented his sexy, strong wrist. "Some of us have more important things to do than wait around for you to grace us with your presence."

She leaned back, curling her lip with irritation. No. Not strong and sexy. The asshole. His wrists were too big, attached to huge hands that were more like bear paws.

"Will. Chill out," Jacob admonished. "She's less than an hour late. For Cindy, that's almost on time."

The other man scoffed. He was growing more unattractive by the second.

"See, I'm barely late."

Greta raised one perfect brow. "You're late. And that's even after I lied, telling you we'd be here at one."

*Thanks, sis.*

Laughing, Cindy took her seat. "Come on now. I knew that meant you'd be here at one-thirty."

Greta's gaze flicked to her cellphone resting on the table. "It is nearly two-thirty." She didn't sound mad, more resigned.

"Jet-lag. I overslept. I've only been home from Europe for two days," Cindy said, sort of telling the truth.

She was merely leaving out the part about stopping at Nordstrom's before meeting them. No sense mentioning it when Jacob's brother was treating her like an errant toddler.

As if he had room to judge her. From what she knew, he didn't even have a house, let alone a glass one to be throwing around stones.

The server arrived, asking Cindy for her drink order, and saving her from further interrogation. She ordered a Merlot, though before the waitress could leave to retrieve it, Will stopped her.

"Could you also take our order?" He glanced at Cindy, displeasure oozing from him. "I've been sipping on my water for almost an hour waiting for you. We need to move this along. I need to stop at work tonight."

"It's a Friday. Take a break, Scrooge." Cindy scoffed, annoyed at being rushed. She told the server to give her another minute.

It was a lie. She planned on ordering her usual but was getting a kick out of irritating Will.

When the waitress returned a few minutes later with her drink; Cindy asked for another minute. Will sighed and drummed his blunt fingertips on the glass table.

She sipped her wine, asking Greta how her day was going. Before she could answer Will cut in, "Are you going to even look at the menu?"

She was surprised to find he appeared slightly amused.

She gave him her sweetest smile. "No. I know what I want."

He sighed, but the amusement was still in his eyes as he drawled. "Weekends might be when *you* flutter from one debutant ball to the next, us common folk have to work—"

"Hey," Jacob interrupted. "As thrilling as it is to listen to you two snipe at each other, could we focus on why we are here? The wedding."

Cindy let go of the snarky retort she had for Will. "You're right. Anyway, I'm growing bored with his tedious chatter." She sniffed.

In truth, a small part of her was enjoying their sparring. Most men fell over themselves to please her. This was at least interesting.

Will was looking heavenward, muttering something under his breath. Cindy swallowed a smile. This was fun.

"Okay." He faced his brother. "As your Best Man, what do you two need?"

*Guess we're done playing. Damn.*

"We wanted to talk about our bachelor and bachelorette parties. We have an idea," Greta began, then stopped to glance around the table. "Although, after this lunch I'm not sure it will work."

Cindy was intrigued and a little ashamed. The last thing she wanted to do was put a damper on her big sister's wedding. "Tell us. Whatever you two want, we'll make it happen." She gazed at Will. He nodded.

Greta smiled, pleasure radiating from her. "Okay. So, instead of a separate night out, we thought it'd be fun to combine our wedding party. To do a weekend at a beach house, here in Michigan. Petoskey, perhaps. The ceremony is at the end of July. We could do the weekend sometime in June. That gives you two months to find a place and contact everyone in the wedding party." She clapped her hands together, clearly excited with this plan. "What do you guys think? Is it something you could do? Together?"

A weekend at the beach sounded splendid. Planning it with Jacob's curmudgeon brother, not so much. She liked trading insults with him, but he didn't seem like a guy who relished indulging in anything fun.

His fingers tapped impatiently on the table, making her want to piss him off more, push his buttons. She refrained for her sister's sake.

There weren't many people she'd put before herself. Greta was of the select few.

Meeting Will's eyes, she knew he'd do the same for his brother.

Cindy faced Greta and Jacob, putting on her best runway smile. "I'm in. It's a great idea."

# Chapter Two

Will flicked on his blinker while checking his GPS. They were less than ten minutes from the lake house. "I'll tell you what, Tim. I can't wait for this damn weekend to be over."

"Three days lying on the beach relaxing, sharing a place with hot ladies. Oh, yes. I can totally understand why you'd wish it to be over," Tim drawled.

"I feel like shit taking off a whole weekend. This is the busiest time for Summer Grill. They need me there. Not to mention, planning this getaway with Greta's sister was a pain in the ass. She was either suggesting houses that were a million a night or couldn't bother to answer her phone."

Tim held up his index finger. "One. You've been working at that restaurant for somewhere around two years. Have you ever taken a day off?"

"Well, no..."

Tim ticked off another finger. "Two. Did you tell her she was useless? That might be a reason she'd skip answering your calls."

*Is he an idiot, or think I am?*

"No. I'm not a complete asshole."

Tim gave a look that said he wasn't so sure. "Okay. I bet she heard it in your tone. Kind of like right now I hear you calling me an idiot, loud and clear."

Will laughed. "Heard that, did you?" Stopping at a red light, he faced his friend. "Anyway, her excuse was her work. That's such bullshit. Between posing and smiling for the camera, she can't return my calls, or check into a few houses I'd found?"

True, she was terrible at rental hunting, but at the same time, he'd enjoyed talking with her. Cindy had a quick, sarcastic wit that made him laugh. And laughter was something that didn't come easy to him anymore. Usually, only his brother could manage to bring out his lighter side.

"Oh, I see," Tim said. "She wasn't allowed to give input in picking the house, just do your bidding."

The light turned green, and Will made a left toward the rental at the end of the street. "Listen, if you'd seen the places she'd picked, you wouldn't want her in charge either. I'd have to sell my soul to afford a weekend at the places she was choosing."

"Dude, your dirtied soul couldn't pay for a shack on the shadier side of Detroit."

Will chuckled. "Ain't that the truth. Anyway, it's a good thing Jacob and Greta hired a wedding planner. If I had to organize their rehearsal dinner and reception with Cindy, we'd probably end up strangling each other."

"I've only met the Silverstones once. Briefly, thank god. I get the feeling they aren't the type to be cool with handmade decorations and a potluck dinner."

"Yeah." Will groaned, parking next to his brother's truck in the driveway of the lake house. "I heard Greta's mom, Sophia, tried to convince Greta to have the wedding at Martha's Vineyard. Like they're the Kennedys or something. Shit, I'm happy for Jacob. Greta is great. Dealing with her family..." He took a deep breath. "No thanks."

The house was even nicer than the pictures online. Modern, with large windows on each side and a good-sized recessed, covered front porch with outdoor furniture.

"I don't know. It might be worth it," Tim said, longing wrapping around each of his words.

Curious, Will turned from the house. Their driveway spread across the length of the property, with a small patch of green between the two. Tim was looking off to their right, to a sweet, sporty Audi parked in front.

It wasn't the expensive sports car that held Tim's full attention.

No, that was reserved for the woman bent, half inside her trunk with an ass even sweeter than the vehicle. Will took in shapely legs, tucked into sky-high heels.

Had to be Cindy.

No one else would come to a beach house dressed like a pin-up girl. As the woman straightened, his guess became fact.

Cindy's long blonde hair flowed down her back. She wrestled a gigantic purse onto her shoulder then began struggling with a huge suitcase from her trunk.

"Wait! Let me help," Tim shouted, sprinting from the car.

Will laughed, getting out much slower. Cindy glanced over her shoulder at Tim, offering him a smile Will was sure made most men into her lapdog.

Hell, when she aimed it at him, he had to force his feet not to rush forward.

Not that he was needed. From Tim's love-struck expression, she already found her perfect puppy.

"Hey, Princess," Will called, unable to resist sparring with her. "You know we only rented the place for two nights."

Her eyes narrowed as her gaze raked him. Something in her perusal made him think she liked what she saw.

Until she spoke.

"I assume from the way you're dressed you just crawled from your cardboard box. Did you even bother to bring a change of clothes?" She lifted her chin, looking down her nose at him. "Or are you one of those guys who flips his underwear inside out and calls them clean?"

Tim's sharp laughter drifted to them from halfway up the sidewalk as he carried Cindy's suitcase to the house. Will ignored his friend. Coming around his car, he leaned against it, crossing his feet at the ankles. "Nah, I don't bother with underwear."

Her widened gaze drifted south, staying a beat too long. His freaking dick woke under her inspection. Needing to break whatever the hell this was, he opened the backseat door and grabbed his duffel bag.

"Let's get inside. I want to see how Jacob and Greta divided the rooms," he said. "Stake our claim before the others arrive."

She nodded, heading for the house. A small part of him was disappointed. Her sharp wit was entertaining, and he couldn't remember a time he was this amused.

He shook his head. Wanting anything from Cindy was a mistake. Not only was she Greta's little sister but one of those spoiled women who feed off guy's attention. She needed to have every man want her.

She was trouble, and he'd collected enough of that to last a lifetime.

Will passed Cindy on the sidewalk, and she followed, resolutely *not* staring at his ass. Instead, she traced the outline of the muscles on his broad back, wondering if his skin was warm from the sun or cool from the AC in his car.

Her concentration was so complete, she nearly walked into him when they'd reached the porch. She'd expected him to open the door, stepping inside. Instead, he held it open with his palm, waiting for her to go inside first.

He was so close she caught his scent. Damn, it smelled nice. Sandalwood mixed with a delicious spice she couldn't name.

She cleared her throat, dislodging the need to run her tongue along his skin to see if he tasted as good as he smelled.

"Aren't you a gentleman. What a surprise," she snapped, needing to return to their comfortable, teasing territory.

"Nah. More like I'm worried you're going to trip in those ridiculous heels and fall on me. I'm getting out of the way," he retorted.

Striding past him, she notched her chin high in the air. "I'm a model. I know how to walk in—"

Her heel snagged on something along the bottom of the door. She lurched forward, and her heavy purse slid from her arm and banged to the floor. She was seconds away from joining it when a pair of strong hands gripped her waist.

"You okay?" Will asked, inches from her ear.

For a moment she couldn't speak. Being so close to him did funny things to her body, warming places he had no business heating up.

"Damn it," she muttered. Her freaking heel was stuck between the door's sill and the start of the hardwood floors. "I'm stuck."

"Hold on." He squatted, then with surprising gentleness, he removed her foot from her shoe. "Lean on me, I'll get the shoe. Shit. It's really wedged in there."

She could've held on to the door's frame, but she desired to know if he was as firm as he appeared.

Two earlier questions were answered. He was warm beneath her palms, and *very* defined.

Leaning on him, she had nowhere to look except at his ass. Well, she could have checked out the house, but his backside was more appealing.

"Shit. The damn thing is jammed in worse than a nail hit with a hammer," he grunted, yanking harder.

Everything became a blur. She heard something, probably her shoe, smack against the floor. Will shot up, stumbling forward at the same time.

She steeled herself for the painful impact. Instead, an arm went tightly around her waist while the other gripped the back of her head. Somehow Will managed to brace himself so his weight didn't suffocate or break her when he landed on her.

His eyes were wide, his mouth inches from hers. "Sorry. Are you okay?"

Her gaze traveled to his lips. "I'm fine."

She was more than fine. His body fit perfectly on hers.

"What the hell are you two doing?" Jacob asked from somewhere above them.

Will jerked back, shooting to his feet. "Helping Cindy not break her ankle." He offered her his hand.

"By throwing yourself on her?" Jacob sounded confused.

She stood with the help of Will, saying, "And by helping, he means knocking me to the floor, then crushing me with his ogre bulk."

She was proud at how calm her voice sounded. It was at odds with her racing heart and thrumming pulse.

Jacob laughed. He picked up her discarded soft pink peep-toe heel. "Not exactly beachwear, Princess."

"I brought other shoes," she said defensively. She wasn't as smart as her sister, but she practically lived from her suitcase. Packing was second nature to her.

Will chuckled. "Yeah, going by the bag Tim dragged in for you, I'd say you brought at least fifteen pairs."

The Grimm brothers were annoying. Taking a deep breath, she held out her hand to Jacob. He handed over her heel. After sliding it on, she asked, "Where am I sleeping?"

He pointed past the open concept living room and kitchen, to the left of the house. "Your bedroom is on the left. You'll be sharing it with Rae and your cousin, Harper."

"Damn it, Will. You couldn't find a place where we had our own rooms? Great," she clipped. "It will be like Girl Scout camp."

In truth, she didn't care. Her job usually required her to share a room with the other female models.

It was more that Will and Jacob were treating her like a spoiled princess. She might as well play the part.

"Ha," Will barked. "You. A Girl Scout. Isn't there something in their pledge about helping people? That seems against your nature."

She had been a Girl Scout from elementary school to her freshman year in high school. She'd loved it, and it broke her heart when her mother made her quit because it got in the way of modeling.

Instead of admitting this, Cindy smirked, taking Will's faded T-shirt between her thumb and index finger. Letting it go, she said, "I help people. In fact, I'm pretty sure last time I was in the city, I dropped a dollar or two in your change cup."

Sauntering past the brothers, she heard Will's quiet laughter and Jacob mutter, "Is it going to be like this all weekend with you?"

She didn't bother to wait for Will's response but hoped the answer was yes. It had been a while since anticipation tickled her heart and made her blood race.

# Chapter Three

Hoisting her beach bag on her shoulder, Cindy started for the back patio. Last week had been airports, photoshoots, filled with too many late nights and early mornings. Relaxing on the beach with a good book while listening to the waves lapping on the shore of Lake Michigan was her version of heaven.

Cutting across the open living room, she caught someone moving around in the kitchen and paused. Will's back faced her as he sorted through the bags covering the counters.

She debated. Stay and help, or head for the sand. The sun called to her.

After taking two more steps, guilt stopped her at the glass sliding door. She let a deep sigh out through her mouth. "Why are you inside, Will? Everyone's out on the beach."

He turned, his hands filled with potatoes. He set them next to a wood cutting board on the kitchen's island. "It's after four, I figure people will be hungry soon. I'm going to cook tilapia and potatoes on the grill."

He grabbed a knife and began slicing. His movements were quick and efficient, almost graceful. Watching him work was fascinating.

A man who knew his way around the kitchen was sexy.

"You know we could order a pizza or something. You don't have to cook. Take a night off. Relax."

"Nah. It's Greta and Jacob's weekend. I want it to be perfect for them."

Damn it.

*He found this place while I barely lifted a finger to help. Now he's going to cook for ten people as I sip on a gin and tonic under the lovely summer sun enjoying a perfect Michigan day.*

The battle taking place within her was fierce; selfish desires or being a decent person. Self-indulgence was way more fun. So was relaxing.

In the end, she let her bag slip from her shoulder. She couldn't leave him to do all the work.

Okay, she wasn't being completely altruistic. Watching Will cook would be a decadent delight.

She walked through the living room, past the huge driftwood table, stopping next to him. "What can I do to help?"

He paused, facing her with a brow raised. "You want to help? You might break a nail."

"You know what? Forget it." She pushed off from the counter, anger running along her spine. "I'm not skipping a perfect afternoon at the beach to have you cut me down."

His warm grip encircled her wrist, making her stop short. She glared into his brown eyes. They reminded her of cinnamon and coffee. He was talking, but his words didn't get past the ringing in her ears.

*Damn it. Focus, Cindy!*

"What?" she spat, holding tight to her irritation, refusing to let it turn into another sort of heat.

"I'm sorry. I'd love your help."

She admired a man who knew when to apologize. It deflated her ire, and she smiled. "That's better. What would you like me to do?"

He released her wrist, making her miss his touch. "Do you have a seasoning you'd like to use for the tilapia? Or I could come up with something."

"Um. I was thinking more along the lines of cutting the potatoes. I'm not much of a cook."

A grin flickered at the corners of his mouth, though he didn't tease her. It disappointed her.

"Slicing potatoes would be great. Thanks." He handed her the knife, then opened a cupboard, rummaging through a shelf stocked with different spices.

"What are you doing?" she asked.

"Seeing what's here that'll make a good rub for the fish."

"You're not going by a set recipe? You make it up on the spot?"

Will nodded, grabbing jars and canisters, bringing them to the counter next to her. "If you don't make your own meals and eat out all the time, how do you stay so fit?"

Cindy warmed at his off-handed comment. She liked the way he said it. He wasn't trying to get in her pants with mindless flattery, merely stating a simple fact.

"Even when I used to order from restaurants a ton, I was careful with my choices. Now, my friend Emma lives with me. She loves to cook." She began slicing the potatoes. "Although she follows recipes, doesn't throw stuff together like you."

He stopped mixing the spices and studied her, like he was waiting for her to tease him or make a joke. She was tempted. Instead she played nice, offering a slice of truth. "Hey. I'm not knocking it. I've eaten at Summer Grill a handful of times. The rotating menu is always excellent. If that was your cooking, don't stop what you're doing."

"Thanks," he said.

She felt his gaze and tried not to bask in it. However, as the seconds ticked by, the silence began to eat at her confidence. "What? Why are you watching me?"

"I'm wondering what the hell those potatoes ever did to you."

*Okay, maybe not checking me out.*

She looked at the cutting board. Sure, her slices weren't exactly even, but it's not like she'd been stabbing them.

Like she might do to Will.

He inched closer to her, placing his left hand on top of hers. "First hold the potato like this." He made her fingers curl in. "Then you won't cut off a nail or the tip of your finger."

Reaching around her, his front briefly pressed into her back. Goosebumps rose along her skin.

"Here." He handed her a different knife. "Use this one instead. Also, try to slice them the same size, so they'll cook evenly on the grill."

She twisted her neck to face him, a smart retort at the ready. Then stopped. His mouth was mere inches away.

Holy hell, he had the type of lips she loved, wide and full. A bottom lip begging to be bitten.

He cleared his throat and swallowed. The dip of his Adam's apple was fascinating. She wrenched her gaze to his eyes.

The spark of humor was replaced with a different sort of heat, and it was molten hot. The need to taste those beautiful lips had her starving.

"Hey, Cindy," called Tim.

Will took a quick step to the side, returning to spices and fish. She blinked. Had she actually considered kissing uptight Will Grimm?

"Yeah. I'm in the kitchen." Her voice sounded false, a tad too cheerful.

Tim came through the living room to the kitchen, holding two greenish-yellow drinks. "Our neighbors are joining us on the beach. They have a margarita machine. I brought you one." He took a sip, handing her the other.

She tried it and moaned at the tarty, sweet bliss. "Wow. This is good." Feeling magnanimous, she asked Will, "Want to try it?"

Tim cleared his throat. His expression became an odd mixture of guilt and embarrassment. What had she said?

"I don't drink," Will replied mildly.

Cindy scrunched her nose. "Never?"

"Not anymore."

Hmm. From scattered comments and conversations between Greta and Jacob, Cindy knew Will had moved back home after his partying had gotten a little too crazy. She remembered Mother mentioning something about an arrest. Cindy figured he'd gone wild for a few years, right after high school, as some kids did. Maybe got caught with something illegal, like weed. She couldn't imagine someone as controlled as Will having a drinking problem.

Tim cleared his throat, shattering the thick silence. "Your sister is asking for you."

"Is it important? I'm helping Will with dinner."

"I'll take over." Tim set his drink on the counter. "Visit with your sister, Maid of Honor."

"Hey," Will cut in, "I'm the Best Man. I should be exempt too."

"Ah. No," Tim said. "No one's looking for you, and I'm more of a caterer. I prep and serve, not cook. I need your direction, Chef Wilhelm."

Cindy giggled. "Is that a nickname or something?"

Will groaned. Tim let out a bark of laughter before answering, "No. His mom was a Grimm Brothers fan. That's their names. Jacob and Wilhelm Grimm."

"Really?" She smiled. "Your mom sounds like a cool woman."

"She was," Will said, with a trace of sadness, reminding Cindy his mom had passed away some years back. "Still. Don't call me Wilhelm. It makes me sound like I'm a hundred and fifty years old."

Cindy smirked, wanting to chase away the lurking sorrow in him. "I should. It suits your personality. You're an old man stuck in a hot guy's body."

Oops. She hadn't meant to say that last part.

One of his brows ticked, the only sign she'd surprised him. He leaned against the counter, crossing his feet at the ankles. All cocky and smug. "You think I'm hot?"

Cindy gave a half shrug. "This house is full of good-looking guys." She cut a glance to Tim. He preened.

She suspected women gave him plenty of attention. However, he didn't compare to Will. Not that she'd ever admit it to him. Or anyone. She winked at Tim before returning to Will.

A flash of disappointment played over his face before he covered it with indifference. Her slight flirt with Tim bothered Will. Good to know.

Playing it cool, she teased, "Anyway, once you open your mouth, you become a cantankerous old man."

Will snorted. "Cantankerous. Big words for a beauty queen."

Cindy shrugged, handing Tim her knife. She did her best runway strut to the patio door. Stopping to get her beach bag, she looked over her shoulder. Both men were watching her. "What can I say. I have beauty and brains."

Will shook his head, appearing amused. "You're also a huge pain in the ass."

"Perhaps." She paused at the sliding door, smiling. "But I'm worth it."

"I second that," said Tim.

The sound of the waves crashing against the shore swallowed Will's response.

# Chapter Four

Will looked from the back patio's small jacuzzi to the massive lake about eighty feet in front of him. He wouldn't mind ignoring the revelry, grabbing the book he'd started weeks ago but never had time to read, and sinking into the hot tub with it.

He sighed, stepping from the back porch. This weekend was his little brother's bachelor party. Will didn't want to be the antisocial asshole. Or, what did Cindy call him? Ah yes, cantankerous.

Thinking of her made him smile, though it fell away as he got closer to the bonfire flickering midway between the house and lake. There were way more people than just their wedding party.

*Shit.* The houseful of guys from next door was back.

They'd wandered away to their own house when he and Tim called their group in for dinner. Will saw the hunger in the men's eyes, and it wasn't for the food. No, they wanted a taste of the women in Greta's wedding party. He'd suspected they'd return at the first chance.

The one Will had tagged as the leader was dancing with a woman slightly shorter than him. When they spun around to the music, Will realized the guy's partner was Cindy. His bad mood intensified. He considered turning around.

"Hey, Will!"

He spotted Tanner, his old friend from the neighborhood, waving him over to where he stood by the fire. He must've arrived after dinner when Will had gone for a short run.

Lifting a hand in greeting, he maneuvered around people lounging on blankets, making his way to Tanner. He was sitting by the fire next to Jacob.

"How've you been?" Tanner asked when Will sat.

"Good. I'm working like crazy, but I'm now the head chef."

"That's great, man! You haven't been there very long, yet every time we talk, you're getting promoted."

Never comfortable with praise, Will changed the subject. "How's Maggie?"

Tanner's face practically glowed at the mention of his girlfriend and lead singer of their popular band, ThreePence. "Crazy as ever," he said with affection. "You remember our drummer, Lincoln?" Will nodded. Hard to forget a man who looks like Cobain. "She talked him into getting a motorcycle. The two of them are riding to Louisiana to visit some friend who used to be in the band. They should be back next week."

He nearly missed the last part when someone turned up the radio. Rae, Harper, and Greta stopped in front of the men, swaying their hips to the music.

"Come on, guys, let's dance," Rae said, reaching for Tanner. "I have a nine-month-old at home. This is the first time I've had the chance to let loose in months. I heard you're the music man, so you're my dance partner."

Tanner laughed, standing. "I write and play music better than I dance to it. Still, I'm game if you are."

"Sure am. You can't possibly dance worse than my husband, and I've never abandoned him on the dance floor."

Greta and Jacob were already swallowed up by the dancing crowd. Harper held out her hand to Will. "What about you, handsome?"

Will hadn't danced in years. Wasn't sure he wanted to now. It brought him a little too close to his wild days.

Yet, Tanner and Rae were waiting expectantly, as was Harper. She was already swaying to the beat.

*Damn it. I'm such a people pleaser.*

"Sure. I'd love to."

Cindy shook her hips, letting the music seep into her soul. There was something to be said about dancing on a beach. The sand between her toes, the waves, and wind in harmony with the melody blasting from the speakers was bliss.

Her dance partner, Terry, brought her against him. He wasn't as magical as the beach music. His drunken sweat and warm breath on her neck were unpleasant.

With each refill of his drink, the more handsy he became, but she was a pro at dealing with unwanted advances. It was time to take a break. Maybe grab a water to counter the vodkas she'd finished off, and in the process, get rid of her groping dance partner.

Glancing around, she momentarily forgot her plans. The site of the water lapping against the shore and the bonfire reaching for the stars made her fingers itch for her camera. She wanted to capture the flickers of flames from the fire along with the bodies dancing hedonistically in the backdrop.

Terry ground against her. "Hey, baby, am I losing you? I hope not. We're just getting started."

*Oh, honey, more like being disqualified before crossing the finish line.* He was becoming a sloppy drunk. Plus, he was boring. He didn't make her laugh or challenge her. Like a certain man with chocolate brown eyes and a reluctant smile.

Cindy caught a flash of Harper's long black hair swaying with the music. Maybe if she turned, Cindy could get her attention. Her favorite cousin would lend a hand if needed.

Harper raised her hands, letting them fall on her dance partner's shoulders. *Will.* She was dancing with Will? He danced?

Cindy crushed the spike of jealousy that rose, unbidden and unwanted. He was good; easy, sensual grace without clinging to his partner.

Unlike hers.

Hell. Terry was nuzzling her neck.

She pushed lightly on his shoulders. "Um, I need a break. Let's get a drink."

He didn't let go of her. "Come on, baby. Don't leave now."

*Ugh. Did he just lick me? Gross.*

Shoving him a harder, she searched for an escape route. Instead, she found Will. He was watching her.

He looked pissed.

She mouthed, "Help me."

His lips pressed into a thin line. He said something to Harper, then made his way over. He gently gripped her elbow. "There you are, Cindy. I need you for a minute."

Terry didn't let go. "Who the hell are you? Her boyfriend?"

"Nope. A friend who needs to talk with her." Will stared back, not seeming the least bit intimidated. Even though Terry had the build of a guy who spent way too much time in the gym and maybe liked steroids.

"She's busy," Terry spat at Will.

"It's fine. Let me see what he needs." Cindy took another step. Terry's grip tightened. *Shit.*

She put on her shiniest smile and added a little flirt in her voice. "You've warmed me up. I could really use a drink to keep me going. Would you be my hero? Get me something cold while I find out what my friend needs?"

Terry's drunken gaze shift from her to Will. "Friend, huh?"

"Actually, he's my brother-in-law." She ran her fingertips along his arm. "A drink. Please."

"Fine." Terry sulked, stomping toward the margarita blender.

"Such a gentleman," Cindy muttered.

Will snorted. Those lovely lips that had been thin with displeasure earlier were now biting back a smile.

She giggled. "Don't say a word."

"He's your hero, huh?"

"Shut up." She smacked his chest.

He raised his hands as if surrendering. "Hey, no judging. Seeing you bend him to your will was impressive. Damn, fascinating to watch."

"Yeah, yeah. Can we leave before he comes back?"

Will pointed with his thumb, back to their house. "I was thinking of cutting out. Maybe trying the hot tub. Want to join me?"

Like that was a difficult choice. Hangout here waiting for Terry to return and maul her, or get the chance to see Will shirtless?

She grabbed his hand, heading for the house. "Let's go."

When they reached the patio, Cindy whipped off her bathing suit cover, throwing it on the nearest wicker chair. She climbed the two steps to the jacuzzi and sank into its hot, soothing waters.

It was heaven.

Taking an elastic band from around her wrist, she gathered her hair into a messy bun before resting her head on the edge of the hot tub. She took a deep breath, filling her lungs with the scent of night air and chlorine.

After a minute, she cracked her lids, wondering what happened to Will.

He was standing at the entrance of the patio, staring at her.

She sat straighter. "What? Is something wrong?"

His gaze traveled down her neck, maybe following the trails of water. Before falling to her breasts, he shot back to her face. "Um, no. When you want something, you dive right in, huh?"

"Yes. Why not? Let me tell you, this is bliss. Between dancing in the sand and my graceful fall earlier, this is heaven on my muscles."

He was still watching her like she'd lost her mind. All she did was get in the freaking hot tub.

She huffed. "Are you getting in or not?"

He nodded.

"Could you first turn the jet higher?" She indicated with her chin the control panel near him.

"Yeah." Gripping the back of his T-shirt, he removed it, tossing it next to her bathing suit cover.

*Whoa.*

The man was gorgeous. Lean torso, beautiful veins running along his arms, and biceps begging to be touched and stroked. All of that, combined with the strong legs of a runner was one helluva sight.

However, what caught her attention was the spreading tattoo on the left side of his chest. A skeleton's body started right about where the heart lies, reaching to Will's collarbone. It held a scythe above his head as if ready to swing, and on its back were wings made from sharp, wicked arrows.

Will messed with the dials, turning up the jet. The hot water and air hit all her sore parts. She moaned in appreciation, the tattoo vanishing as her lids slid closed.

"Shit, woman. Where exactly are those jets hitting you?" His words were teasing, his tone lava.

"Right where I need them," she purred, facing him, wanting to know if the heat in his voice reached his eyes.

It did.

He shook his head. "You're trouble, aren't you?"

"Maybe, but a little trouble is always fun."

She wasn't sure why she was trying to tempt him. Jacob's stodgy brother. All frowns and seriousness.

Her gaze ran over him, drifting to his smart-ass, quirky mouth before traveling to his chest. Then lower. *Damn.*

Okay, the steady heat gathering between her legs might be the reason she wanted to entice him. She couldn't remember the last time someone intrigued her. This enigma of a man had her full attention.

Would he be up for a weekend of fun?

She saw hesitation battling with his desire and backed off. He didn't seem like the man who did anything impulsively. If she pushed too hard, he might shoot down the idea, not even consider it.

And now that she'd thought of it, she wanted it. A lot.

"Don't worry, old man," she said, falling back to their easy, teasing rapport. "I'll keep my trouble on my side of the tub. I don't want you to have a stroke."

He rolled his eyes, his shoulders losing some of their rigidness. "I'm not worried about my heart. More like you trying to drown me if I let down my guard."

"I have always wondered if it's true what I've read. If five minutes without oxygen leads to brain damage." She stretched her arms across the back of the jacuzzi. "For Jacob's sake, I won't discover the answer tonight. So close to the wedding, it'd be added stress on him to find a new Best Man."

"Sometimes you're a scary woman, Ms. Meier." He sat on top of the tub, on the ledge. "There. Happy?"

"That is not inside. What? Are you afraid of a girl?"

He snorted. "When the girl is you, yeah."

She sprang forward, grabbing his legs.

"Shit!" he squawked, as she pulled him into the water.

Once he was in, she let go. Moving back, she laughed maniacally.

"Oh, you think that was funny?" The gleam in his eyes was diabolical. "You're going under, babe."

Panic leaped into her chest as he started toward her. Her hair would frizz, and oh God, everyone would see her without make-up. *He'd* see her without make-up. No one ever saw her without her carefully applied mask.

"You can't!"

He arched one sexy brow, inching closer. "Oh? Why not?"

"I have contacts," she lied. "The chlorine might damage them."

He stopped. "Really?"

"Yup."

Letting out a breath that rang of disappointment, he floated into a seat across from her. "Fine."

She smiled, leaning against the edge, waiting for an awkward silence to saturate the space between them. One she'd be compelled to fill with needless chatter. To her surprise, he closed his eyes, not seeming to expect anything from her.

Whatever speck of tension she held, drained away as she took in the sky. The night was clear. Beautiful, full of stars. Snippets of poems and prose trickled into her head.

She glanced at Will. His relaxed position hadn't changed. Figuring he wasn't paying attention, she mumbled a few of her favorite lines, hoping it'd help her remember them until she had her notebook.

"Are you talking to the voices in your head?"

*How the hell did he hear me over the freaking jets?*

"Yes," she quipped, covering her embarrassment. "They're telling me to drown you. I'm telling them no."

He leaned closer. "Liar. What are you really doing?"

She looked away. "Nothing."

"Come on. Tell me. I promise I won't tease."

She saw his sincerity, and took a chance, believing him. "I like to write little verses or poetry. The night is inspiring."

To her surprise, he didn't laugh, instead appeared intrigued. "Will you tell me them?"

Hell. No.

She shook her head.

He slid across the tub, sitting next to her. "Why not?"

"Because guys don't like that stuff. You'll think it's stupid."

"What, because I have a dick I can't appreciate beautiful words?"

Well, she sure appreciated the way he said dick. Blunt and strong. Made her mind wander...

She shook her head, trying to dislodge her X-rated thoughts and shrugged. "Maybe."

He leaned in closer, those chocolate eyes full of challenge. "You're afraid."

"Of what?"

He studied her. She waited for him to tease or crack a joke. Again, he did the unexpected.

*"She has a pretty cover, but she's a closed book/Her story is beautiful yet she's unwilling to share her pages/Terrified to show her prose, her poetry/Afraid her words are shallow, as skin-deep as her beauty."*

She swallowed her shock and discomfort. His words hit too close to the heart. However, this side of him also melted her. Made her want to cuddle and ravish him.

The challenge written in his words spoke to her competitive side. Her response fell from her mouth with surprising ease.

*"She's a closed book, but she'll spread her pages for him/If he promises to savor each line/Every story."*

He sucked in a breath, his nostrils flared. "Damn, woman. You don't have to worry about people finding your words trivial. They're liable to set the world on fire."

She licked her bottom lip as if his compliment had fallen from his tongue to hers. It tasted sweet.

He zeroed in on her mouth, tilting his head. They were so close his breath tickled and caressed her needy desire.

"There's my dance partner who deserted me," called Harper.

Will blinked as if waking from a dream. He twisted around while simultaneously putting space between them. "Hey, Harper. Sorry. We needed a break from the neighbors."

"I get that," came Tim's deep voice. "It's the same reason we're escaping."

Cindy buried her disappointment in a false smile, watching most of the wedding party troupe to the patio. "Did you at least grab me a margarita before leaving?"

Tim shook his head, grinning and pointing his thumb over his shoulder. "There's some dude name Terry stumbling around carrying one, asking for you. You want me to go and get him?"

Her smile became genuine as laughter filled her belly. Will appeared just as amused, saying, "We're going to find him in the morning, lurching along the shore calling for you. A margarita in one hand, his love for you in another."

An unladylike snort escaped her. "Shut up, Will."

His grin widened as he stood and helped Greta into the hot tub. Followed by Jacob, Tim, and Harper. Cindy wasn't thrilled when her cousin took the spot next to Will.

"Where's everyone else?" he asked.

"The rest of them are still dancing," answered Jacob.

Greta sat next to Cindy, bumping her shoulder. "You and Will seem to be getting along much better."

Suddenly fascinated with the bubbling water, she ignored the unspoken questions radiating from her sister. Ones Cindy had no idea how to answer.

# Chapter Five

Cindy grabbed her tennis shoes before closing her shared bedroom door and tip-toeing to the patio. The sun was beginning to crawl over the horizon, lighting up Lake Michigan and the sky in the loveliest shades of yellows and orange.

Something moved by the steps. Her heart jumped into her throat, she stumbled back into the glass door.

It stood, becoming the silhouette of a man. "Who's there?"

Will.

*Shit.* She wasn't wearing makeup. Hadn't even bothered to brush her hair. She'd set her alarm super early hoping to get in a run before anyone woke. So, of course, the man she wanted to seduce would be awake to see her in all her morning glory.

Had she even remembered to brush her teeth?

She was tempted to hightail it back inside, but there wasn't time. He was moving fast toward her.

"It's me. Cindy."

He stopped. "Why are you up?"

"I'm going for a run." She strode past him, hoping he didn't get a close look at her.

"Wait. I'm doing the same. We can run together."

*Oh, come on.*

Before reaching the sand, she dropped her shoes and slid her feet into them. She bent at the waist to tie her laces. "I like to run alone."

"Afraid you can't keep up?" he teased.

*As if.* She'd run cross country in high school, always placing in the top ten. In the years since graduating, she hadn't dropped her speed or endurance. Finishing her laces, she faced him.

He was staring at her ass.

"Like the view?" She wiggled her bottom a little.

His gaze shot to her face. She swore a blush darkened his cheeks. He cleared his throat. "Well, you did shove it out there. What else was I supposed to look at?"

She quirked a brow, eyeing the glorious sunrise before turning to him. "Yup. Nothing to see here. I get it. My ass is outstanding. Even prettier than the rising sun."

He flashed a smile full of the devil. "Damn, woman. Your ego is even bigger than your ass."

Her mouth fell open. *He did not just say I have a big butt.*

Laughing, he took off for the beach. "I bet you run like a girl too."

She started after him, yelling through her smile. "You bet I run like a girl. Which means I'll pass your lumbering butt in two seconds flat, leaving you in the dust and sand to weep at the sight of my magnificent ass."

True to her word, she shot past Will in less than a minute. She was also correct about her ass. It was glorious. He was tempted to go slow just to continue admiring the view.

The first time they'd met at that French restaurant, he'd found her pretty enough but she hadn't made his pulse race. She was polished and flawless; too perfect. The stylish, expensive outfit she'd worn showcased her body with class and sensuality. Her hair and makeup were as immaculate as if she'd stepped from a magazine to their table. She was like a beautiful painting, something to be admired from a distance. Never touched.

Now, with sweat trickling down the side of her makeup-free face while her strong legs pounded the sand in comfortable, old shorts, she was real. And stunning.

He wanted her.

Okay, fine, he wanted her yesterday too. When she let some of her perfected façade slip, she was incredible. It had taken all his self-control not to kiss her, especially when her eyes begged him to do it.

The old, impulsive Will would've acted on it in a heartbeat. He'd never pass up a good time, no matter the consequences.

He wanted to believe he was wiser now. Not stupid enough to go after his brother's sister-in-law.

Not for a fling.

With their polar-opposite backgrounds, they'd never be more than a fun distraction. Hell, forget the past, they had nothing to offer each other now. They were way too different. She liked excitement and fun. He needed calm and steady.

Also, what if they went for it and she wanted more? He wasn't boyfriend material, especially in her expensive, manicured world.

Hell, he was barely out of the hole he'd dug for himself, carrying more baggage than an international airport. He was a weak man who should never be responsible for another person's happiness.

His rambling thoughts were taking off faster than Cindy's long legs. He'd gone from fling to boyfriend in nearly the same breath. He shook his head at his stupidity.

"You're quiet. Are you dying, old man?" She sprinted past him again.

He smiled, catching up. Damn. She was beautiful. "Ah, no. You're panting pretty heavily. I didn't think you *could* talk."

"Oh, I could run circles around you."

He didn't doubt it for a second. Her endurance was a surprise. She kept pace with him better than any of his running buddies. Shit, she was pushing him.

Did she have this much stamina in the bedroom? Would she go all night, take charge? *Stop.*

He ran faster, trying to outrun his desires.

She easily kept pace with him, making him laugh. She was burrowing into his mind while never leaving his line of vision. The two were creating a dangerous combination.

Okay, next plan. Exhaust them both. She'd be too tired to tempt him. He'd be too spent to move.

"Want to make a friendly bet?" he asked.

"If it's me racing you, I'm willing to make an unfriendly bet. Since I know I'll whip your butt."

He laughed. Well, more like wheezed. He was going to lose, and didn't care. Her smile and light-hearted laugh made it worth it.

He pointed. "From the blue house back to ours. The first one home is the winner."

"What does the winner get?" Her gaze roamed over him, full of naughty suggestions.

Damn. She was going to be the death of him. "What do you want?"

She focused on his mouth.

He waited for her answer with equal parts apprehension and anticipation.

"If I win, you have to go dancing with us tonight."

Will groaned. Yesterday, during dinner the group had decided they wanted to go clubbing. He'd offered to drop them off, returning to drive them home when they were done. In the end, they'd decided to walk to the bars. He'd been relieved to skip it.

"I don't dance. I don't drink." He slowed to a jog.

"What were you doing last night with Harper?"

"Fine. I don't bar hop anymore." It brought back too many bad memories.

They stopped running but kept a brisk pace. "Come on, Will. Rae claimed Tanner as her dance partner. Which leaves me with Tim or Terry. You move better than both of them."

His spike of jealousy at the thought of either man touching Cindy was replaced with pleasure from her compliment. "You like my moves? Think I got game?"

"Ha!" She crinkled her nose, and he wanted to kiss it. "My three-year-old cousin has more game than you. I said you dance better than Tim and Terry, but I don't know, maybe Terry would be better when sober." She picked up the pace to a jog. "If you win, I guess I'll find out."

Shit. She was good. It didn't matter who won. No way did he want handsy Terry all over her. She'd managed to box him into going to a freaking club.

Acting like it made no difference, he asked, "You never told me, what do I get if I win?"

"Honey, there's no sense discussing it. I always win." She took off running.

# Chapter Six

Tim stood over Will, blocking the hot sun. "I have to leave."

Will placed his index finger in his book, closing it. Tim's shoulders were pinched, and he wore an uncustomary frown. Hell, everything about him was tense.

"What's wrong?"

Tim ran his fingers roughly through his hair before gripping the back of his neck. "My mom. She's in the hospital."

Before Will could ask, Greta and Cindy spoke to his right. "Is she okay?"

"She wasn't well when I left. My sister just called, told me they're on the way to the hospital. Mom's vision is blurry, the pain is getting worse. She's so weak my sister practically carried her to the car."

Will gathered his towel, book, and water bottle. "All right, give me ten minutes to get ready."

"I'm sorry. I feel like shit. It's your brother's weekend, and I'm making you bail on him."

"He'll understand."

Greta nodded in agreement, but Cindy held up her hand in a stop motion.

"What?" Will asked.

"Why don't you let him take your car, and you stay?"

"Neither Tanner nor Jacob are heading to Detroit on Sunday. I need to be home and back to work on Monday."

"Um, hello, asshole, I could give you a ride home." Her tone oozed 'duh.'

"Oh." Why hadn't that occurred to him? "Would you?"

"Yeah." She turned the word into two syllables as if speaking to the village idiot.

He ignored her snark, asking Tim, "Are you okay with driving my car?"

"Yeah, if you don't mind. It'd let me leave sooner."

Will shrugged. "It's all yours."

Tim clasped Will's shoulders briefly. "Thanks, man." He took off running toward the house. When he reached the patio, Will faced Cindy.

She was lounging on her towel, propped on her elbows with her toes buried in the sand. There was a challenge clear in her eyes.

In truth, he found it hard to focus when she was in that damn teal bikini again. The material caressed her breasts in an X then wrapped around to tie at her back. The bottoms were no better. Small with ties on the side. Ever since she lain next to him on the beach, he'd pretended to read. In reality, he was fantasizing about tugging those strings on her bottoms with his teeth.

Keeping his gaze firmly on her face, he lifted a brow. "Asshole?"

"Well, yeah," she huffed. "Here I am suggesting you stay, yet you think of asking anyone except me for a ride home."

He pressed a hand to his chest. "Yesterday, you called me homeless-looking, questioning if I change my underwear on a regular basis. You'd allow me to sit in your fancy car?"

Her indignation morphed to glee. "I can find an old blanket or something to throw over your seat."

He laughed as Greta gasped. "Cindy!"

She blinked her oh-so-innocent blues, but her smirk gave her away. "What? Not a good idea? Oh, I know. I could run inside and get a bar of soap, demanding he wash up in the lake?"

*That's it, the funny lady needs to cool off her smart, little mouth.*

"Great idea. Though it has been a while since I washed, I've forgotten the process. I might need some direction." He bent, scooping Cindy into his arms.

She yelped, gripping his neck. "What are you doing?"

"We're going for a swim. You're going to teach me how to bathe."

She squirmed, kicking and twisting. "No! My makeup. My hair!"

He held tight, making his way to the lake. "Seriously, Princess, you won't melt." He paused. "Well, sometimes you are more wicked-witch than Glinda."

"Put me down," she screeched-laughed.

He waded to his waist, with her butt dipping in the water. He wanted her to loosen up, enjoy herself. To not always worry about looking perfect. However, he wasn't a complete dick.

"Can you swim?" he asked.

She scoffed. "Of course, I live in a state nearly surrounded by water." She let go of his neck, sliding her hands into his hair and pulled. The mischievous glint in her eyes made his pulse race. "I just don't like being manhandled by a scullion."

He stopped. "Wow. The socialite is using her big vocabulary again. I'm surprised you know any titles used for kitchen workers. Have you ever even been inside one?

"Eew. No. I don't want to touch dead carcasses and dirty dishes. Ugh, you do all the time. Your hands are probably covered in germs, and they're touching me. Gross."

He smiled so big it hurt. "Oh, no. We can't have that."

"You better not!"

He heaved her up, tossing her in the lake.

She broke the surface seconds later, laughing and sputtering. "Damn it, Will. I'm going to have to hide out here until everyone goes inside. You better sleep with one eye open tonight. Paybacks are a bitch."

His laughter mixed with hers. "I'm shaking in my shorts. Why the payback? You're still gorgeous."

She dropped her chin, giving him a yeah, right look.

"Honest. It's nice to see your natural beauty under all the prep and perfection."

"Really?"

"Yup." He smiled, knowing he shouldn't poke a bear, but unable to resist. "Even with the mascara dripping down your cheeks, mixing with your snot."

She slapped a hand over her nose and dived under the water. He laughed harder, then seconds later yelped as an ironclad grip snaked around his ankles yanking him right off his feet. He went under swallowing a mouthful of Lake Michigan.

He emerged, coughing lake water and hearing delighted laughter. He was hit upside the head with Cindy's beauty.

Her hair was slicked back. A light spatter of freckles he'd never noticed before was scattered across her nose, tempting him like sprinkles on ice cream. However, what made his heart hammer was her honest, gleeful smile. A guy would be tempted to sell his soul to taste it against his mouth.

*What the hell. They could barely stand each other.*

He shook his head, dislodging crazy thoughts and dove, coming up right in front of her. She squealed and tried to jump back. He was faster, catching her around the waist. Heaving her over his shoulder, they headed deeper into the water.

She slapped his back, "Let me down. Take me back." She laughed and screamed.

"Oh no, little mermaid. We're going deep."

She stopped moving, making him look to see why. Bad idea. Her suit, small to begin with, had ridden up during their struggles. He got an eye full of her ass. It was freaking perfect. His body responded. He thanked his lucky stars she was over his back and couldn't see he was half hard.

"Please, I'm no Ariel. I'd never leave my swanky kingdom for some sea captain. Cindy-rella wants her Prince Charming."

He scoffed. Of course, she'd want some rich dude who mommy and her wicked step-father would love.

*Again, what the hell do I care? Let the pampered princess have an equally pampered prince.*

"One. Eric was a prince. He just didn't want to sit around the castle playing with his crown, so he explored. Two. I should've called you Ursula. That mean sweep was diabolical. I'm going to be blowing lake water from my nose for the rest of the day. Probably tomorrow too."

"You sure know a lot about the Little Mermaid, are you—"

The rest of Cindy's words were cut off when she shrieked like a banshee and bucked, shoving herself up, away from the water. Her ass flexed tight, directing his gaze there once again. How could he ignore it? It was a bite away from his mouth.

"Shit, Cindy!" His wet grip loosened, and she wiggled down his front, struggling in earnest.

"What the hell was that, that touched me?" she gasped.

Paying more attention to the shape of her perfect ass than where he was going, he didn't notice what he'd waded into until now.

"Seaweed." They were now almost to his armpits in water. He let go, figuring she'd swim farther away, putting more distance between her and the green slime. Instead, she wrapped her legs around him and climbed.

"Calm down," he said. Although with her screech and a loud boat passing nearby, he doubted she heard.

She continued climbing him, pressing her chest into his face. It was sweet, tortuous heaven.

"What?" she panted from above his head.

"It's seaweed." He closed his eyes. It didn't matter. The vision of her wet soaked breasts was forever burned into his retinas. "Not the damn Loch Ness Monster."

"Oh." She stilled, loosening her death grip, sliding down but not completely letting go. When they were face to face, she whispered, "Sorry."

"It's fine."

It wasn't. At all. He was hard as a rock, and her legs were still loosely around him. If she shifted an inch or two, she'd know the effect she had on him.

So, of course, the waves from the passing boat crashed into them, pushing her into him. Her sexy mouth formed into a sexy "oh" of surprise.

*Fuck.*

Her lips shifted to a cocky grin. She didn't let go and focused on his mouth.

*Move away, Will. Move, asshole. She's trouble. Move.*

"Hey! Cindy!" shouted Jacob from the shore, causing them to spring apart. "Is my brother trying to drown you?"

"More like the other way around," Will shouted back.

"Oh, yeah?"

His gaze flicked back to Cindy. Her self-satisfied smile was firmly in place. Was she gloating or thrilled? Did it matter?

No.

A fling with his brother's sister-in-law was a terrible idea.

"Yes, oh yeah. You held on tight enough, I think I might have a cracked rib," he joked hoping to ease the heat flickering between them.

She swam closer. "I don't think it is your ribs causing you discomfort. Do you need some relief?"

"Cindy," he warned, as his body screamed to bring her closer. "Bad idea."

"Bad ideas are the most fun."

He used to think that, until shitty ideas piled up like bricks, building him a life worse than death. A handful of those bad choices flashed through his mind, cooling some of his desire.

"No, they aren't." He hated how serious he sounded, the way the playfulness drained from her. However, he needed to stop what was smoldering between them. "You and I would be a disaster together."

"Who said together?" She scoffed. "I was talking about a little fun. Nothing more, but I forgot. Fun is forbidden with you." She turned, swimming to shore.

# Chapter Seven

Tying the sash on her wrap dress, Cindy peered at her reflection in the bedroom's full-length mirror. She twisted around to view the back. The cut and color suited her. The deep red complimented her sun-kissed skin, the plunge in the front and back was sexy without crossover into the land of slutty.

Someone tapped on the closed door, followed by Greta's friend, Susan, asking, "Can I come in?"

"Sure." Cindy stepped to the dresser, grabbing her hairspray.

She'd decided to wear her hair up. The night was hot and muggy, she didn't want anything on her neck while dancing.

"Rae told me I could borrow a pair of her earrings." Susan stopped, then whistled. "Damn, woman. You're hot."

*Would Will think so?*

Cindy wanted to kick herself for such a stupid, errant thought.

*Who cares.*

"Thank you." She faced the mirror, spraying her hair.

In the reflection of the glass, she watched Susan pick up a pair of earrings from Rae's nightstand. Sitting on the edge of her bed, Susan met Cindy's gaze. "Hoping to snare Will in that outfit?"

Cindy's heart skipped a beat, and she looked away. "What? No."

Susan was Greta's best friend, but when she and Jacob had split last year, he'd contacted Cindy, asking for help. She, in turn, called Susan. The two of them had hatched a plan to get a sullen Greta out of her apartment and to a nightclub where Jacob was waiting. Since then, the three women formed a tight bond and tried to meet at least once a month. Cindy considered Susan a close friend. One she learned could smell a bullshit story from a mile away.

Didn't mean she was going to admit her embarrassing and odd attraction to Will.

Busying herself with checking her makeup, she asked, "What makes you say that?"

"You two seemed cozy in the hot tub last night. Also, today in the lake."

Yeah, that was before she'd acted like a fool, throwing herself at him. Then got pissy when he refused her.

Her pride was still stinging.

"Most definitely not for Will," Cindy huffed. "Besides, I'm sure his boring ass isn't going with us."

After her attitude in the lake and the way she'd given him the cold shoulder for the rest of the day, she was certain he wouldn't stick to his end of their bet.

*Good. He's a wet blanket. I don't need him dampening the fun.*

Susan leaned back, resting on her elbows. "You sure? You want to bet on it? He isn't dressed for a night in."

Cindy shrugged, even as her pulse kicked up a notch. "Whatever. Makes no difference to me. I'm not dancing with him." The last part was the truth. No way would she make an ass of herself again. She opened the door. "Ready to go?"

Susan nodded. They made their way to the living room. Will was leaving his bedroom, texting someone.

She almost stumbled in her heels again. He was stunning. He'd give the male models she worked with a run for their jobs. His tan linen slacks weren't the baggie, shapeless style. They hugged his hips and thighs in the most enticing way. He'd paired them with a slim-fitting casual white cotton shirt; the top buttons were open, the sleeves rolled to the elbows. The combination was deadly sexy.

"Is everyone ready?" Greta called out.

His gaze snagged on Cindy. She could almost feel it. It was warm and carnal. He wanted her as much as she did him.

*So, what is his deal?*

Not her problem. He'd had his chance.

She turned to Greta. "I'm ready."

Will's fingertips tapped an irregular beat on the wooden table, his annoyance growing. Why had he kept his end of the deal with Cindy? It's not like she gave two shits he was here, in this crappy-ass club.

He sighed, resting into the comfortable leather backing of his seat. The place wasn't shitty. The restaurant side sported plush booths and solid oak tables. Even the food was good. The DJ and dance section were top notch.

Cindy seemed to agree, spending most of her time there dancing with every guy. Rae and Harper tried to get him to go with them, but he wasn't in the mood and refused. Eventually, they gave up.

As the hour ticked by, his sullenness grew. Now it was a beast sitting next to him, whispering discontent into his ear.

Part of his problem was the atmosphere. It brought back memories of his partying days. If it were five years earlier, he'd already be half in the bottle and best friends with the local drug dealer.

He could still spot them. A woman by the restroom. The blond man standing off to the left of the glass top bar. The one who kept watching Cindy with open lust.

*Fuck. I'm leaving.*

He started to scoot from the booth but paused when he saw her coming toward him. She was probably stopping by to order another drink and ignore him.

He should dodge her. Get out before she arrived. Instead, he sat studying her approach.

She was correct about one thing; the woman knew how to walk in a pair of heels. If sex had a walk, it would be hers.

She slid into the booth next to him. He caught a whiff of her perfume. It was a little vanilla and a lot nice.

"Where are you going?" she asked.

"Oh. You're talking to me now?" He sounded like a damn bratty teenager.

She seemed to let it bounce off her, saying mildly, "Yes. Are you finally going to get off your butt and join us?"

"No. I'm going back to the house."

"Why? It's early. Have a drink with me. After we can dance."

"I don't drink. And your dance card is already full."

"Are you jealous?"

*Yes.*

"No."

She smiled, leaning closer. "Liar."

Damn it. Forget vanilla. She smelled like seduction, of heated nights and hot kisses.

*Stop.*

She was his brother's sister-in-law. Not someone to have a casual fling with. He needed to remember that important fact.

"Who's your pick?" Will stretched his arms across the back of the booth, acting like the question didn't taste like dirt.

Her perfect brows rose. "Excuse me."

"Who's the lucky guy you're going to take home?" He wanted to take back the rotten question before he even finished speaking it.

Her eyes flashed. She looked like she wanted to set him on fire.

"What? Because I dance with a man, I have to sleep with him? Good thing I didn't accept any offers to buy me a drink. Then I would've had to take them to a dark, deserted corner to show my appreciation." She smacked the table, probably wishing it were his face. He wouldn't have stopped her, not with the crap he just said.

"No. I'm sorry. That was an asshole thing to say."

"Yes. Yes, it was," she agreed.

He rested his hand on top of hers. "Let me buy you a drink as an apology."

"No," she said sternly, yet didn't move from his touch.

"Please."

Her glare softened a fraction. "No, but thank you. I've reached my limit for the evening. I was going to get water."

"Okay, let me get it for you. If you're willing to dance with me after, I'd love to."

She nodded, then leaned in closer. "Though, to warn you, I'm only agreeing because I'm hoping to stab your feet with my stilettos."

Will winced, accepting his fate. "Fine. I deserve it."

She waved him off. "No, I'm kidding. You don't have to dance with me because you feel bad about your jerk comment. My feet hurt, anyway."

*I'm such a prick.*

He got the waiter's attention, ordered two sparkling waters. When he left, Will patted his lap. "Put your feet here. I'll rub them."

The corner of her mouth twitched. "Wow, guilt must be eating at you. I've been dancing for hours. My feet probably smell like death."

"Oh, right. Never mind," he joked. Sort of.

"Too late."

Her heels hit the floor, seconds later her feet with sexy, deep red polished toes rested on his lap. He sighed, pretending he was put out. Running his thumb along the arch of her foot, he pressed, moving them in slow circles. Her eyes closed, and the groan of pleasure that escaped between her lips shot straight to his dick.

He cleared his throat. "You know, I've wanted to dance with you all night."

She opened one eye. "Then why have you been sitting at this table, pouting?"

"I'm not pouting," he muttered, before going with complete honesty, "because if I dance with you, I'll want to do more."

Her entire focus was now on him. She seemed shocked at his confession. "Will, I practically threw myself at you this afternoon, you shot me down. Called me a bad idea."

"Not you. Us together. We'd end in disaster. I don't do relationships, plus you're my brother's sister-in-law. Not the best choice for a fling."

She gave him a once-over before dropping her feet and moving closer. "Earlier, I wasn't asking you to be my boyfriend. I get we wouldn't be good in a relationship." She slid a hand up his thigh. Everything inside him tightened, heat thumped in his veins, heavy and hard. "I'm willing to bet we'd be good in other ways."

Hell. She was right. When she'd fallen on top of him yesterday, she fit against him perfectly. Her body branded him. He wanted more, so much more.

He scanned the dance floor. Jacob and Greta were dancing, happy and oblivious.

Cindy rested a palm on the side of his face, making him look to her. "It's not about them. We are two adults who know the rules of this game. Let's play."

Maybe she was right. Neither was filling the other's head with false promises. She didn't seem to want more than he could give. Still, it wasn't like after tonight they could walk away and never see each other again. There'd be holiday gatherings and such.

But that mouth. Those curves. The way she was watching him didn't have him worrying about what-ifs or the future. He couldn't think past wanting her right now.

Damn it. After all the mistakes he'd made, he should have better impulse control. Instead, he could almost hear his resistance crumbling.

He gave one last weak effort at reining in the possible train-wreck. "We can't leave. Jacob and Greta will know."

Cindy shrugged one delicate shoulder. "So?"

"Ha! They would totally cock-block. You and I together is trouble for them." Will smirked. "My brother can think with his other head. Unlike me, when I'm around you."

Her hand inched higher, running her fingertips along the zipper of his slacks. The slight contact with his dick through the cloth made him groan.

"Oh, you think it's bad now. Wait until I get my hands on you without anything between us," she purred.

There was a clink of glass on wood, diverting their attention. The waiter was dropping off their drinks. Will stopped him. "Could I have the bill?"

The other man nodded, getting the receipt from his apron.

"Hold on, please." Will opened his wallet, handing over his credit card.

Cindy stood. "I'm telling Greta we're leaving."

"Good luck." Part of him hoped she'd talk some sense into her sister, another part of him wanted to grab Cindy and run before anyone could stop them.

Their waiter returned with the credit card receipt in seconds, passing her on the way to the dance floor. Will finished with the bill as Greta and Cindy talked. She didn't seem steady on her feet.

Had she drunk more than he realized? If she were even slightly buzzed, he'd put on the brakes. He was not taking advantage of a drunk woman. Not only would it be a sleazy thing to do but brought back memories of careless fucking and boozy, sloppy kisses.

Those reminders killed some of his heat.

As she reached the table, her brows drew together. "What's wrong?"

Her gaze was sharp. Still, he had to ask. "Are you drunk?"

She laughed, low and throaty, making him think dirty thoughts. "No. That was a little act for Greta. I told her my drinks aren't sitting well with me, and you offered, reluctantly, to walk me back home. So remember, help me but don't look happy doing it."

He swallowed his smile when he caught sight of Jacob watching them. "You are quite a devious woman."

She did her sexy one shoulder shrug, again. "Have you met my mother?"

Oh, yes, he remembered Sophia. Her disgust for the Grimm family was impossible to forget. What had she called him when they'd met briefly last year? Ah, yes. The lowlife screw-up.

Shit. He was. He had no business with someone like Cindy. She had her life together. The stains of all his fuck-ups and disastrous choices would dirty her.

She leaned down, giving him the most glorious view of her breasts. Grabbing his hand, she pulled him up. "Wilhelm Grimm. Stop over-thinking everything."

He groaned and laughed at the same time. "Quiet, Cindy-rella."

She placed a hand on each of his shoulders. "Act annoyed as you help me to the door. Helm."

He gripped her elbow gently. Giving Jacob a sharp nod of his chin in goodbye, they started for the door. "Don't call me Helm either."

"Aren't you bossy."

"You think this is bossy? Wait until I get you home." He looked at her, wanting to gauge her reaction at his declaration.

His breath caught in his throat. Her cornflower blue eyes were fully dilated, focused on his mouth.

He needed her outside. Now.

# Chapter Eight

Cindy stepped through the doorway Will held open for her. He rested a tentative hand on her waist, as if unsure she welcomed his touch. She did and let him know by relaxing into him.

A light scent of seaweed and lake water carried on the evening breeze. It did nothing to cool her. Not with Will so close, his desire mingling with hers.

They weaved around other couples out enjoying the pleasant night, turning off the main street they found their street deserted. He leaned in, running his nose along her neck, his light stubble tickling and enticing her.

"I've wanted to do this since you fell on me yesterday. You smell so damn good. Vanilla, woman, and sass."

"Sass?" His words made her giggle. His touch sent her pulse racing, while her feet couldn't seem to move.

"Yes," he whispered as she twisted to face him. His lips found her collarbone, igniting her with need. She tilted her neck, giving him more access. "You're brazen, mouthy, and incredibly sexy."

"Oh, I think you like my mouthiness."

He straightened, zeroing in on her lips. "I do like your mouth."

They were centimeters apart. She closed the distance, brushing her lips against his. "Do you?"

Instead of answering, he kissed her. It was gentle, somehow assertive, and pure sinful heaven. She opened her mouth slightly, inviting him to take more, and oh, he did.

His arms went around her, bringing her flush against his deliciously hard body. She ran her hands up his back, around to his solid chest, digging her nails into the cotton of his shirt. He groaned; it tasted like desire.

He kissed her one more time lightly before glancing to their house at the end of the street then to the lit, crowded Main Street. If he was having second thoughts again, she was going to scream.

Leaning his forehead against hers, he said, "Um. Listen. I've been to my doctors recently. A clean bill of health but, um, I didn't bring condoms."

She breathed a sigh of relief. "I've got us covered on every angle. I'm on the pill, have condoms, and my doctor's blessing to go forth and have fun."

Will laughed. "Did your doctor actually say that?"

"Yup. Told me all my tests were negative. Handed me some condoms, told me to have fun." She ran a finger down the front of his shirt. "And you, sir, are my fun."

He kissed her once, hard and quick. Then picked her up, one arm under her legs, the other supporting her back.

"What are you doing," she squeaked, loving his strong embrace.

"Those heels make your legs look a mile along and your ass even more amazing, but I can't take this slow pace anymore."

His long strides were surprisingly smooth as his determined steps ate up the sidewalk. She played, running her lips along his neck to his ear. Once there, she nibbled and kissed.

"Are you trying to get us arrested for indecent exposure. I swear, you keep that up..."

"You'll what?" she challenged.

He set her down. They'd arrived home.

Gripping her waist, he brought her deeper into the shadows of the porch. His hands slid to her backside, slid farther, and gripped the hem of her dress. He tugged it, exposing her lacy panties to the night air.

"I'll take you right here," he growled. "Let the neighbors and moon hear you scream every time I make you come."

Wow. She loved this domineering, almost cocky side of him.

"Multiple, huh?"

"Yes. Once with my fingers." He let go of her dress, one hand skimming over her hipbone and resting briefly at the top of her panties, before dipping inside. Shivers of pleasure broke along her skin. "Then, with my mouth." He kissed her. Against her lips, he whispered, "last with me inside you."

Holy hell, with his words and the strong, enticing rhythm of his fingers, she was damn near on the precipice of her first orgasm. She rocked into his hand, unable to stop a needy moan from escaping.

"Are you almost there?"

She nodded, falling into his heated gaze. He switched his tempo slightly while kissing her like a starving man. That did it. Hot pleasure raced through her, and she slumped into him, whimpering as waves of ecstasy ebbed and flowed from her head to her toes.

Will switched from determined strokes to gentle caresses. Eventually, she found her breath again. He gently withdrew his hand from her panties, bringing her to him in a tight embrace.

"Damn, woman, the sounds you make. I could get off on them alone."

She ran her palm along the front of his slacks. He wasn't kidding. He was hard as granite, thick and long. Her hunger bloomed. She wanted to taste him.

He arched into her touch but stopped her when she reached for his zipper. "Let's get inside."

"Are you too modest? Even though you don't mind exposing me to the neighborhood" she teased. "I touch you, you try to run inside."

Smirking, he pulled the keys from his pocket. "Not at all. Its more, what I want to do to your body will be too difficult here. And you'll have splinters in places you'd rather not have."

As he twisted around to unlock the door, she admired his broad shoulders, her gaze traveling to his fine ass. A thrilled tremor raced through her. He was all hers tonight, or at least until the rest of the wedding party returned. She didn't want to waste a moment.

The lock clicked; her pulse jumped in anticipation. "Let's go to my room. I have condoms in my travel case." *No sense playing coy at this point.*

With a dip of his chin, he indicated she lead the way. She wanted to sprint toward her room but managed to slow her strides and put an extra sway in her hips. She wanted him as inflamed as her.

It worked. He moved behind her, lightning-quick. His arms went around her waist. Running them up her stomach, he palmed her breasts, teasing her nipples through the silk of her dress. The combination was heaven.

"If you keep swinging your ass like that, I'm going to bend you over the couch," he rumbled in her ear.

"If you keep playing with my body, I guarantee I'll make it worth your wait."

"Woman—" was all he managed.

When he cleared the doorway to her room, she twisted from his hold. Kicking the door closed with her heel, she tugged the tie at her waist. The dress fell open, revealing her light pink lace panties and matching bra.

He ran his fingertips along the exposed tops of her breast, his touch as light as a butterfly's wings. "You are gorgeous."

Men complimented her all the time, but something in his voice made it feel like more than a toss away praise. Like he saw more than her surface beauty.

*Don't overthink this. It's one night, nothing more.*

Running his fingertips along her shoulders, he slid the straps off, and the dress fell. It pooled at her feet. She reached for the waist of his slacks.

He stilled, surprising her by letting her take over. She wondered how long that would last.

She popped the button then dragged down the zipper, taking her time, unwrapping her gift. His pants dropped to the ground, revealing muscular thighs and the present she really wanted, taunting her in a flattering pair of boxer briefs.

Using his feet, he kicked off his shoes while she started on his shirt. Kissing her, he cupped her face gently and began walking backward, in the direction of the bed. When the backs of his legs hit the mattress, she'd freed his last button. Slipping her hands under his shirt, she pushed it from his shoulders. It fell onto the bed. Seconds later, they were on top of it, hips to hips and lips to lips.

His body was delicious and hard, everywhere. He tasted like her favorite dessert, one she wanted to feast on for hours.

She wanted to taste and lick him until he melted like fine chocolate in her mouth.

He gripped her bottom, and she grinded against him, wishing they were already naked. He groaned her name, making her tighten with desire. She needed more, more of his heated skin against hers, inside her. No more playing around.

She stood. He tried to bring her back.

"Where are you going?" He sounded pained at the separation.

"Condoms. They're in my shower bag."

His hands dropped away. She hurried to the bathroom, flipping on the light. With three women, sharing a room, it took some time locating her bag. Then there was a moment of panic when she couldn't find her stash. They were wedged behind a packet of face wipes. Grabbing a few, she returned to the bedroom, leaving on the light.

She found Will sitting on the edge of the bed. He must've heard the click of her heels because he looked at her.

*Shit.* Indecision was back.

"Damnit, Will. Get out of your head."

He smiled, but it was weak. His gaze traveled from her stilettos to her eyes. "Woman, you are so damn beautiful."

She came closer, standing directly in front of him. "Then why so forlorn? What happened in the minutes I was in the bathroom?"

"I'm a mistake, Cindy. Everything I touch turns to ash. We shouldn't do this."

"What the hell are you talking about?" She came closer. His warm breaths caressed her stomach. He didn't move away. "Your touch has heated me but cool your ego. You won't burn me."

He laughed quietly. "I didn't mean it like that."

"I know." Another step, a whisper away from his lips. "It's one night. Don't deny us this. Something that feels this good can't be wrong, right?"

He didn't answer with words. Instead, he kissed her stomach. She dropped the condoms on the bed to run her fingers through his soft hair. His trail went lower while his hands glided up her thighs, gripping her panties, sliding them off.

She lay on the bed, her legs hanging over the edge, warmth gathering and thrumming between her legs. He rested between them, claiming her with his mouth. She gasped at the sudden onslaught of pleasure.

Hell, he might be better with his mouth than his fingers. He sucked, licked, and kissed her into a panting mess. Taking his time, driving her wild.

She grabbed his hair, moving him where she needed him. From the way his mouth became hungrier, he must have appreciated it, even liked the direction.

Her legs started to shake as her climax built. When she was on the razors-edge of orgasmic bliss, he stopped. She sat up on her elbows to find out why. He'd tilted back on his heels, watching her. A devilish smile played on his gorgeous wet lips.

"Why did you stop?" she demanded.

Again, he didn't answer. He leaned forward, kissing her stomach. She wanted to scream, needing his mouth lower, offering her the relief his tongue had nearly provided.

His kissed along her body until he hovered inches from her. Using his lips, tongue, and teeth, he played with her neck while removing her bra. He bent, lightly biting each breast.

She liked it. A lot.

He straightened and demanded, "Sit up."

For once, she obeyed.

He studied her like she was a priceless piece of art. "Middle of the bed. Now."

Her gaze dropped to his erection. She didn't want to listen. She wanted to taste him.

"Damn it, woman. Don't look at me like that, or this will be finished before it starts."

The desire stamped on his every feature. From the lust whirling in his eyes, to the way he licked his lips, amped-up hers.

She reached for him.

He took one step back. "I owe you another orgasm."

Through her molten lust, she managed to smirk. "I thought you said I'd get three."

"Yes. My greedy woman. Three it shall be."

*My woman.*

She liked that, Will's woman.

No. Not happening.

They had this night. One night. Why did she have to keep reminding herself? He didn't do relationships, and she didn't want one.

"Now, listen to me. Move up the bed. Or I will tease you on the edge of orgasm for hours." His tone told her he wasn't kidding.

For half a second, she considered pushing him. Making him work harder for her submission. In the end, she wanted what his voice promised and did as he demanded.

Resting one knee on the bed, he took one of her ankles and kissed it before removing the heel. He did the same for the other. Spreading her legs, he crawled between them, moving along her body. His delicious heat mixed with her desire.

Sliding a hand inside his boxer-briefs, she wrapped a hand around his erection. He groaned, rocking into her grip.

"Come here," she whispered.

It was his turn to listen. He went down onto his elbows, his mouth meeting hers. She opened her lips, and he took the invitation, his tongue tangling with hers.

She let go of him, tugging on the waist of his underwear. He took the hint and shifted to his side, removing them.

Returning, he laid on her and thrust. His erection glided on top of her with the perfect amount of pressure. Her nails scraped along his broad back as the razor edge of her climax quickly climbed back, coiling tight.

"Please," she begged against his lips, hoping he'd understand what she wanted. More of him. All of him.

He patted around on the bed, followed by the crinkle of a packet. He shifted onto his side. Watching him roll on the condom was incredibly erotic.

She gripped his bicep and brought him back on top of her. He drove into her slowly, as if wanting to give her time to adjust.

It was considerate, given his size, but damnit, she was impatient for him. She crossed her legs around his waist, and using her feet, gripped him under his ass and pushed him all the way inside.

The sweet bit of pain mixed with so much pleasure had her nearly screaming his name. He didn't give her the chance to catch her breath. He kissed her while moving his hips, deep and smooth. In less than a minute, she was coming apart. Pleasure washed through her, making her toes curl and calling out less-than-ladylike words.

He didn't stop his perfect rhythm until her body pieced itself back together again and her shouts turned to whimpers.

Opening her eyes, her gaze met his. He appeared quite pleased with himself.

"That's two," she panted. "One more."

His smile was all wicked intent. "Sure you can handle another one?"

*No.*

"Yes."

Rising a little, he grabbed a pillow. Putting it under her, he took her feet and placed them on his shoulders. Leisurely, he slid back inside. And wow.

*Wow.*

The angle was almost too much, yet his rhythm was unhurried and controlled. The only thing giving away his struggle at keeping his desire in check was the tight clench of his jaw and the way his hands dug into her skin.

She wanted to break his control, but the position restricted her movement. All she had were her hands, and she used them. She never broke eye contact while running her fingertips over his cheeks, down his neck, to his chest, using the pads of her thumbs to circle his nipples. His breath caught, and his thrusts became rougher.

"Like that," she pleaded, tight pleasure coiling around her.

His control slipped a notch. She clutched his biceps; a light sheen of sweat covered his skin, along with the rise and fall of his chest from his quick, uneven breaths. The sight was an erotic image she wanted burned in her mind forever.

His hand gripping her waist slid to where their bodies were connected. Her third promised orgasm ripped her apart in the most delicious way.

She reached for his neck, wanting his lips, his body plastered against hers. He came willingly, and her legs went around his waist, needing him close as possible.

"Cindy," he growled.

She gripped him tighter, urging him to lose control. The last of his restraint broke away as he slammed into her, taking all she had to give, and she wanted him to have everything. Her body. Her passion.

Hell, maybe even a small piece of her heart.

# Chapter Nine

Cindy was tucked under him, with him still inside her. The last thing he wanted to do was go. However, she'd been clear this was about sex, not cuddles and closeness.

"I should leave," Will whispered into her soft, satin neck, careful to keep the bulk of his weight off of her.

"Do you want to?" She traced lazy circles on his back with her nails.

He decided to go with honesty. "No."

"Then stay. They'll probably be out for a couple more hours, and I'm not done with you."

"Damn." He chuckled, reluctantly leaving her to dispose of the condom. "Three orgasms, but you want more? You're a greedy woman."

She gave him a look at said, "So?"

He smiled, feeling it to his soul. "I like it."

Going into the bathroom, he brought her a washcloth. "You want me to, or you?" he asked.

"Would you?" Her gentle, guarded gaze nearly broke him.

Had no man ever wanted to care for her after sex? Assholes.

Her sweet sighs and warm eyes made him want to cradle her in his arms and take care of her for the rest of her nights.

He shook that crazy-ass thought from his head. Who was he kidding? He couldn't take care of himself, let alone someone else. His proof was his past.

Plus, Cindy only wanted him for tonight.

He'd take what he could get, knowing it was more than he deserved.

Scooting onto the bed, he sat next to her, running the warm cloth between her legs. Flipping it, he trailed it up her body, over her breasts. The last part was unnecessary, he just wanted a reason to touch her, and she seemed to like it.

Her eyes fell shut, and an exhale of contentment fell from her lips. When the heat leaked from the washcloth, he went to the bathroom, tossing it in the sink. Returning, he found her nearly asleep.

He hesitated and considered leaving, letting her sleep. Fuck it. He wanted a few more minutes with her.

Sliding in under the light sheet, she cuddled into him. Resting her head on his chest, he found she fit perfectly. It made his heart ache in longing, begging for more than one night.

Impossible. But a little longer couldn't hurt.

He promised himself he'd get up in five minutes.

*Shit.* Why the hell was Cindy poking at his shoulder?

He opened his eyes to find Rae and Harper standing over him. *Double shit.*

"I think you took a wrong turn, Will," Rae said, impish mirth dripping from each word. "Not sure if you noticed but you're in the girls' room."

Cindy muttered something, twisting away, taking the freaking cover with her. He snatched the edge of it before he flashed the two women.

Rae's smile widened. "Looks like you lost your clothes too."

Harper rested a hand on her hip. "Friday night, I thought we might hook up this weekend. This is a surprise twist."

"It sure is," Rae cut in. "Seems the Meier sisters have a taste for Grimm."

Both women started giggling, waking Cindy. Gazing at Will, then her friends before muttering, "Well, shit." She ran a hand through her mussed hair. "Are Greta and Jacob home too?"

Rae rubbed her hands together. "Oh, the plot thickens. Is this a secret tryst?"

"How can it be? In two months, he," Harper pointed at Will, "will be Greta's brother-in-law. Kind of hard to keep dating a secret. And why bother?"

Cindy answered, "Because we aren't dating. It's a one-time thing. We'd rather skip the lecture from our siblings."

Her matter-of-fact tone hurt a little, even if she spoke the truth.

"Oh, so like, Friends with Benefits?" Rae quipped.

"You mean, family? Eew. That sounds wrong." By the time Harper finished, she and Rae were leaning on each other, laughing their asses off.

Cindy was biting her bottom lip, amusement dancing in her eyes. He dipped his chin, giving her an are-you-kidding-me-look. Though in truth, their drunken glee was funny.

When Rae was able to speak again, she said, "No, Greta and Jacob aren't here. Just us, along with Tanner."

Will sat, still clutching the covers. "I'll leave. Let you ladies get to bed."

"If you want," Rae said with a small shrug. Neither woman moved.

He cleared his throat. "I'd prefer not to have an audience while I get dressed."

"Oh! Sorry." Rae swiveled around, her cheeks turning a bright red.

"Fine," Harper pouted. She headed to the bathroom.

After putting on his clothes, he glanced at Cindy, not sure how they were supposed to say bye.

The side of her mouth quirked. "Come here."

He didn't hesitate, placing a knee on the bed and leaning in. She met him halfway.

If it was supposed to be a simple kiss, it dove into erotic with a swipe of her tongue. He rested a hand at the side of her neck, relishing her taste.

One of her hands wrapped around the arm holding him up, as if trying to get him back on top of her.

Someone cleared their throat.

Time to go.

Before he could stand, Cindy whispered against his lips, "Meet me in the morning. Let's run together."

"Same time?" he asked.

She glanced at the alarm clock. It was a quarter after midnight. That was it?

"Yes, six-thirty is good."

He nodded a distracted goodbye to Rae.

Was Cindy hoping a run would put them back in order? As sort of friends. Or, was she like him, craving more time together?

Either way, he'd be there.

# Chapter Ten

Will rolled over, snatching his phone to check the time. *Again*. He was worse than a kid at Christmas.

Ten after six. *Close enough.*

Grabbing a T-shirt and shorts he'd tossed on a nearby chair last night, he shuffled into the bathroom, trying not to wake Tanner. Although the chance was slim, Will remembered during their adolescent sleep-overs, soon as Tanner's head hit the pillow, he slept like the dead.

Will was thankful for it last night. He hadn't relished the idea of having another possible conversation like the one with Rae and Harper.

Ready in less than five minutes, he headed for the back door, trying to decide where they could run. He hoped he could talk her into running to the end of the beach. They could try the trails in the woods. Not that he was trying to get Cindy alone, away from curious eyes.

Nope, no impure, tantalizing thoughts swirling around in his mind. At all.

Sliding closed the patio door, her voice floated from somewhere near the stairs, startling him a little.

"Morning," she called quietly.

"You beat me out here."

He took in the sight of Cindy leaning against the railing, one ankle crossed over the other. The sun was just starting to rise. It was a stunning backdrop of pinks and purples, yet he found it dull next to her.

"Yeah. Lazy ass, I was thinking of leaving without you. You know I have to be back before anyone is awake. I need to shower and put my mask on." She waved a hand in front of her face.

Crazy woman. She was stunning, fresh-faced, and smiling.

Also, he liked she was comfortable enough around him to go without her mask of refinement. Her veneer of perfection.

"Then let's get moving." He started for the steps. "Want to run the trails?"

She nodded before taking off. Damn it.

He ran after her, catching up quickly. "You didn't let me stretch first. If I pull something are you going to nurse me back to health? Rub out the pain?"

"I'm not the nurturing type." Her gaze ran over his body, stopping at his shorts. "Although, if you need me to rub something out…"

He shook his head, chuckling as a shimmer of heat spread low in his belly. So, this run wasn't to return things to the way they were before last night.

*Good.*

When they came to the narrow trail leading into the woods, he let Cindy go first. Conversation came to an end as they had to pay attention. The path was narrow and littered with roots, rocks, and other forest debris. The sun was shining, but its rays didn't reach very far into the trees, the cover too dense.

After running about three miles and tackling a rather steep hill, they slowed to catch their breaths. He took in his surroundings. All around them were deep greens, browns, and flashes of white from the sycamore and ash trees. The only sound was the wind through the trees and the chirping of birds. It was peace personified.

His gaze moved from the trees to her. She was bouncing on the balls of her feet, staring into the forest like she was ready to run uphill for another three miles. She made him feel like an old man.

It made him wonder. "How old are you?"

She twisted to face him. "Twenty-five. What about you?"

No wonder. He *was* old compared to her. He grabbed the bottom of his shirt, lifting it to wipe his sweaty brow. "Thirty-four."

Letting go of the material, he waited for the "old man" comments. She repeatedly said he acted elderly, turns out he was compared to her. Shit, nearly a decade older than her. How could she *not* give him a hard time?

Instead, he found she was staring at what was moments ago his bare stomach. Taking two steps, she stood in front of him, reaching under his shirt.

It was the invitation he hadn't realized he was waiting for. He brought her flush against his body. She was warm, her skin deliciously damp from the run. The combination was pure heaven against him.

His mouth found hers as she slipped her hands into the back of his shorts. The heat of her body and lips against him had him wanting to throw discretion over the side of a steep hill. He longed to take her here, in the open, not caring if anyone saw them.

Breaking the kiss, he murmured against her lips, "You're killing me."

She tilted back an inch, the hunger in her eyes nearly melting him. "It's only fair. I fell asleep replaying what we'd done and woke needing more of it."

He groaned. Fuck. Those angelic blue eyes hid a devilish mind, full of sinful fun.

"It's a little difficult given everyone is back. We have a full house." He tried to be reasonable while his body shouted for him to shut-the-fuck-up.

She reached for his hand, leading him off the trail, deeper into the mix of trees. "I don't need a bed. I need you." She jumped. He caught her ass as her legs encircled his waist, and she planted hot kisses on his neck.

Every part of him begged to remove her shorts, to bury himself deep inside her. Before his last thread of logic snapped, he groaned, "Please tell me you have a condom."

She loosened her legs from around him, and he let go. With a satisfied smirk, she flashed a small square packet from a hidden pocket of her shorts.

He took it from her, bringing her back against him, where she belonged. "Such a resourceful woman."

She hummed, either in agreement or pleasure. The sound merged with his barely restrained need for her.

He growled, kissing her hard and deep as her hands skimmed along his back and up into his hair. She tugged in a way that made him want to mark her, to have her screaming his name into the morning air.

His touch was greedy, moving to her ass, he tugged at the waist of her shorts, wanting, no needing, inside. She shifted an inch, giving him access. He took it, dipping a hand inside her panties.

She moaned. The sound was like a stroke, a lick from her tongue. He wanted to hear it again. Repeatedly.

However, before he could work her into a frenzy with his hands, she stepped away.

"Why—" he began.

"I don't want your hands. I want you." She gripped him through his shorts, taking the condom from him.

He let her take charge. Usually, he never relinquished it, but her demanding ways were so damn hot, impossible to resist.

Shoving down his shorts and boxer-briefs, she took him in her hand, stroking him from base to head. He arched into her hand, groaning in pleasure.

She let go. Ripping open the foil packet, she rolled the condom on him, watching him with eyes dancing with desire.

He needed to take charge.

Taking her face in his hands, he ran a thumb along one of her cheeks before kissing her with care and gentleness, letting the side of him that yearned for so much more make a brief appearance, before his lust and base desires took over.

"Turn. Grab tight onto the tree," he demanded.

The way she whipped around told him she was more than willing to take orders. *Good*.

He ran two fingers along her spine, then along the waist of her sexy pink shorts. As slow as his greedy desire allowed, he pushed them down, exposing her lush ass.

Twisting her neck to face him, she asked, "What are you waiting for?"

He loved her unabashed ways, especially when it came to sex. Still, working her up was half the thrill.

He slid his length between her legs, so close, but not giving her what she wanted. "I'll tell you when."

She huffed. "Tease."

He swallowed a chuckle, bent his knees, with her wet heat begging for him, he sank into her in one thrust.

They both groaned in relief.

The reprieve was short-lived, as his compulsion to move swelled. His fingers dug into her soft skin, savoring her.

She shifted forward, then slammed down, burying him in her addictive heat. Apparently, she didn't want to be savored. She wanted to be devoured.

He complied, causing her to lock her arms against the tree. Finding a pace she liked, he kept it until her panting words became needy pleas for relief. He reached around, between her legs, searching for her spot that'd send her over the edge. He found it. Within seconds, her body stiffened. Her sweet lips caressed his name.

Her warmth, along with the sounds of her pleasure, had his climax crashing through him with shocking speed. Her tight orgasm made him see freaking stars.

His last thought before euphoria raced through him and obliterated everything but the feel of their bodies was how in hell was he going to let this woman go?

# Chapter Eleven

Cindy watched as Will hung up his cellphone, saying, "Thanks, Tim," then focus on her. "He said it's cool. He'll drop my car off at your place."

She shrugged. "I told you, I don't have a problem driving you to your apartment."

The more time with him, the better. Saying goodbye and returning to friendly acquaintances was more difficult than she'd anticipated. She found one weekend wasn't enough.

"It's probably easier for him. Saves him from having to drive to Detroit. His mom's still at UofM hospital, that's what, ten minutes from where you live?" Cindy nodded, and Will continued. "He said his sister could meet him at your place. From there, they're going to visit their mom together."

She sighed. "I'm glad his mom's okay. Appendicitis is scary. It's a good thing they took her to the hospital before it ruptured. And thankfully it wasn't something serious like a stroke or cancer."

She waited, wondering if he would bring up his mom. Greta had mentioned Will and Jacob's mom passed away when they were teenagers.

He only grunted in agreement. So much for a heart-to-heart.

Ah, well, he did say he didn't do commitment. She assumed it meant he didn't go around spilling his hurts either.

So, was it her?

And why did she care?

Serious relationships were not her thing. She traveled too much, and honestly, most guys bored her after a week or two of dating. Why did she suspect this wouldn't happen with him?

She shook aside her wayward thoughts, giving him her address. He texted it to Tim while asking what she had planned for the rest of the day.

"No plans. You?" she replied.

"Nope. Want to grab lunch together?"

Happiness flowed through her, slow and sweet. Maybe he wasn't eager to end things between them either. After they'd come back from their rather adventurous run, everyone was already awake, piled in the kitchen and dining area, eating and talking loudly.

She'd made a beeline for the bathroom. By the time she finished with her shower, Will was in his room with Tanner, packing. She hadn't had a moment alone with him until they'd gotten in her car.

Once on the road, he'd kept the conversation light, never broaching the subject of them. She guessed it made sense. There was no them. They'd kept things from Greta and Jacob for the sole reason the fling would end when they left the lake house.

Will cleared his throat. Oh. She'd never answered his question.

"Yes. Lunch would be great. I didn't eat much for breakfast." She tried not to sound too eager but wasn't sure if she succeeded. "I know a great place, right around the corner from my house. Do you mind if we stop at my condo first? I want to drop off my bags and see if Emma needs anything."

Cindy could call, but she missed Emma and Max. Plus, her roommate never answered her damn phone.

Will shrugged. "I don't mind. Emma? The roommate who cooks?"

She nodded. Just then one of her favorite songs came on the radio, and she turned it up. The rest of the ride passed with easy, light conversation. It seemed like within one tick of the clock she was clicking the button to open her garage, driving past Will's car to park inside.

She shut off the engine. The dim, quiet space made her more aware of his closeness. His scent of male and spices wrapped around her. He was watching her. She wanted him kissing her.

Instead, he opened his door. "Pop the trunk. I'll get your bags."

Disappointment bit at her lonely lips, yet she managed a cheerful tone. "Wow. Such a gentleman. I'd have never guessed it."

His low laughter bounced around in the small area. She loved the sound.

Her garage was under her condo, and she started for the steps with Will following. Reaching the top, she opened the door.

"You could leave them here." She pointed next to the washer and dryer. She figured most of the stuff in her bag needed to be washed. There was no sense lugging it to her room.

The utility room's door was closed. Through the thin wood, she heard a high-pitch squeal. Cindy smiled at the sound. She'd missed Max's exuberant, wet kisses.

"Who…" Will began, but she already had the door open and was striding into the living room.

Max was sitting on the beige rug, playing with some wooden blocks. He twisted in Cindy's direction. Catching sight of her, he let out another squeal of delight and took off in a frantic crawl, coming for her.

She picked him up, kissing both of his cheeks. "My little June bug, how are you?" The tiny toddler grabbed for her hair, but she was familiar with this game, and quickly shoved it behind her shoulders. Those chubby hands could do damage. "Oh, no, you don't. I know your devil tricks."

Turning, she found Will standing a few feet behind her, watching with open curiosity. "Meet Max," she said. "My roommate's gorgeous baby boy."

Will came closer, looking adorably confused. "You didn't mention she had a baby. I thought Max was her boyfriend." He rested a hand on her waist, talking to Max. "Hi, little guy."

Max's eyes widened like saucer plates, then he promptly buried his face in the crook of her neck.

Will chuckled. "Shy?"

"Yeah. He's not around many guys."

"Cindy? Is that you?" called Emma, stepping from her bedroom. "I figured from Max's happy screech it must be you." She stopped short when she saw Will, taking in his hand resting on Cindy's waist.

"Emma, this is Will."

He offered her his hand. She shook it. "Where did you come from? I thought Cindy was spending the weekend with her sister's wedding party."

"I'm part of the party. I'm Jacob's brother."

"The uptight one," Emma blurted. The woman never did have a filter. Well, except when around her ex-husband.

Will didn't seem offended. He just laughed, looking to Cindy with one brow raised.

"First impressions and all that." She shrugged.

Emma leaned sideways, snagging Cindy's gaze. "So...is he now more than Jacob's brother?"

Heat traveled up her neck. "He needed a ride home."

Her friend smirked. "A ride, huh?"

*When we're alone, I'm going to strangle her.*

Running her nose lightly over Max's gossamer soft hair, Cindy refused to meet anyone's eye. "Leave it alone." She wasn't sure what to say. He was clear he didn't want more than a weekend, which ended today. Her pride wouldn't allow her to beg for more. "He's Jacob's brother. Nothing more."

No one said a word, not even a babble from Max. A silence, thick and awkward, filled the room.

Will broke it. "I better go."

*What the hell?*

Needing to get a read on him, she faced him. Something like an electric shock rushed through her. His playfulness was gone, replaced by a face of stone.

"What about lunch?"

"I shouldn't. I need to check in with Mark. He covered my shifts while I was off this weekend. I need to head to work early. Tighten up loose ends before my shift starts."

"Okay..."

It wasn't, but what could she do? He wasn't her boyfriend. She had no claim to him. He could leave whenever he wanted. Even if it felt like he was smothering the sun.

Still, she tried again. "When will I see you?"

He gave a shrug that felt like a slap. "The wedding, I guess. I have a busy schedule these next couple of weeks." Rocking once on his heels, he looked at Emma. "Nice meeting you."

"You too." She reached for Max. "I'll take him. Let you two say bye."

"No need." He kissed Cindy on the cheek. "I'll see you at the wedding."

He left, taking her good mood with him.

She took a deep breath, trying to expel her confusion and hurt. She faced Emma, whose brows rose, damn near touching her hairline. "He was abrupt."

He was, making her hurt shift into anger. He probably never wanted to go to lunch with her, just didn't know how to break away, how to let her down easy.

As if she were some delicate flower who'd die without him. *Please.*

She kissed Max before setting him on the rug. "I guess. Like he said, he has stuff to do. He'd come in to help me with my bags. Not stay for tea, or move in." She started for the utility room, wanting to unpack her suitcase and be alone.

"I heard you mention going to lunch together," Emma called.

*Thanks, friend. Need a hot poker to jab at the sore spots?*

"Yeah, we tossed around the idea." Okay, he mentioned it, she'd jumped at it like an overeager puppy. "This is better. I need to repack. I'm leaving for a show in Miami tomorrow afternoon. Then I'm only home for two days before heading off to Chicago. It will be like this until the wedding. I don't have time for lunch with someone like him."

Emma followed Cindy, parroting, "Someone like him?"

"Yes, barely a friend."

"Uh-huh. I saw the way he watched you. He didn't look at you like a friend. Or touch you like one." Emma leaned against the doorframe. "Did you two sleep together?"

Cindy bent, unzipping suitcase. "Yes, but we both agreed to a weekend. It's over. Plus, he's not my type."

"You have one? You date guys from every nationality."

"I don't mean looks. He's too serious. I'd grow bored with him in a week. And I don't want things to get weird, you know, with him being Jacob's brother."

Max found them. He was probably hoping they wouldn't notice him trying to crawl around them. The kid was a daredevil, wanting to climb everything, including the garage stairs.

Emma reached him first, scooping him into her arms. "Denial can be a lovely thing." She closed the door to the garage and made her way back to the living room.

"Yes, it is," Cindy whispered.

# Chapter Twelve

Frustration swirled through Will as he listened to the cheerful chatter around him while he took in the striking murals along the museum walls of the Detroit Institute of Arts. The tinkle of the silver hitting glasses started again, signaling the guests wanted the bride and groom to kiss.

Digging out another smile, Will watched his brother with his new wife, glad Jacob was happy. He deserved it. Nevertheless, tonight was a reminder of how much Will had screwed up.

Ten years ago, in his early twenties, even with all the partying he'd been certain by the time he hit thirty he and Jolene would be married. They'd have a kid or two. He'd be giving his little brother advice about love and marriage.

Instead, he was crawling out of the wreckage he created, all the while wanting to barrel headfirst into another disaster.

He surreptitiously studied Cindy.

Over the passing weeks, he'd tried to forget her. It hadn't worked.

A dozen times he'd thought to call her. Invite her to a movie or dinner. Anything, to hear her voice, her laughter. Catch that gleam in her eyes right before she cut loose with some sarcastic wit.

He wanted her in his bed, in his life. One weekend wasn't enough. He wasn't ready to let her go.

*You never had her.*

Besides, ending things was for the best. Eventually, one of them would want more. Hell, he already did. He needed to let go. More might cause problems with Jacob and Greta while making things more difficult for Cindy.

There was also her mother, Sophia. Will remembered the shit she'd done when Jacob first started dating Greta. She'd tried to wreck their relationship, and damn near ruined Jacob's business.

Will sighed. That was the last thing he needed. He was fantastic at destroying what he loved. He didn't need the added help of a vindictive mother. And for what? Lust?

A woman like Cindy deserved a man with clean hands, a flawless background, and a whole heart. Even for a temporary fling.

Too bad the reckless part of him didn't give a shit. No, that side was willing to burn everything to the ground, even for a moment, a breath of satisfaction and bliss.

His gaze traveled along her soft shoulder, bare except for the slim, light green strap of her dress. The sight taunted him.

Not that she was trying to tease him. She seemed content to ignore him.

Like she had been all day.

Except for the brief instance when she'd first exited from the limo.

He hadn't been with the wedding party. As a thank you, Jacob rented rooms at a swanky hotel for him and his wife, along with those who stood in his wedding party, less than a block from the DIA. Allowing everyone to enjoy themselves without having to worry about driving home after drinking. A limo would arrive the next afternoon to take them back to Greta's apartment, where the group had met before the wedding.

He'd refused both the limo ride and hotel since he lived close to the DIA and didn't plan on drinking anyway. Plus, he needed his car. He'd offered to drive the newlyweds to the airport, early tomorrow for their three-week honeymoon in Iceland.

Therefore, he'd been standing on the marble steps of the DIA when the limo parked at the curb, and Cindy emerged gracefully from it, her sensual beauty making his blood race. She was stunning in a floor-length, light green dress, her hair done up in some complicated style that showed off her elegant neck.

As if sensing his hunger, her gaze snapped to his. She seemed rooted to the spot, and he swore he saw longing swirling in her eyes. For half a second, he'd played with the idea of closing the distance between them, taking her in his arms, and kissing those lush, full lips.

Then she'd blinked, turning to some guy who stepped from the limo first. The way he reached for her hand, Will assumed the asshole was her date.

The one gesture killed the sliver of anticipation and what-ifs. Well that, and the way she snubbed him. Even, now when they sat next to each other at the main table, she kept her shoulder turned away from him, talking to anyone except him.

Hell, he was surprised she deigned to let him take her arm when they walked down the aisle together after the wedding ceremony.

*It's for the best. Stop whining and move on. Like her.*

He spotted Cindy's date at a table toward the front of the room. The guy was perfect for her. From his immaculate suit to his perfect blond hair. He was hearty handshakes and easy grins. Even from where Will sat, it was apparent everyone at the table was enamored with him.

*Asshole.*

Will noticed his two friends, Lucas and Tim, sitting at the table with The Date. Will had wondered if Lucas would come to the wedding. He was good friends with the groom; however these sorts of things must be difficult for him.

He'd married his college sweetheart, and in less than a year he'd buried her. Two years had passed since the death of his wife, but Will understood all too well those wounds take a long time to heal.

Hell, he was still waiting for his past hurts to scar over.

He stood, needing to get away. They were done with dinner and speeches. There was no reason for him to stay at the head table.

Time to shake his damn mood. He reached Lucas as a couple was leaving. Will took one of the empty seats.

"What have you been up to?" he asked his old friend.

Lucas smiled. It was nice to see it touched his eyes. He'd lost his hollow, deadened stare. "I recently finished a lucrative job and bought a gorgeous building down the street from here. The inside is beautiful, art deco from the 1920s. Updating it is going smoothly. Well, for an old building, anyway."

"Yeah, I bet. Pretty, but brimming with hidden problems."

Lucas nodded. He owned an energy consulting company. He and his brother-in-law also bought up property, turning the buildings eco-friendly then either selling or renting them.

"What about you? What's new?" He asked Tim. "He mentioned you two were thinking of opening a restaurant together."

Cindy took the empty seat next to her date, not acknowledging Will yet something told him she was listening.

He focused on Lucas and Tim. "At this stage, it's all talk. We have a game plan, nothing concrete. I'm not ready."

"Now's the time, business is booming in Detroit, especially culinary," Lucas said, echoing something Tim had told Will probably a million times.

*Don't I know it, but I'm done taking advantage of people. Especially my brother.*

"Yeah. Soon. I hope." Will glanced at his possible business partner. "I better before he finds someone else."

A part of him wished his friend would, then if everything fell apart Will wouldn't have the added guilt of fucking with Tim's life too.

"If you weren't such an awesome cook and managed the staff like a magician at Summer Grill, I would've given up on you last year," Tim replied.

The Date must've been eavesdropping because he leaned toward Tim. "If you get tired of waiting around, my boyfriend is looking for a partner to open a Thai-fusion restaurant." His gaze shifted to Will. "Although I have heard him mention your restaurant and the menu. He was impressed."

The world shifted on its axis. Her date was gay and complimenting Will's cooking.

Hmm. He went from rival to friend in one sentence, even if he was poaching his business partner.

"Wait," Tim said, pointing toward Cindy. "You're not together?"

Cindy shook her head. "Saul is one of my best friends. Like me, he's a model. He's in town, visiting. I asked him to come with me." Her tone was matter-of-fact, but her cheeks were glowing.

Will had assumed Saul was a real date, and he suspected Cindy wanted it to seem that way. Why? To make him jealous or to make him think he didn't have a chance?

"You're gay?" Tim asked. *What the hell is his problem?*

Saul, no surprise, took Tim's question as an insult. "Don't worry. I won't try to molest you. Like I said, I have a boyfriend." He flicked a dismissive glance over Tim. "And you're not my type."

Tim held up his hands. "Sorry. That did sound rude. I don't give a shit you're gay. I'm confused. I thought you were *with* Cindy."

*So, it isn't just me.*

Earlier, Cindy and Saul were holding hands. Also, when the wedding party did the obligatory first dance alongside the bride and groom, Cindy, the Maid of Honor, had to dance with the Best Man, Will. Before the band finished the number, Saul cut in, like a possessive lover. Will had wanted to punch the guy.

He'd also seen them walking to the bar, arms around each other's waists. She'd rested her head on his shoulder while waiting for their drinks.

Her gaze caught his for half a second before turning back to her date, the red on her cheeks deepening. Will narrowed his eyes. She was trying to make him think she was with Saul.

"Though, I have to admit my ego is dying," Tim quipped.

"Your ego," Will echoed, confused and amused. "How does your lack of tact hurt your self-esteem? Oh, and Tim, if we do ever open a restaurant, let me do the talking. You stay in the back."

Tim laughed. "First, Cora shoots me down then Saul says I'm not his type." He tapped his heart. "It hurts, man."

Cora was here? He shouldn't be surprised; she was friends with Greta. In fact, without her help, he'd never have gotten the job at Summer Grill. Will looked for her distinctive red hair.

Saul asked, "Who's Cora?"

"Cora Moore," Tim replied. "She's a friend of the bride."

"I also used to work with Will," came a familiar sultry voice.

Will stood, offering Cora his seat. "She was my boss." *And lover.*

She shook her head. "No, thank you. I hired you, but you didn't work under me. Well..." Her smile twitched.

He cleared his throat, the collar of his shirt suddenly a little warm and tight. He glanced at Cindy. Her beautiful mouth was pressed in a thin line.

"My favorite song is playing," Cora continued, "care to dance with me, Will?"

"Sure," he lied, offering her his arm.

He wasn't positive if his imagination was playing tricks, but it felt as if someone's glare was burning a hole into his back all the way to the dance floor.

The curvy redhead pressed into Will more like a lover than boss and employee. Envy crawled along Cindy's skin. She wanted to cut in, to touch him in a way that marked him as hers.

She wasn't sure where this possessiveness came from; she usually lost interest in a man rather quickly. It didn't matter she'd dated men featured in business journals for their wealth and power or ones plastered on the cover of fashion magazines for their beautiful smiles and perfect bodies, she grew bored within weeks.

Her interest hadn't waned with Will.

When she'd first seen him on the expansive steps of the DIA, her breath caught, choking on her longing. His light brown suit jacket was draped over an arm, showing off his broad shoulders and the snug fit of the sage vest. The color set off his warm, chocolate eyes and had her wishing she could drown in their depths.

He looked delectable. She'd spent the wedding ceremony trying not to stare.

Afterward, when he was no longer distracted, the struggle to ignore him was damn near impossible. Sitting next to him at the wedding table was torture. His heavenly scent of warm spices and man had enticed her way more than the elaborate meal placed in front of her.

She made sure to talk to everyone but him, afraid if she did, he'd see how much she wanted him. A woman needed to hold onto some pride.

Nearly four weeks had passed. He'd never called or sent a text. She had to deal with reality. He wasn't interested in more with her. One weekend was enough.

Still, did his former boss have to molest him on the dance floor? Annoyance prickled under her skin.

The woman's hands drifted from his shoulders to under his jacket to rest on his lower back. By the next song, she'd be groping his damn butt.

"You okay?" Saul asked, making Cindy jump.

She turned from Will and his "boss" to face her friend. "I'm fine. Want to dance?"

The side of Saul's mouth twitched. "Why don't you ask the man you really want?" His gaze rested briefly on Will before returning to her.

*Am I that obvious?*

She raised her chin. "I don't know what you're talking about."

Saul laughed. The jerk. "Then why are you shooting daggers at the pretty redhead?" He placed a hand over hers, holding the flute glass. "The champagne is way too delicious for you to waste by shattering the glass in your angry grip."

She looked at her hand, her knuckles white. Loosening her hold, she said, "Okay. Fine. We had a night. And a morning. My pride is a little bruised at how easily he got over me. With most of my conquests, I contemplate changing my number so they'll leave me alone. He never called once." She studied her nails before muttering, "Whatever."

"Uh-huh. Is he the reason you kept checking your phone when we were working in Miami?"

She glared at her friend, embarrassment coursing through her blood.

His teasing smile softened. "Oh, honey, he's not over you."

Her gaze shifted to the dance floor. Boss's hands were no longer inches from Will's lovely ass. One was back on his shoulder, the other clasped in his. However, there was barely a sliver of space between them, and her smile oozed seduction. "Saul, I love you, but are you blind?"

"Don't look at her. Focus on him. His back is ramrod straight as if trying to find distance. See his hands, the one not holding hers? It's stiff. Like he's dancing with his mom or cousin. Go dance with him. You'll understand the difference."

She studied them more closely. Okay. He did seem rigid. Though, it probably had nothing to do with his dance partner. It was more he hated parties.

"And," Saul continued, "the way you're watching her, with murder in your pretty eyes, is the way he was looking at me earlier. Before he learned you and I are only friends."

Now that caught her attention. She was about to ask him to elaborate when the redhead rose on her toes, whispering something in Will's ear. While also sliding a hand down his torso, hooking a finger inside the waist of his slacks.

*Oh. Hell. No.*

Cindy stood.

Saul slapped her lightly on her butt. "Go get him, Tiger."

She twisted around, running a hand through his hair because he hated when she did it. He swatted it away. "Stop. Don't mess with perfection."

Smiling, she headed for the dance floor. As her steps brought her closer to Will, her pulse thrummed, her heart pounded faster than the music.

Setting herself up for rejection was something new.

# Chapter Thirteen

"Mind if I cut in?"

Will tried to hide his shock. Cindy had ignored him all day, now she wanted to dance. With him.

What the hell?

Cora's lips tightened as if she was going to object. She was already annoyed. Right before Cindy's arrival, Cora asked if he wanted to spend the night with her. He'd declined, saying he needed to get up early to take Jacob and Greta to the airport.

It was a shit excuse. They had plenty of late nights together at work and in each other's beds to know he was fine on a couple hours of sleep.

He wasn't sure why he turned Cora down.

*Liar.*

Letting go of Cora to dance with Cindy, he knew damn well why he'd refused. He couldn't sleep with one woman while wanting another.

"Let me know if you change your mind." In an unexpected territorial move, Cora kissed his lips lightly before leaving.

Frost dripped from Cindy's gaze, yet she took one of his hands. He rested the other on her waist. She felt right in his arms, even if it was so wrong.

She squeezed his hand. Hard. "Your boss? Really?"

"Your point?"

He sounded mulish but didn't care. He'd endured weeks of silence and today's indifference. She had no right to question him.

Her blue eyes were ice. "I don't have one, I'm just wondering why you didn't bring her as your date."

"We aren't dating."

"Only fucking," she jeered.

That was the first time she'd dropped the f-bomb. Combined with her venom, he was surprised enough to answer honestly. "We haven't been together in months."

She huffed. "I'm sure if you'd invited her, she'd have put out."

Her spite was uncalled for. Cora was a good woman. True, their relationship had been purely physical, but it was what they'd both wanted. She didn't deserve scorn any more than him.

Will leaned back to study Cindy. She wore a haughty expression, one that reminded him of her mom. It drove him crazy, and not in a good way. He wanted to wipe it from her face.

"What makes you so sure we don't have plans after the wedding?"

The color drained from her face, making him regret the shitty jibe.

"You are such an asshole," she spat, stalking off the dance floor.

"Cindy! Wait!"

Damn, how could a woman move so fast in sky-high heels? He chased after her as a fast song started. All the weaving around everyone slowed him.

Jacob was watching, his brows furrowed, but Will didn't have time to worry about his brother. Cindy was exiting the reception room.

By the time he reached the inner courtyard with the Industry murals, she was through the iron archways and down the stairs, almost to the doors. He called to her again, and again she ignored him.

He followed her, flinging open the door. She was gone.

Then her voice floated from the shadows. "What do you want?"

He jerked in surprise. She was leaning against the building, nearly hidden in the dark. "Why did you take off?"

"Because." She sighed, sounding miserable. "I don't want to hear about, nor picture, you spending the night with another woman."

Confusion and hope played tug-a-war with him. "I don't understand you. You haven't contacted me once since the lake house—"

"Neither did you."

He nodded, coming closer. "I thought you didn't want me to."

"That's the same reason I didn't call you.

Will smiled, hope gaining the upper hand over confusion. "Today, you barely deigned to look at me."

She raised her hands, then let them fall to her sides. "It made me want things I couldn't have. Remember? You don't do relationships and didn't seem interested in continuing with our weekend fling."

"Didn't you tell me the same thing?" he asked. "You said you didn't want more than a night. Hell, at your condo I was introduced as 'the brother.'"

"I didn't know what to call you. You aren't my boyfriend." She quirked a saucy smile. "Should I have introduced you as my boytoy?"

He snorted in a lungful of laughter. "It sure would have been better than the lame-ass introduction I was given." He rested an unsure hand on her hip. "What am I to you?"

Her beautiful cornflower blue eyes studied him, apprehension flashing through them. When she spoke, her voice quivered. "I don't know, Will. The only thing I'm sure of is one weekend wasn't enough."

He suspected all the time in the world wouldn't suffice for him. For that reason alone, he should walk back inside.

Instead, he gripped the hand resting on her hip tighter, getting rid of more space between them. "I agree, but I don't know what to do. I don't want to cause trouble between Jacob and Greta. Or your family."

"I don't want your hand in marriage," Cindy joked. "Just more time with you. We are attracted to each other. Let's enjoy the flame until it burns out."

His conscience screamed, no, his mouth said, "Okay."

That one word carried so much weight, because for the first time in years he wanted more than sex and easy conversation with a woman. He brought her against him.

They'd be fine because she didn't want more, only his body. Never would. She had everything going for her while he offered nothing except a mountain of mistakes and an uncertain future.

Her soft lips met his. He hesitated for half a second, then kissed her back with everything he had, quieting his worries.

He held her tight. Letting his body understand she was back.

She seemed to need the same. Her hands clutched his sides before sliding up his back. Her heat and vanilla scent had him wishing they were all the way in the shadows. Or better yet, at his house, in his bed.

Someone cleared their throat. Loudly. Reminding him they were in public, making out.

He kissed her lightly before glancing at their intruder.

*Shit.* Of all the people to wander outside, it had to be Greta.

She studied them, but Will couldn't get a read on her. Couldn't tell if she was upset, happy, or indifferent.

"So. Yeah. It's nice to see you are now getting along. Um, we're getting ready to toss the bouquet and garter. The Best Man and Maid of Honor should be there." She started for the door, then stopped. Facing Cindy, she said, "Will you meet me in the ladies' room?"

Will's stomach plummeted. Greta was going to tell Cindy to drop him.

Sure, Greta liked him as a friend, maybe even a brother-in-law, but not the man for her little sister.

She knew his past. What happened to those he dated.

"Greta—"

She cut him off. "Jacob is waiting for you. Will you let him know we stopped to freshen up?"

He glanced at Cindy. She nodded. "I'm fine. Go ahead."

What could he do? He went inside to find his brother.

As soon as the restroom door shut, Greta dug in. "What are you playing at, Cindy? Does Will have to be one of your conquests? Your throwaways?"

*Ouch.*

"What the hell, Greta! I've had boyfriends."

"You have guys you date or who accompany you to events. Have any of them meant a thing to you? Will is a good guy. He's had some rough years. He needs more than what you're willing to give."

"One," Cindy bristled, anger and indignation beginning to boil, "you have no idea what I'm willing to give. Two—"

"I get it." Greta rolled her eyes. "You enjoy men, have fun with them, but Will isn't like the guys you normally go after. He's serious. What if he wants more?"

"He doesn't. He has been very clear on that point."

Her sister crossed her arms, her body language screaming she didn't believe a word Cindy said.

"We hooked up at the lake house." She held her hand in a stop motion when her sister started to open her mouth. "He told me he didn't do relationships."

"Bull," Greta cut in. "He was with Jolene for something like five years. He was probably telling you what you wanted to hear."

Cindy paused, then waved aside the revelation. She'd delve into that later. "Listen. Stop interrupting." She waited for some sign her sister was ready to listen.

Greta made a zipping motion with her hand along her mouth.

"We'd agreed on one weekend. The problem is, it isn't enough. We want to see more of each other but keep it casual. *And* you weren't there. I was. I'm telling you he isn't feeding me a line of bullshit. He doesn't want a girlfriend."

She wasn't sure if it was her as a girlfriend, or if something that had happened with this Jolene that made him loathe commitment in general. It didn't matter. She didn't have time or patience for a boyfriend.

"Will wants se—"

"Stop." Greta shook her head. "My sister and my brother-in-law. I don't need to hear the end of your sentence."

Cindy laughed. "Okay." She decided to bare a sliver of her soul to her sister. "Listen, I like him. Sure, he's prickly, serious, but being around him... It's nice. He's my opposite yet seems to understand me. I get it's odd. He's your brother-in-law, and he'll always be around. However, we're adults. When it is over, I won't let things get weird. I promise."

There. That was it, and most was true. The part about not feeling much might be a small lie. She pushed it aside, waiting for her sister's response.

She hoped Greta would accept the situation. Although, honestly, it didn't matter. This was between her and Will. No one else.

As if reading her thoughts, Greta threw her hands up, clearly exasperated. "Like it matters what I think." Her expression softened. "Hell, maybe you two will be good for each other."

Her admission surprised Cindy. "What makes you say that?"

"Will could use a little of your laughter and free spirit. You could use some of his calm, his perseverance."

Okay, she hadn't needed her sister's acceptance but couldn't deny it was nice. "Thanks," she whispered.

Greta opened her arms. Cindy walked into them, hugging her. "Love you, sis. Please don't break Will."

"I make no promises." Cindy laughed, wondering if it would be the other way around. Stepping back, she said, "All right, we better get back before people start to wonder if the bride took off."

Opening the door, Greta said, "Plus, it's time for the bouquet toss. You better be out there." She wiggled her eyebrows. "Will might catch the garter."

"Uh. No thanks. Did you hear the part about neither of us wanting anything serious?"

Greta's smile widened. "Yeah, well, neither did I or Jacob."

Cindy scoffed. Although, deep down she admitted to herself, the idea wasn't appalling. Maybe even nice.

She shook her head, following her sister, wondering what the hell was wrong with her. Men were too much work, and Will seemed to be holding on to some heavy baggage.

Seconds after returning to the reception, an announcement was made for the single women to gather on the dance floor. Cindy stood in the back, not eager to catch the flowers or get in the crosshairs of Kimberly, her stepfather's sister. She was newly divorced and on the prowl for husband number four. Heaven help anyone who got between her and Greta's bouquet. More than nails would end up broken.

So, of course, when the flowers were tossed, they hit Cindy squarely in the chest. She instinctively grabbed them. For half a second, she was certain Kimberly was going to tackle her. Cindy scowled, and the other woman seemed to change her mind.

Good thing too, because Will caught the garter.

He placed it rather high on her thigh. Thankfully, the sounds of wolf whistles and clapping covered her gasp when his fingertips brushed across her panties.

As he helped her stand, she saw Greta leaning into her husband, whispering. His eyes widened. He looked at his brother, then Cindy. Catching her watching, he smirked.

Yup, he was going to tease her, and in truth, she deserved it.

Back when Greta started dating Jacob, Cindy had told her sister he was only for fun, not long term. She believed his background was all wrong for someone like Greta. In the end, she was the one wrong. However, even after accepting the relationship, Cindy loved to tease Jacob about his working-class ways.

She shrugged, willing to take his taunts if it meant he was okay with her seeing his brother. His smile told her he was fine with it.

# Chapter Fourteen

The evening flew by as if time had a fast-forward button. Cindy loved the ending way more than the beginning. Not the wedding party. That was perfect from beginning to end. It was more her state of mind. At the start, she'd ached and dreaded seeing Will.

When she had, her longing for him was so deep, it hurt. However, with it ending with his lips on hers, his smile directed at her was bliss.

Not that they'd done much kissing. They'd kept the PDA to a bare minimum, not ready to have everyone know their business. Especially since they could not even define it. Were they a couple, dating, or just sleeping together?

Best not to overthink it, and without discussing it, they decided to keep it friendly in public. However, when he'd put the garter high on her leg and lingered a beat too long, some of the guests might have guessed.

Now the hour was late, and she was tired of holding back. Yet, here they were still at the wedding party. Being the Maid of Honor and Best Man, they'd felt obligated to stay until the end. However, if people didn't get their butts moving quicker, she was going to start shoving them out the damn door.

Stepping from the reception to a deserted hallway, Cindy pressed a palm against the cold stone wall and breathed in deeply, trying to relieve her aggravation. As if her longing called out to him, Will's hands slid around her waist from behind. She leaned against his firm, comforting body. Resting her head on his shoulder, she sighed. She fit perfectly.

"Come home with me," he said.

"Remember, Jacob got everyone in the wedding party rooms at that old mansion? The one converted into a hotel? Stay with me. Mine's closer. Oh, didn't you say you were taking them to the airport?" She felt him nod. "You won't have to get up as early to get them since we'll be at the same place."

"Closer works for me." He nipped her neck, sending shivers everywhere. "It means I'll have you naked and underneath me sooner.

She twisted around, resting her hands on his chest. "You are mighty sure of yourself. What makes you think I'll be under you? Checking in my room this afternoon, I saw the four-poster bed. I'd pictured you on it. Spread out and tied up." Heat flared in his eyes, touching her everywhere, compelling her to continue. "Your tie for one wrist, belt for the other. What should we use for your ankles?"

He opened his mouth to answer. Before he could, Jacob stopped next to them, already talking. "This is weird. You know that, right?"

"Why?" Cindy asked, holding tight when Will tried to break their embrace.

"Besides the fact I thought you guys couldn't stand each other?"

Will shrugged. "People change."

"I guess, but what could you two have in common?" Jacob asked, and when Cindy smirked, he held up his hands. "Never mind. Don't answer. Anyway, I came looking for you because your *lovely* mom is asking after you."

Cindy groaned, leaving Will's arms. Mother had certain criteria for the men she wanted her daughters to date. The Grimm brothers did not meet her standards. Usually, Cindy didn't worry herself with Mother's skewed view. However, Mother was on edge, struggling to accept Jacob. Seeing her only other daughter with his brother, well, she might freak.

She wouldn't cause a scene here, but Cindy was willing to bet all she owned Mother would arrive at her hotel room in full rage mode. That'd put a damper on the night's plans.

It'd also make having Will tied up and naked a tad awkward.

"I better go deal with her. Will you give me ten minutes?" she asked.

Will nodded and thankfully did not offer to join her.

She was back in five, taking Will's hand. He led her from the DIA to his car. Once there, he opened the passenger door for her. Before getting in, she kissed him on the cheek then on the lips.

He gripped the back of her neck, keeping her close. She didn't mind one bit and deepened the kiss. He tasted fantastic, like peppermint and dreams.

Tires squeaked as a car came around the corner of the parking lot. They stepped apart, and Cindy slid into her seat. Will closed her door, coming around to the driver's side. Before getting in, he took off his suit jacket, hanging it on his seat.

"The wedding group planned on meeting in the lobby for drinks," she said. "Most of them left about an hour ago. I wonder if they'll still be there."

"Why? Do you want to visit with them, or is it more you don't want to be seen walking in with me?" he asked, not sounding upset.

His question and the delivery of it surprised her. She wasn't ashamed to be seen with him, why would he think such a thing? Also, why didn't the possibility piss him off? He asked it like it was a reasonable question.

"We agreed to be discreet tonight, so it wouldn't take away from Greta and Jacob's night. You know people will gossip and tease." She faced him. "Do you think *I'm* embarrassed to have people know we're dating?"

He shrugged, and it fractured a piece of her heart. "I'm not the business tycoons and models you date. Your mom hates me even more than Jacob. Have you forgotten all the shit she put them through? Why would you want to deal with her games if we aren't even in this for the long term?"

She shook her head, even though it bothered her the way he had them over before things barely started. She was also confused. How did her mother know of Will's past, while she knew nothing? "My mom hates you? How does she even know you?"

"That night she had Jacob arrested, I ran into her at the police station. Let's just say it wasn't a pleasant introduction."

Huh. Interesting.

She wanted to ask him or Greta about that crazy night, but resisted. Right now wasn't the time. There wasn't room in the car for her mother.

She rested a hand on his arm as he put the key in the ignition. "Good thing you're dating me, and not Mother." Will's eyes widened like the thought was terrifying. Cindy couldn't help laughing. "Listen, I don't know much of your past. Greta has always been protective of you, never saying much. But I know this, you aren't your past. And I like the man you are now."

He offered a flash smile. His lips barely twitched, let alone reach his eyes.

Fine. She switched tactics, willing to try anything to chase away his ghosts. "Okay, let's set that aside for now. Let me answer your first question. No, I don't want to visit with our friends. I want you. In my bed. Possibly tied up, definitely at my mercy."

Finally, his smile became genuine. Letting go of the steering wheel, he took her hand, entwining their fingers. "I'm beginning to think you have a kink with the rope. But, honey, even without the ropes, I'm at your mercy."

Damn. He had a way with words.

He nipped on two fingers before letting go to shift the car in reverse. The touch of his teeth, the heat of his words, reached her everywhere.

Thankfully, the place Jacob booked was a block over. They were parking out front in less than five minutes. Their steps from the sidewalk to the large, wraparound porch and through the front door were quick, both eager to be alone.

The woman at the front desk smiled at them, wishing them a pleasant night as they passed. They waved, as Cindy tried not to run.

*Oh, it would be.*

She led him up the stairs, to the end of the hallway. When she removed an old-fashioned key from her evening bag and slid it in the lock, Will ran his nose and lips along the back of her neck. Her skin pebbled in anticipation of what was to come.

As the lock clicked, he tugged the thin zipper hidden at the back of her dress. By the time they were in the room, he had it at the dip at the base of her spine. She set the key and her purse on a table next to the door. The flick of a nearby switch lit a lamp next to the bed, filling the room with a soft glow. She turned, needing to see him.

He brought his hands to her shoulders, brushing the thin straps aside. The dress fell, pooling at her feet.

"Damn," he whispered, cupping the side of her face.

His mouth crashed against her with a groan of satisfaction. It set her growing desire on fire.

He walked her backward until the backs of her legs hit the bed. She tumbled onto it, taking him with her. He let go, bracketing his arms at the side of her body, as if not wanting to crush her with his weight.

She wanted it. To be engulfed by him. His scent, his taste, his weight. All of it.

Gripping his shirt at the waist, she tugged. "Take it off."

He stood, working the buttons of first his vest, then his shirt. In his impatience, he popped off the top two. The tiny metal disks clinked and rolled when they hit the wood floors. Tossing the shirt on a nearby chair, he started on his belt buckle, moving to her with a predatory gleam in his eyes.

It warmed her in all the right places.

"I wanted to take this slow. I have you sprawled on the bed before me, like I've fantasized nearly every night these last weeks. My plan was to savor every inch of you. Instead, I'm going to feast on you like the starving man I am."

She unsnapped her strapless bra, throwing it aside. Leaning back, she crossed her legs at the ankles. In only her cream high-heels and barely-there lace panties, she smiled. "If you think you can handle me, then please, indulge. Devour me."

He cursed under his breath as he shucked out of his remaining clothes. Standing before her in all his naked glory, he was exquisite.

Gripping her ankles, he uncrossed them, drawing her to the edge of the bed. Then he stilled

Hungry for him, she took over, grabbing his waist and taking his erection into her greedy mouth. A groan filled with carnal need tumbled from him, feeding her lust. She yearned to hear it again. She took him deeper, finding a rhythm that had him digging his fingers into her hair and pulling, telling her his control was slipping. She wanted to make it crumble.

Before she could, he grated her name and stepped away. "I might not be able to take it slow. This time. But I want to be buried inside you, watching you flood with pleasure as we come apart. Together."

She rose, her heels clicking on the hardwood floors as she made her way to the table with her purse. Getting a condom, she asked. "Want me to put it on?"

"Hell yes." He shook his head. "Wait. Better not. I'm so fucking worked up right now. I'll do it. Instead, get your sweet ass out of those panties."

"What about the heels?" She bent, taking off her silk bottoms.

"Leave them on. It makes you the perfect height." He stood directly behind her, palming her ass. "Go to the dresser. Bend and hold on to it."

She did as he demanded. His tone made heat and desire, pulsate through her, pooling at her core.

He ran his erection between her legs, not giving her what she craved, teasing her. "Bend over. Hold on."

"Will, please…"

"Please, what?"

"No playing. Not now. I need you here with me. In me."

"Always, for as long as you'll have me." He thrust deep and hard.

She whimpered from the soul-shattering pleasure of him. However, instead of taking what they both wanted, he stilled.

"What?" Her voice came out husky, breathless

She twisted slightly to look at him. For some reason, worry tugged tight at the corners of his gorgeous mouth.

"Are you okay? Am I hurting you?" he asked. "We can move to the bed."

Her heart melted at his concern.

"I am more than fine. Right now I want to touch heaven." She slid along his length. "Will you take me there?"

His hands dug deeper into her waist, and buried himself in her. She moaned, pushing back. It was all the encouragement he needed. Her palms pressed into the dresser at the force he drove into her. She loved it, her pleasure coiling, tight at the base of her spine. He reached around, leaning into her, his skin slick from his exertions. He cupped her breast briefly, tweaking each nipple before skimming a hand down her body, between her legs. The sure circular motion of his finger mixed with his heady rhythm sent her over the edge. If his other arm wasn't around her and his legs strong, she'd have taken them both to the floor.

Her body shook and pulsated around him, taking him even tighter. From the way his breath became more erratic, he was close to his release. So, it surprised her when he broke their connection.

"Why—"

"Turn around."

As she did, he grasped her waist, setting her on the dresser. "Scoot forward, put your legs around me."

Again, no argument from her. He slid back inside her, kissing her mouth hard. She'd feel the press of his lips well after the sun rose.

"What am I going to do with you?" he whispered, taking her in a way that was far from gentle. The motion was perfect. "I want you all the time. In and out of bed."

"And I, you." She leaned against the mirror digging her heels into his backside, her fingers raking his biceps, spurring him on, loving the way his arms shook the closer he edged toward his release. "Let's enjoy each other. We'll worry about where this is headed, later."

The heat, longing, and lust in his gaze squeezed at her heart. She wrapped her hands behind his neck, bringing his mouth back to her lips.

The taste of them, along with the slight shift of his hips, had her second orgasm building at lightning speed.

"Oh, Will, I'm going—" A wave of pleasure engulfed her making words impossible.

This time, his climax chased hers. The room filled with the sounds of their bliss and satisfaction.

Afterward, they stayed entangled on the dresser until their breathing returned to normal. Then he told her to hold tight, clasped her bottom, moving them to the bed. Once there, she let go, falling back on to the soft mattress.

It was much more comfortable than a wooden dresser, made even sweeter when he crawled into bed. Happiness warmed her. Unlike at the lake house, this time he'd spend the whole night with her.

The contentment blanketing her at having Will back in her arms and bed scared her. She already liked him way too much. Needing, or worse, trusting him, terrified her. He'd see her weaknesses.

Keeping her fragility hidden from everyone was a must. She learned at a young age, with her mother, sharing meant exposing her heart for others to hurt. No way.

If he stayed around long enough, her imperfections would show. Her weak and jealous side would make an appearance. What if he found her shallow and empty-headed as many believed? It didn't hurt her when acquaintances said such stuff. However, if Will did, it'd cut like a knife.

What they had was new, yet he had her respect along with a small piece of her heart.

All this frightened her, but also filled her with a weird mixture of delight and trepidation. She slid an arm under him and rested the other on his hip. He scooted closer, kissing her with tenderness instead of lust.

"Do you want to come with me when I take Jacob and Greta to the airport?" he asked.

Cindy nodded, cuddling into Will's chest. They drifted off to sleep talking of the next day and unimportant matters, like a real couple. She'd never had this sort of thing. With him, it was nice. More than nice. Perfect.

# Chapter Fifteen

Leaning against his car, Will waved to Jacob and Greta as they stepped through the automatic doors of the airport. Cindy was standing next to him, doing the same. He twisted to face her, asking, "Do you want me to drive you to Greta's to get your car? Or you want to come back to my place?"

*Please pick the last option.*

She started for her side of the car, running her fingers along the hood. "Hmm. I have to leave on Tuesday for Miami. For work. I'm home for one day before heading to London."

His good mood slipped a little. She was the jet-setting model. Of course, she had more important things to do than hang out with him all day. Opening his door, he slid in, then started the car.

She rested a hand on his thigh and squeezed. "Do you mind if we get my car later? We could go to your place now. Emma is home, and since I'll be gone for a while, I'd love to have time alone with you. No one else."

Damn, his mood shifted so fast it made him light-headed. He leaned in, kissing her. "I'd like that a lot. I'll make you breakfast, if you don't mind a quick stop at the grocery store."

"Having Chef Grimm cooking for me sounds perfect."

He put the car in drive heading toward the departure ramp toward I-94. "Don't expect much. I'm starving. Think along the lines of fast and filling. At this point, I'd almost be happy with a bowl of cereal."

Hell, he was hungry enough to eat a freaking bear. Not only did the newlyweds have an early flight, what little time he'd set aside to get ready and find breakfast, was spent fooling around in bed with Cindy. Every part of his body except his stomach agreed the time was well spent.

Traffic was light since it was early Sunday morning and they made it to the grocery store a block from his apartment in less than a half hour. They were out of the store in even less time.

On impulse, Will made a right on John R Street. "Want to see the place I want to rent some day?"

Cindy's brows drew together. "Are you moving?"

"No. I'd love to open a restaurant." He shrugged, somewhat embarrassed his pocket-sized dream was so big to him. "Nothing extreme. At least not at first. Tim and I were thinking a small lunch bistro. Something simple, but tasty."

"Is that what you were talking about last night?"

Will nodded, oddly nervous. Her opinion meant too much, more than it should.

"Yes! Show me." Her excitement warmed the cold edges of his heart.

He parked his car in a free spot on the street, right in front of a quaint corner shop sporting a lease sign in its massive window. Through it a sturdy wooden bar could be seen, running the expanse of the shop. He loved it. It would allow customers to enjoy the view of the bustling street while eating lunch.

"It seems you two have given it some thought. What's holding you back?"

*Me. My past, and all my many, stupid mistakes.*

"I owe Jacob some money. When I pay him back, I'll consider the restaurant." The idea of leaving his comfortable job with good pay made his stomach hurt, but some risks are worth sleepless nights and stress. Or so he's been told.

"That's shitty of Jacob."

He peered at Cindy, confused. "What? Why?"

She folded her arms over her chest. "He doesn't seem hard up for money, yet he's making you pay him back before you move forward with your business."

"Oh, he isn't making me. I'd made the decision. I'm already a shit for having my little brother literally pay for my mistakes."

"There is nothing wrong with leaning on people from time to time."

"Yes. However, there was a difference between accepting help and using someone as a crutch."

"How?"

It was too soon for this conversation. They were keeping things between them light, so there was no reason to dive into his ugly past.

Sure, he was being a pussy. He should lay out his mistakes, but damn, he didn't want her to leave.

And she would.

He pulled back onto the street, away from his dream. He needed distance from his yearnings and mistakes.

"Tell me, when have you ever needed help?" He hoped to move the questions away from his past.

"Seriously?" she scoffed. "I wouldn't be anywhere without my mom. It was her networking that got me my first modeling job. She also co-signed for my condo. Paid for these." From the side of his vision, he saw Cindy grab her chest.

*Wow. Really?*

"Your boobs aren't real?"

"Nope. My mother knows the best surgeons."

"She supported you getting an unnecessary surgery? Why?" He tried to keep the judgment out of his voice, but what mom told her daughter she wasn't born perfect?

"Support it? She suggested, hell, insisted. Said my chest was too small, the size wasn't symmetrical with the rest of my body and it'd make it difficult for me to get modeling jobs."

Stopping at the last light before his apartment, he turned to Cindy. "How old were you?"

"Sixteen. Right before I started modeling."

Sixteen? What the fuck. She was a freaking kid, her body growing, maturing.

"Don't look at me like that. My boobs are perfect. It's not like I went porn star big."

She thought his problem was with her size and not with a parent pressuring her young daughter to fit some mold of what society believes is perfect. As if he gave two shits about her bra size.

He faced the road when the light changed. "I didn't say they aren't nice, but there isn't anything wrong with small breasts."

"You seem to enjoy what I have."

His cheeks warmed. "Well, yes. Though, believe me, I'd adore them no matter the size."

"Whatever. Guys like big boobs, butt, and small waist. It is the ideal."

Her flippant comment depressed him. Have all the guys she dated only see her surface sheen, missing the beauty underneath? Her sarcastic wit, the devilish spark in her. The way she took on the world, did as she pleased. That was what made her sexy.

Wanting her full attention, he didn't answer until parked at his apartment. Removing the key from the ignition, he twisted to face her. "Your looks are secondary to me. What I find attractive is your boldness, humor, zest for life."

She rolled her eyes. "Please, I'm a sure bet. You're going to get lucky this morning. The flattery is unnecessary."

Stubborn, blind woman. "Listen, lady. I didn't find you all that pretty until I'd dunked you the lake and you had snot running down your face."

"Stop." She laugh-shouted, holding up a hand. "We don't speak of that."

He hooked two fingers around her wrist, bringing her palm to his lips. "There is no denying your body is hot-as-fuck, but what turns me on is your smart mouth, your feistiness."

She peeked open one eye. "You're a strange man."

"This is true. Now come on, let's get you inside. I promised you breakfast." Before letting go of her hand, he lightly bit the tips of her fingers, knowing she liked it. "And you mentioned something about you being a sure thing…"

Cindy reached for Will's hand that wasn't holding the bag of groceries. While they rode the elevator to his top floor apartment, her mind replayed their recent conversation. What he said made tears gather behind her lashes.

It never bothered her when people noticed, or that men loved her looks. She'd always taken good care of herself. Exercise and shopping were damn near her religion. Hell, it was her bread and butter. It paid her bills. Most importantly, it allowed her to travel. Exploring was right up there with writing, photography, and great sex.

Yet, Will noticing beyond her polished surface and liking what was there filled her with the warm fuzzies. Leaning on tip-toes, she kissed his cheek as the elevator door opened.

Lifting their clasped hands, he kissed hers before releasing it and stepping into the hallway. His apartment was at the farthest end.

Unlocking the door, he asked, "What do you want in your omelet?"

"Whatever you're having," she said, more interested in checking out his apartment.

His place had an open floor plan. From the front door, the kitchen was to her right. Straight ahead was the living room.

It was obvious what he cared about was the kitchen. Everything there was top of the line and pristine. Meanwhile, the living room couch and chair were clean but definitely not high-end. Nothing hung on the walls, not even a TV.

A sliding door on the opposite wall from her snagged her attention. He didn't have blinds or curtains. Outside, on his balcony, was a wall of green. Plants grew everywhere. Pots spilling with vegetables lined the ground and vines grew up the two walls.

She walked toward it, asking if he minded her wandering around. With his head practically buried in the fridge, he told her she was welcome to go wherever she wanted.

The natural snoop in her wanted to make a quick left into an open door just past the kitchen. She'd spied a messily made bed and a nightstand with a lamp. She was bound to learn something interesting in there.

She didn't stop. Partly because the whispered conversations between Greta and Jacob regarding Will made Cindy hesitate to know too much, but mainly because his balcony looked like a freaking garden oasis.

Pulling open the door, she was met with the most enticing scents. Almost every inch of the small area spilled with herbs and vegetables. Pots everywhere, overflowing with parsley, cilantro, onions, and many more she couldn't name. Two trellises were on both sides of the balcony, offering privacy and food. Along the balcony's floor, vines crawled with maybe watermelon or cantaloupes.

Leaning into a huge container, she buried her face in green leaves and inhaled deeply. Yup, mint.

She squeaked, almost falling face first in the plant when hands were suddenly on her bottom. Thankfully, he grabbed her waist before she tumbled.

After righting herself, she twisted around, swatting his chest. "You nearly gave me a heart attack and a face full of dirt. I go from peaceful Zen to horror-movie racing heart in less than two seconds."

He nuzzled her neck. "Sorry. I needed to get stuff for the omelets but was gifted with the sight of you bent over. I couldn't resist."

The mention of food made her stomach growl, begging.

Stepping away, he patted her belly. "Wow. I better feed you."

She nodded. There was no sense denying it. She was starving.

He plucked a couple of tomatoes from the vine, handing them to her. Then pulling a pair of scissors from his back pocket, he snipped some tall pointy herb that smelled like onions. "Come on," he said.

Following him back inside, they made their way to his kitchen. She sat in one of comfy, black leather chairs at the small, round wooden table. Every inch of open space was covered with delicious smelling food: bacon, a big bowl of fruit, coffee, and purple berry smoothies.

"Wow. I want to say you went overboard, though at this point, I could probably eat it all."

"Dig in," he said, from the stove. "I'm nearly finished with the eggs."

She took a sip of coffee, closing her eyes in pleasure, letting the flavor dance across her tongue. It was even better than the cups she'd drunk in Italy. "This is amazing. Why does it taste like it is from my favorite coffeehouse?"

"I get the coffee from a local coffee shop. They have the best selection and roast their beans throughout the day." He pointed to a large machine on the granite counter. "Plus, that grinds each cup. Makes a huge difference."

"I'll say. If breakfast is half as good as this, you're in trouble."

He walked to the table, carrying two plates. "Oh, why is that?"

"Because I'm never going to leave. I'll lie here eating until I'm eight hundred pounds."

He shrugged one broad shoulder. "That much weight might make you uncomfortable, but I'm cool with it. You could be my taste-tester. Help me select Summer Grill's fall menu."

"Or one for *your* restaurant."

He looked away, clearly saying he didn't want to pick back up the topic. Fine. She'd let it go. For now.

Taking a bite of her omelet, she moaned, sounding a tad orgasmic. It fit because the taste was like phenomenal sex to her taste buds. "That's it, Will. I'm moving in. You were holding back at the lake house."

He chuckled, after swallowing his bite of food said, "Yeah, well, I didn't have my balcony garden. Fresh herbs and veggies take any meal up a notch."

They ate in companionable silence. Cindy couldn't bother with conversation as she was having a deep love affair with breakfast. After she polished off her eggs, bacon, and was peeling an orange, she found her words again. "I wish I didn't have to go back to work on Tuesday."

She wanted to spend days, hell weeks or months in bed, with Will, only leaving it to shower and eat.

"Yeah, your job does get in the way of you moving in here to gain a thousand pounds."

"Hey!" She threw an orange slice at him. "I said eight hundred pounds."

He somehow managed to catch the fruit and popped it in his mouth. "Thanks."

"What are your plans for the week, while I'm gone?" she asked. "Besides pining for me."

He snorted. "Hmm. I guess between my lonely crying fits I'll work. The summer months are crazy. I damn near live at the restaurant." He shrugged. "With the few days I do have off, I don't know. Usually, I'll run, play some pickup basketball, go to a meeting or two."

The last one caught her attention. "Meetings? For what?"

He sighed deeply. She guessed he hadn't meant to say the last part.

"NA. Narcotics Anonymous."

Her heart dropped, her breakfast turning to lead. "You're an addict?"

"Greta never mentioned any of this to you?"

Not the answer Cindy wanted. "No. She said you had some issues in your past, but it wasn't her story to tell." She was surprised at how steady her voice sounded.

*She could've told me after finding out I'd hooked up with him.*

"Issues," he muttered, shaking his head. Crossing his arms across his chest, he said, "I haven't used in over five years."

Her distress halted. "Wait. You haven't used drugs in more than five years?"

He nodded.

She was confused. "Then why do you call yourself an addict? Also, so much time has passed, why do you still go to meetings?"

He leaned forward, resting his elbows on the table, placing his chin on his hands. A mixture of pride and despair seemed to swirl around him. "Think of addiction like cancer. I'm in remission, with the chance it could come back at any time. The NA meetings are my check-up appointments. Going to them helps clear away dangerous thoughts trying to burrow into an addict's mind." He sat back, defeat in the slope of his shoulders. "Listen, I get if this is more than you signed up for. Do you want to end things?"

*What? No.*

Sure, his revelation scared her, but he was speaking of his past, not present. She came around to where he sat. "Push back your chair."

He did as she ordered, and she straddled him. "I'm not ready to go anywhere. Okay?"

"Okay," he whispered.

She ran a hand through his hair, gripping the back. "After that huge breakfast, I need to burn off some calories. Any suggestions?"

He ran his hands down her back, stopped at her ass, kneading it. "I have many suggestive suggestions."

# Chapter Sixteen

Standing on Jacob and Greta's porch, Will said, "You must be beat from the flight. It was, what, over ten hours? You sure you don't want me to make you guys breakfast or an early lunch?"

Jacob shook his head. "Thanks, but we're good. Dad dropped off some food. Greta and I are going to have cereal then crash. Get Cindy home. I think she's worse off than us."

Will looked inside the car. Cindy's eyes were closed. She was fast asleep. After Will picked her and the newlyweds up from the airport, she'd kept drifting in and out of sleep during the drive. He needed to get her home.

By a stroke of luck, Cindy arrived home from London twenty minutes after Jacob and Greta's flight from Iceland. After hugging her sister and brother-in-law, Cindy kissed Will with enough heat it made him wish he'd rented a room next to the airport. Greta had sarcastically suggested it.

However, once in the car, Cindy was asleep before they even left the airport. She needed sleep, not sex.

"Yeah, you're right. How about when you international travelers are over your jet lag we meet for dinner? I want to see your Iceland pictures."

Jacob chuckled. "Sure. That'd be great, if not a little weird."

"How so?"

"The last time the four of us met for dinner was back when we wanted to talk over the lake house idea with you two. You could barely tolerate Cindy."

Will snorted. She'd arrived almost an hour late and acted like a spoiled princess. Man, he'd pegged her wrong. Her cover was good. He suspected she used it to keep people from getting too close.

He understood the need all too well.

"I guess first impressions aren't everything." He slapped Jacob affectionately on the shoulder. "Good to have you back home. Call when you feel human again."

"Will do," Jacob said, clapping Will on the shoulder.

Returning to the car, he opened his door, trying not to make a sound. Not that he needed to worry. Even when he started the car, Cindy didn't stir. He figured being quiet wasn't necessary.

Tapping her address in the GPS, he was glad he'd had the foresight to ask Greta for it. He'd been there that one time, after the lake house, and hadn't been driving. He couldn't remember how to get there.

Listening to the radio on low, he drove to her condo. Since it was the middle of the week and past the morning rush hour, he made it to her place in Ann Arbor in less than an hour.

After parking his car, he leaned over the gear shift, running his thumb along her cheek. Her eyes fluttered open, and she stretched like a cat in the sun.

"You're home," he whispered.

She brought her seat to the full upright position. "Come inside," she said before kissing him.

When she tried to deepen it, he stood, and held out his hand to her. "Let's get you some food first. I don't want you passing out on me. Again."

"Sorry. With the different time zones, I didn't sleep until the last leg of the flight, and it was fitful."

"I'm kidding. I'll make you something quick then leave, letting you rest."

He didn't want to leave. He hadn't seen her in nearly two weeks, though they'd talked almost every night. It seemed their earlier agreement to keep things light and hook up when convenient was not happening. He cared for her and could tell she did as well.

It scared the shit out of him. The last person he loved ended horribly. He shoved aside thoughts of Jolene.

Tried to do the same for love because, hell, fondness and love were two different things. He'd make sure one didn't become the other. For him or Cindy.

"I won't refuse food. All I had today was a smoothie at the airport." Her gaze seemed to taste him. "I'm starving. Your arms are starting to look tasty."

He chuckled. "Good to know I'm more appetizing than airport food."

"Oh, you are more tempting than my favorite restaurant." She ran a hand up his inner thigh. "In fact, you're my favorite meal. My sweetest dessert."

He shifted, giving her more access while reaching for her. Kissing along her neck, he murmured, "Mmm. You do have a way with words."

She opened the door. "First, I need a shower. I smell like regurgitated airplane air and B.O." She offered a sexy smile over her shoulder, adding, "Not mine, of course, I am too much of a lady to sweat."

Will laughed, shaking his head. He went around the back to grab her luggage, after shutting the trunk, he came to her.

Nuzzling her neck, he said, "I bet in an hour I will have you sweating and saying some rather unladylike things."

The way she melted into him, her body knew the truth of his words, even as her lips issued a challenge. "We shall see."

Cindy started up the stairs to her condo. Once inside, she made a beeline for the shower.

"Where do you want your bags?" he called to her retreating back.

"Would you leave the big one there in the laundry room and bring the smaller one into my bedroom?"

Following the sound of her voice, he found her bedroom. He pushed the door the rest of the way open and heard the sounds of the shower from the master bathroom.

Her room wasn't what he'd expected. He'd pictured frills and fluff. Instead, he was met with muted green walls, a crisp cream bedspread on a simple, beautiful wooden bed frame. The only fussy adornment was a chandelier-ish light fixture. Some type of light blue fabric circled crystals giving it the appearance of falling raindrops or water. It was the perfect accent for the stunning photos hanging over her bed.

He knelt on the comforter to get a closer look. There were four, and the theme was reflection. One had a wineglass in the foreground with a vineyard mirrored in the wine. The background was muted and slightly blurred. To its right was a close up of a puddle on an old cobblestone road. Reflected in the water were the pillars of what might be a Roman or Greek ruin. The other middle photo was taken at some park where a bridge spanned a small river. A variety of trees dotted the bank. The focus was on their reflection in the early morning water. He recognized the last photo, The Bean in Chicago. It had some other formal name, but he couldn't remember it. Anyway, the way the photographer reflected the cityscape and sky off its metal surface was spectacular.

He could stare at these photos all day, dreaming of adventures abroad or down the street.

"Will?" she called from the shower.

"Yeah," he replied, reluctantly leaving the photos.

"Would you mind opening the suitcase you brought in here and bring me the small purple bag inside it? It has my favorite face cream."

He dropped her luggage by the door, walking in a daze to stare at the art over her bed. Shaking his head, he returned to her travel case. After finding what she needed, he made his way to the bathroom.

"Where did you get those photos?"

She stuck her head from around the shower curtain. "What are you talking about?"

"The pictures over your bed. Where did you find them?"

She looked at the tiled floor as if shy. "They're mine. I took them."

*Huh. Color me impressed.*

"Cindy, those are stunning."

Her gaze flew to his. "Really? Mother told me they were tacky. Said I should get real art for my walls."

Damn. The more he learned of Sophia, the less he liked her.

"By chance is your mom the type who judges art by its fame or price tag, instead of raw talent?"

Cindy giggled. "Maybe."

"I figured as much. Don't listen to her. Because, woman, you've got talent."

A lovely pink crept along her neck to her cheeks. Made him wonder if she was pink anywhere else. "Need help?"

She shook her head. "No. I'm about finished. I have a feeling if you get in here, we'll stay in until the water runs cold and I pass out from starvation."

Oh shit. "Yeah. Sorry. Does a sandwich work for you?"

She nodded, and he left the bathroom. Passing the open luggage, he paused. There was a leather notebook stuffed with photos. Wanting to see more of her work, he called out as the shower shut off, "Do you mind if I look at the sketchpad thing in your suitcase."

Her sigh was so heavy he was going to tell her to forget it. He didn't want to pry or make her uncomfortable, but before he could, she spoke. "Sure, if you promise to be gentle."

Gentle? Was the book old? He ran his thumb over the supple leather. It wasn't old.

Opening it, he found the pages covered with words. Some described the time and place of a photo inserted between the sheets. Others were poems and proses. She'd mentioned at the lake house she liked to write, but damn. Apparently, Cindy had as much of a talent for words as she did with the camera.

He sat on the edge of the bed, engrossed in her writing, forgetting about everything except her words. Her poems were a feast for the imagination. Her travel descriptions made him want to apply for a passport.

"Geez, I'm dating a chef and practically starving, yet he can't even make his girl a sandwich."

*Shit. Food.*

Standing, he set the notebook on the nearest nightstand. Pulling back the comforter, he said, "Lie down. Rest. I'll make us something. Give me five minutes."

The admiration when he first looked from her writing had filled Cindy's heart to the brim. He hadn't even noticed her body, which was wrapped in a tiny blue robe. The awe was for her written words.

It was as if the man truly did see past her body. She could barely fathom it. He was unlike any man she'd ever dated.

She went to her suitcase, grabbing the notebook where she'd written her musings. Rifling through pages, she read a few different entries. Writing was cathartic, but to have someone besides her sister call her talented made her dream of the possibilities.

Tossing the notebook on her nightstand, she tried to extinguish the embers of her fanciful aspirations. She didn't have time for whimsical fantasies. Quitting her career wasn't an option. Nor would she chase after something that was bound to fail.

Untying her robe, Cindy set it on the cushioned bench at the end of her bed. Wearing her favorite silk nightgown, she slid under the soft cotton sheets. The combination was heaven. She groaned in appreciation as Will came in caring two plates piled high with food.

He quirked a brow. "What are you doing under those covers?"

She pulled back the comforter on the other side of the bed. "Why don't you come here and find out?"

"Yes, ma'am."

He handed her a plate before setting his on the nightstand. When he tried to climb into the bed with his jeans on, she stopped him. "Oh no, mister. Strip."

"Um. What about your roommate and her kid?"

"They're gone for the day. Emma went to her parents' cabin for a few days. They aren't due back until tomorrow night." She studied her plate, not wanting him to see her vulnerability. "I remember you telling Jacob you didn't have to work tonight. Will you stay? I've missed you."

The quiet sound of his jeans hitting the floor caressed her ears. "I was hoping you'd ask. Hold on." He walked to the bedroom door in this T-shirt and boxer briefs, closing it. Smiling sheepishly, he said, "In case your roommate comes home early."

*He's so freaking cute.*

"Oh, yes, you better. You don't want her to come in and catch us..." she widened her eyes, "eating."

The smile he gave her as he got into bed was downright sinful. He reached for his plate, saying, "Honey, this sandwich isn't all I plan on eating." His gaze traveled leisurely down her body, searing her with its heat.

She debated setting her food aside and bringing him to her. She craved his touch.

As if sensing her indecision, he pointed at her sandwich. "Sustenance first."

He took a bite of his, and she followed suit. The explosion of tangy and spicy hit her tongue, turning her ravenous. She ate half of it in nearly three bites. Then managed to slow and eat like a lady instead of a starving animal.

"How in the world do you manage to make a simple sandwich taste this good? You need to open your restaurant."

He shrugged. "Someday."

"No. Seriously. You needed to open it yesterday, not someday."

There was a challenge in his stance. "What about you?"

She paused, her sandwich midway to her mouth. "What about me?"

"You have a notebook filled with travel details and pictures. Why?"

*He saw too much.*

Embarrassment heated her cheeks. She didn't want to discuss her stupid daydream and muttered, "I don't know. It's just something I like to do when traveling."

"No way. Your pictures look professional, and the details surrounding the destinations are too specific. These aren't mindless musings."

His warm brown eyes seemed to beg, asking her to share. Nerves ate away the last of her appetite. She set her plate aside.

He was going to call her dream fanciful. Or silly, like her mom insinuated whenever Cindy shared her ideas. Still, he'd opened up a little regarding his past and told her about his dream to open a restaurant. Not that his was implausible, like her stupid fantasy. She was a model, not a writer. A photographer.

"Fine." She raised then dropped her hands. "I want to write a travel book. Or start a blog detailing my travels. Maybe sell some of my photos online. I want to share my pictures, my travel experiences. Right now, modeling works for me, but at my age, I don't have many years left. Plus, something to express my creative side would be nice."

"What's holding you back?"

He sounded so matter-of-fact. As if it wouldn't end in failure. "Why don't you open your restaurant?" she countered.

"I told you. I owe Jacob. I have to pay him back first."

"That's an excuse. I'm willing to bet my car he doesn't care if you open your business first."

Will smiled, setting his empty plate on the nightstand. "You'd risk your fancy Audi?"

"Yup."

"Well, we're talking about you, not me. Seriously, Cindy, you are talented." He shifted, reaching for the notebook. She stopped him, placing her hand over his.

His words caressed her deepest dreams, saying what she'd always wanted to hear. However, she was too tired to think. All she wanted was her pillow and his arms around her. "Please, I'm exhausted. Let's talk about it later when my brain isn't mush. I need a nap."

"Deal." He slid his hand from her notebook and brought her into his arms as he lay down.

"Wait." Needing the warmth of his skin while drifting to sleep, she tugged at his T-shirt. "Take it off."

"You are one demanding woman." He gripped the back of his shirt, yanking it off. Tossing it aside, he opened his arms wide. "Come here."

Now, there was a command she was more than willing to obey.

# Chapter Seventeen

Opening his eyes, the first thing Will noticed was the sun was much lower in the sky than when they'd fallen asleep. Wanting to know the time, he stretched with his free arm for his cellphone, trying not to move the rest of his body. Cindy was snuggled into his chest with a leg thrown over his waist. He didn't want to jostle her.

He stretched another inch. She muttered something and rolled away from him.

*Damn it.*

He picked up his phone. The screen showed it was a little after five in the evening. They'd slept around six hours. Working late nights, he had no problem falling asleep in the middle of the day. However, if Cindy wanted to get over her jetlag and back to her normal schedule, she needed to wake up.

Glancing to her side of the bed, he took in an enticing sight. During their nap, they'd managed to kick the covers to the end of the bed. Her sexy, short silky nightshirt had risen exposing a pair of sheer panties.

He gently ran a palm down her side, reaching her ass, he slipped his hand under the material. Her skin was smooth as the silk.

She shifted onto her back, a sleepy smile on her lips. "What time is it?" Her drowsy voice sounded like sex and dreams.

Settling on his side, he skated a hand to her breast, cupping it then teasing her nipple with his thumb. "After five."

She arched into his touch, wrapping a hand around his neck, bringing his lips to hers. His hand slipped from under her nightshirt, falling onto his back, bringing her on top of him.

"My dreams were filled with you. And you were doing some rather naughty things," she said against his mouth.

"Let's make those dreams come true." He kissed her deep, digging his fingers into her hips while she rocked against him.

He'd awoken hard, wanting her touch, needing to bury himself in her heat. Already losing control, he debated pushing her panties aside and taking her in one thrust.

"Condoms?"

"Nightstand. Next to you," she panted, trailing kisses down his torso.

He opened the drawer, feeling around, refusing to take his gaze off her. Finding the box, he grabbed it just as she reached into his boxer-briefs. She stroked him from base to head, licking her lips.

He dropped the box of condoms. They hit the floor with a quiet thump, at the same time the click of the front door made them freeze.

*Shit.*

Cindy slithered up his body. "Don't worry. Emma must be home early. I'm sure she saw your car. She won't come in here."

He hoped Cindy was right because stopping right now might kill him.

Retrieving the condoms, she took one before placing the box on the nightstand. "Now, where were we?"

"Right here." He gripped her ass and hitched his hips.

She grasped the hem of her nightgown. Right before she took it off, the bedroom door swung open.

"Why didn't you call me when you got in this morning? We're supposed to meet Matty and Jim for lunch," Sophia's voice rang though Will's lust, making his heart nearly stop.

Cindy rolled off him, yanking the sheet over them. "Mother! Seriously, you don't waltz in without knocking."

Sophia huffed, not seeming to care she'd walked in on her daughter in bed with a guy. "I thought you were sick. It's not like you to neglect plans we've made."

"You could have called. You know, instead of barging into my bedroom," Cindy retorted, sounding irritated. "Now, Mother. Please, a little privacy. We'll be out in a minute."

Yeah, that's what he wanted, a sit-down with Sophia. It wouldn't be awkward. Not at all.

They'd met twice. Once when Will was picking up Jacob from jail, after Sophia had jumped to conclusions that ended with his brother's arrest. Then at the wedding. Neither time had she bothered to hide her disdain.

"Fine. Fine." She started to leave, then glanced at the bed. Her gaze locked on him, and she froze.

*Here it comes.*

"You have *got* to be kidding me, Cindy," Sophia shrieked. "I've bitterly swallowed the reality of Greta marrying someone beneath her. But you? With this one? Hell, at least his brother has a job. A career. All this one has is a police record and track marks."

"Mom!"

The disrespect for his brother pissed Will off. However, Sophia was right about him. Cindy could do better.

"I should leave." He grabbed his jeans.

Cindy's hand gripped his shoulder. "No. Stay. She has no right. This is my home."

"Who found you this place and co-signed?" her mother asked, voice dripping with venom.

"Are you threatening me?'

"Merely reminding you."

"No problem. I'll move." She twisted to face Will. "Think they have a place available in your building?"

Sophia made a choking sound. He almost smiled. He admired Cindy's defiance, even if it was misplaced.

"Oh? What will happen to your stray? With a baby, it will not be easy for her to find someone else to mooch off of."

A flash of worry cross Cindy's face. Will stood, clutching his jeans. Even then, Sophia didn't turn away, merely continued staring daggers at her daughter.

He couldn't fathom how Cindy and Greta had grown into such strong, thoughtful women with Sophia for a mother.

"No. I'll go. I don't want to cause any problems." He reached for the shirt he'd tossed on the floor last night. Back when something with Cindy seemed possible.

Sophia's irritated gaze bored into him. "You are nothing but a problem."

He slammed his lips together, swallowing a million angry retorts, yanking his T-shirt over his head. He berated himself enough. He didn't need this woman's help.

"Mother. Leave."

"Cindy—" he began.

Sophia cut him off. "You are making a mistake. He is a mistake." She pointed, making sure her daughter understood, without a doubt, who she was condemning.

"Who I date is none of your business."

"Dating. Is that what you're calling it?" Sophia scoffed, glancing at the box of condoms on the nightstand. "Whatever this is, I hope to God you get this little rebellion out of your system before it's too late. You don't know him. He destroys everything he touches."

"Leave," Cindy repeated.

Sophia inhaled deeply through her nose. "Fine. I'll reschedule our dinner with the Montagnes. We *will* talk later. I'm not going to let this get as far as it did with his brother. No way. Not with this one." She spun on her heels, not waiting for either of them to respond.

Will had nothing to say anyway. Sure, he was offended, yet part of him agreed with her.

He took a deep breath, defeat in every word that followed. "Your mom is right. I'm no good for you. I understand her wanting a better man for you."

"Please, my mother is about as deep as a puddle. Her concern isn't for my wellbeing or happiness, it's more on how I represent her. She wants me with a guy who's been on the cover of *Forbes*. Or at the very least, *Vanity Fair*. You see how she is with Jacob. Are you saying he's not a good man?"

"Hell. No. And, I agree, your mom loves the superficial shine." He sighed. "But what lies under my imperfect surface is even worse. I'm dirty and rusted. All the way through."

Cindy came around from her side of the bed and knelt. Taking him into her arms, she rested her head on his chest. "I haven't known you long, but I'm certain that isn't true." She quirked a saucy smile. "Plus, I like dirty."

Her body was heaven against his. She had a way of soothing his demons.

However, it was time to introduce them to her. At least a few.

"Christ, Cindy, we are worlds apart. You date cultured and polished men who have beach houses in the south of France. I don't even own a passport."

She leaned back, looking insulted. "So? I don't need to date a rich man to fly me around and buy me stuff. I do well enough on my own, thank you very much."

He nodded. She was a strong woman who didn't need a man's support. It was more that she deserved someone better than him. He stepped back. "I agree. You also don't need one who's OD'd multiple times. Someone who's been rushed by ambulance to the ER so many times the staff knows him by name." Her eyes widened. He ran a thumb along her brow. "For the last five years, while you were spending your free time traveling and partying with friends, I was in rehab or NA. Your mom might have co-signed on your condo, but when you were moving in and paying your bills, I was crashing at my little brother's because I was jobless and broke. Broken."

"It's your past," she whispered.

"Not that far in my past. An addict in recovery is still an addict." His honesty hurt, humiliated him, but his feelings didn't matter, she needed to understand. "The chance of relapse is always there."

"You are the strongest man I know. I'm willing to risk it." She tightened her grip on his waist. "I'm not ready to let you go. Let's not worry about future what-ifs. We both aren't after anything serious. Let's have our fun."

The problem was, she was becoming more than a fun distraction. She was burrowing into pieces of his heart he'd thought were too scarred to feel. He'd been wrong. "But if this is just a pleasant diversion, why cause a problem with your mom?"

"Because I'm a big girl." She stuck out her bottom lip like a pouty kid. "My mommy isn't going to tell me what to do."

He chuckled, pulling her lip between his for half a second before letting go. "Oh, I see. It is what she said. I'm your youthful rebellion."

"Ha! I'm too many years past my teens to be rebelling against my parent. I'm too young for a midlife crisis." She hooked her fingers through the belt loops on his jeans, bringing him closer. "I like you, Wilhelm Grimm. I have no intention of letting you go until I'm done with you."

He cringed at his birth name, but let it pass because her innocent-looking blue eyes were clouding with heat and sin. "What do you plan on doing with me?"

She cupped the front of his jeans before standing on her tiptoes. Running her lips along his neck to his ear, she whispered, "Whatever I want."

He let her.

# Chapter Eighteen

Freshly showered, Will stepped naked from Cindy's ensuite bathroom. The smell of bacon and coffee accentuated his hunger.

Stepping into his boxer-briefs, he peeked from around the bedroom door, checking to see if Cindy was alone.

When he didn't hear Emma or Max, he padded past the living room to find Cindy at the counter. Her back was to him, and she was washing dishes, wearing only a cream pair of panties and a light blue T-shirt that barely covered her backside. In fact, when she shifted to place a pan on the drying rack, the cotton came up, playing peek-a-boo with her superb ass.

He spent a few seconds admiring the glorious view before sliding his arms around her waist and nuzzling her neck. "Good morning. Why didn't you wake me? I'd have helped."

She leaned her back into him. "I was tempted. Cooking for you is intimidating. It's never going to reach your standards." Turning, she hooked her hands behind his neck. "But you looked peaceful. I didn't have the heart to wake you. So, if it tastes like shit, appreciate the extra sleep."

"Yes, I was tired. Someone wore me out last night. Anyway, it'll taste great just for the fact I didn't have to make it." Except for a full pot of coffee, the table and counter were empty. No food in sight. "Um, did you eat it all?"

Letting go of him, she went to the oven. "No. I've been keeping it warm until you woke, Sleeping Beauty." She removed an egg casserole dish that smelled like heaven.

"I'll pour us coffee. Where are your cups?"

She pointed to a cupboard.

Will was a little unnerved with the way this domestic moment kissed at his heart. The last few years he'd kept everyone at a distance, not realizing how lonely his life had become. Having Cindy in it was like a light, summer breeze. Beautiful and invigorating.

As they sat, he asked a question that had clung to him since this morning. "Can your mom do anything if you don't fall into line? Make you leave somehow?"

Cindy cut into the casserole, placing a slice on his plate. "No, probably not. She isn't paying the rent. She co-signed, not signed for the place." She tilted her head. "Although her best friend's husband owns the building, so maybe. Anyway, I think it's an empty threat. And if it isn't, I'll move. Making the rent isn't a problem. Plus, I could probably find a place for Emma, Max, and me somewhere closer to a park. Or where rent isn't so crazy because of the address."

"If you can't find a place, you guys could stay with me," Will blurted, then froze. *What the fuck? Where had that come from?*

She paused with her fork midway to her mouth, her eyes wide as the plates they were eating from. "What?"

He backtracked. "You know if you need to until you find another place to live."

*I need to slow down. I'm freaking her out. Shit, I'm freaking myself out.*

She waved off his offer. "Forget it. My mother makes a lot of empty threats. I want to talk about something else."

He took a bite of his omelet. An explosion of breakfast goodness celebrated on his taste buds. Bacon, eggs, onions, and mushroom. "Wow. This is great."

"Thanks. I found it on one of those online websites."

They dug into breakfast. Will didn't say much, he was too busy enjoying the food. He hadn't realized how hungry he was until he'd taken a bite.

When most of Cindy's plate was empty, she reached for her coffee cup, saying, "Back to what I'd wanted to talk about yesterday."

He hoped she wanted to discuss her talented writing and photography but doubted it. "What's on your mind?"

"Your restaurant."

*Damn it.*

"Where I work? Summer Grill?"

"No. *Your* restaurant. The place you showed me on the way to your apartment that first time I came over."

He sighed, his sliver of hope dying. "It is a long way off. I still have to pay back Jacob."

"Really? Why? Is he charging you interest?" she pushed.

Annoyance slithered along his spine. She wouldn't understand.

*He doesn't even want it back.*

"No. That isn't the point. A debt is a debt."

"Pay him back after you open your restaurant."

"What if I make no money? What if it's a bust? Then I'll owe the bank on top of Jacob."

Frustration was soaked in his every word. She either didn't notice or care. "Oh, I see the problem now."

He set down his fork, his appetite evaporating. "Please, do enlighten me."

"You're so afraid of failure, of making a mistake, you aren't willing to take any risks."

*Not true.*

*Or was it?*

Will took his plate to the sink, giving himself a moment to wrangle in his temper. "You're one to talk," he shot back.

Coming up behind him, she dumped her dish in the sink, setting her mug on the counter before leaning against it. "What are you talking about?"

"I've read your journals. I saw your photos. I know where your passion is. It isn't in modeling."

"Those are hobbies." She shrugged, looking away. "My job pays good and allows me to travel."

"Who cares. Don't you want to share your travel stories and advice? Sell them, along with your photographs. I get it, you're beautiful and the camera loves you, but you love it too. Being behind it. I'm telling you, you need to submit those journal entries to travel magazines. Hell, you need to write travel guides, showcasing your amazing pictures. At the very least, a blog."

She somehow managed to appear both pleased and pissed off. After a few beats of silence, she said, "You have my life figured out. What about yours?"

He smirked. "Managing other people's lives is always easier than our own."

Drumming his fingers on the counter, he mulled an idea over in his head, not sure he wanted to travel such an intimidating path. In the end, he was willing to if she agreed. Her talent was too strong to keep hidden in her pretty notebooks and hung on walls no one would ever see.

"Want to make a deal?" He waited to make sure she was listening, his heartbeat gathering speed, nerves racing. She made the go-ahead motion with her hand. "Have your sister set you up with a killer website showcasing your photos. Start a blog, using those journal entries. Submit your work to a couple of magazines or online journals. If you do that I will talk to Tim and Jacob. Check more into the property I showed you."

Cindy moved closer until she was flush against him, the heat from her body mingling with his. "Oh, I have to do so much, and you only have to talk?"

"I'll do more than chat with people. I'll figure out what's needed to get my restaurant open. Tim and I will meet with the banks. We'll talk with the realtor who's leasing the property. I'll ask my friend Tanner to help me with the bookkeeping. Maybe I can hire him, or he'll recommend someone."

Cindy broke into his ramblings. "Wait. Isn't Tanner a musician? Singer. Plays the guitar, right?"

"Yes. He's also a CPA."

"Huh, that's an odd combination."

"It is, but he's great at both. What do you say? Deal? Seal our pact with a kiss?" He stooped, his mouth less than an inch from hers, waiting for her answer.

She gave it with her lips. They met his, tasting of coffee and risk.

It was an exhilarating combination. He ran his tongue along the crease of her mouth. She opened, inviting him in, running her hands up his back, using her nails. The sensation never failed to make his blood race south.

Groaning, he gripped her ass, bringing her closer. As he was deciding if he should lift her on the counter or carry her to the bedroom, the front door swung open.

Emma shouted. "Cindy, you home?" Catching sight of them half-naked in the kitchen, she halted, then smirked. "Well, hello, 'just brother of Jacob.'"

Cindy turned, tugging at the hem of her T-shirt. At least she had on one. He was standing in nothing except underwear with a rapidly fading hard-on. To make it worse, Max was laughing and waving from Emma's hip.

"Shut up, smartass. Emma, meet my boyfriend, Will."

Okay, being called hers helped. Still, a pair of shorts would be nice.

He had to smile when Emma stumbled back in an overly dramatic fashion, making Max's giggles become shrieks of delight. "Boyfriend. Cindy Meier has a boyfriend? I haven't heard you refer to a guy as a boyfriend since the third grade. Bill Mumford." Her gaze traveled from Will's bare toes to his red face. "Though I see why she's made an exception with you."

A fierce warmth rushed up his neck, covering his cheeks. "I, um, I'm going to get dressed."

"Clean towels are under the sink. Oh, you might want to lock the door. Emma's eyeing you like you're the tastiest thing on the menu," Cindy teased.

"It has been a while, and you know I have a thing for tattooed men with broad shoulders," the other woman retorted.

Cindy leaned against the counter, crossing her ankles and reaching for her coffee mug. "Um, who doesn't?"

He shook his head, scooting around the women. "They say guys are bad. I feel like a piece of meat."

As he headed for the bedroom, Cindy called after him, "You are a prime cut, babe."

Laughing, he closed the door.

# Chapter Nineteen

Will's cellphone rang from somewhere in his apartment, but his whole body protested him leaving his comfy seat on the balcony. The call ended, only to begin screaming again, two seconds later. Swearing, he got up.

Yesterday morning he'd spent with Tim going over plans for the restaurant. In the afternoon he worked a shift at Summer Grill. They had been slammed, and on top of it, he was training his replacement as head chef.

He'd come home exhausted, stripped and fallen face first into his bed. When he woke in the morning, he dragged his ass to the kitchen for coffee, then to his favorite spot. He hadn't moved since.

Unable to remember where he dropped his phone, he followed the sound, finding it in the slacks he'd worn the night before.

Seeing the number on his phone, the previous day's stresses were forgotten. "Morning. How was yesterday's shoot?"

"Not bad," Cindy replied. "Quick and painless. Plus, I don't have another job until next week."

"Now that is the best news I've heard in a long time."

"Really? Even more than the bank telling you, you were approved for the lease?"

"Hell, no. Extra time with you wins. Hands down."

Between their work schedules and side projects, they'd hardly seen each other. They'd had a couple of late-night dinners and one very hot night at his place. Today, they were both free and planning on spending it at Jacob and Greta's for an end-of-summer party.

He'd get the whole afternoon, along with the possibility of another scorching night at his place, followed by a lazy morning with Cindy. He was a lucky man.

It occurred to him, for a temporary lover, he missed her more than he should. Wanted her near him too much.

His good mood wouldn't allow him to ponder this conundrum for too long.

"Aren't you a charmer? Do you mean it, or are you sweetening me up for a spicy night?" she teased, a lick of heat carrying over the phone line.

"Um, both."

"Mmm, delicious. Tell me more."

"You want more of the sweet or the spice?"

There was a light click of her tongue. He'd learned this meant she was considering her options. He waited, unsure which answer he wanted.

"I'm going to go with spicy. You have a smooth deep voice. It's perfect for phone sex."

He coughed out a surprised laugh. "Do I?"

"Oh, yes," she purred, the sound promising so much erotic delight.

He'd never done it before but imagining Cindy's breath catching or touching herself because his words turned her on had him considering. He searched his mind on where to start. Before he could, she muttered. "Crap. Harper."

He was confused. "What's that now?"

"She's calling me. I told her I'd pick her up for the barbeque, forgetting my Roadster only has two seats. Dumb, I know."

"She's going to the barbecue?" *Shit.* He'd forgotten now that Jacob was married, his wife's family would also be there, including her parents. "Will your mom and Nigel be there?"

"Dad might. I doubt my mom and stepdad would deign to go to a simple backyard gathering."

Thank Christ. He wouldn't have to deal with snide remarks or their disgust of him.

"Anyway," she continued. "I think something's going on with Harper and your friend Lucas."

"Lucas and Harper?" Will echoed. *No way.*

He could be dating again. His wife had passed away over two years ago.

Although, Harper seemed an unlikely choice. Lucas went more for the quiet, bookish types.

Then again, if someone had told him back when he'd met Cindy they'd be dating by the end of summer, he'd have laughed his ass off. Yet, here they were, and he hadn't felt this alive since, well hell, he couldn't remember.

"Yes. Your Lucas, my Harper. She asked if he was going to be at the party. Like I'd know."

"Doesn't mean they're dating. Maybe your cousin just has the hots for my friend." He shook his head. They sounded like two gossiping teenagers.

"Doubt it. She said if he's there, she isn't going. To me, it sounds like a woman scorned, not enamored." Cindy paused. "Damn. She's calling again. I need to answer. But before I hang up, do you want me to swing by with her? We could drive together in your car."

"Nah, go ahead. I'll meet you there. I have to stop at the realtors to drop off paperwork. I'm not sure if I'll have to stay and fill out more shit. I swear, I feel like all I've been doing these last weeks is signing my name. Anyway, no sense dragging you two along. Get to Jacob's, start celebrating."

"Will do."

He heard disappointment in her voice. "Do you want to come with me?"

"Hell, no. Sounds about as exciting as watching paint dry."

Was he imagining the gloomy undertone in her voice? "Is everything okay?"

"Yes." She sighed. "Don't mind me. I'm just being a baby. Things are moving lightning-quick for you. Meanwhile, I got my first rejection for a piece I submitted to a travel journal."

"Oh, shit. I'm sorry, babe."

*I'm an asshole boyfriend. So caught up in my crap, I forgot to ask how her writing was going.*

"No worries, I'm told it's part of the process. I guess another is me pouting," she said with a weak laugh. "Oh. Harper is calling again. I'll meet you at Greta's."

"Okay. Can't wait to see you."

"Same."

"Do you think your car will be okay?" Harper asked. "You should have told Greta to save you a spot in the driveway."

Cindy glanced around the neighborhood. Trimmed green lawns, a mix of middle to upper-class homes, with cars to match.

She clicked the lock on her Audi. "It'll be fine. It's not like the area we drove through by Eastern Market."

Recalling the boarded up and burned out homes, she shuddered. The desperation, hopelessness, and violence brewing under the surface had her praying she didn't get a flat tire. Growing up in Petite Bois and later moving to Ann Arbor, she hadn't spent much time in Detroit. She was discovering the city was an odd mix of extreme poverty and wealth. Her sister's neighborhood was the perfect balance between these extremes.

"Besides," Cindy continued, making room on the sidewalk for Harper, "if you were so worried about getting a good spot, why'd you take an eternity getting ready. I sat around at your place *forever*."

Harper didn't answer. She seemed to find her coral painted nails the most interesting thing in the world.

*Huh.* Something was up.

"Any reason you took an eternity getting ready for a backyard barbecue?" Cindy probed.

"No. I always want to look my best." Harper shrugged, still not meeting Cindy's eyes.

They walked up the driveway, spotting Will's car. He'd managed to beat them here. Good thing he hadn't waited for her.

Opening the gate to the backyard, she turned, wanting to push Harper a little more.

As if knowing it, she raised a hand. "Please, let it go."

Fair enough. It wasn't long ago they were at Lake Michigan, and she had her secrets with Will.

Cindy nodded at her cousin, scanning the backyard. It was so different from the lush estate she and Greta grown up in, but the coziness and the obvious care of it made it more special. There was a detached garage in the back, shaded by a huge maple tree. Off to the side was a large fire. Tables and chairs were lined up along the house. Next to the patio door was Will, manning the grill.

She pointed to him. Harper waved, saying she was going inside to find Greta. Reaching Will, Cindy inhaled deeply. The smell of summer food lightened her soul and made her stomach rumble.

He leaned closer, kissing her neck. "Was your sigh of bliss for me or the food?"

"Well, both are rather delicious."

She was lying. He was way more tempting than food. He was fine in tan shorts, worn blue T-shirt, frayed around the collar, and leather flip-flops.

There weren't many weeks of warm weather left. Soon they'd be buried under layers and snow. The thought depressed her.

It also reminded her October was right around the corner which meant her mother's annual party.

"So…"

He was slathering barbecue sauce on a rack of ribs and stopped. "Why does that one word sound loaded?"

*Because it is.*

"My parents have this annual Halloween party. I was wondering if you'd go with me? The food is amazing, the costumes are fantastic with everyone trying to outdo each other, and the decorations—" She stopped babbling and waited for his refusal.

Instead, he asked, "If this is such a big deal, how come I've never heard Jacob or Greta mention it?"

"They didn't go last year. They'd gone to the Masonic Temple for this creepy-cool masquerade called the Theatre Bizarre."

Cindy suspected they'd made other plans on purpose. At the time, things were still really tense between Jacob, Nigel, and Mother. An arrest tends to put a strain on things.

"Are they going this year?"

She smirked, hiding her nerves. "Why? Will you only go if your little brother is there? You can't handle my parents on your own?"

She found she really wanted him to go. It had nothing to do with a desire to get a rise from her parents. Sure, she'd played those games when she was younger, but now she wanted him to be part of the things she loved.

So much for keeping things simple. Oh, well, he didn't have to know about her growing attachment. No sense freaking him out.

"Ha! I'm not sure I could manage with my whole family as backup." He moved the ribs aside before lining potatoes next to them on the grill, then turned to her. "Though, I'm not going to lie. It'd be nice to have some friends in my corner."

She gripped his elbow lightly, waiting for him to look at her. "I'm always in your corner."

His soft, answering smile was beautiful. "Yes, I'll go."

Clapping her hands, she did a quick happy dance. "I love Halloween. The dressing up, parties, handing out candy. What do you want to go as?" Ideas flooded her. "Oh, what about gangsters? I'll be a Flapper? Or Cleopatra and Mark Antony."

"Um, didn't they end up doing a Romeo and Juliet?"

"Good point. Morticia and Gomez Addams?"

"Or," his grin was full of devilish mischief, "I go as a convict, you as my warden. Your parents would shit."

Cindy laughed. "They would, so it has my vote. If," she looped two fingers around his closest wrist, "you let me handcuff you."

He nipped her ear before whispering, "You can handcuff me anytime you want. We don't need Halloween."

The image of him naked and at her mercy bloomed hot and delicious in her mind. She pressed in closer. "Anytime?"

"Hey! There are kids here," Jacob called out, his voice full of humor.

He wore the same troublemaking grin as his brother, holding a beer in one hand and red wine in another. He offered her the wine. "Here. Greta said this is your favorite."

"Thank you." She took a sip. The crisp, fresh flavor spilled over her tongue.

"Nice brother I have. I come to his house, cook for his party, and he can't even bring me a cup of water?"

"Let me see how you do with the ribs. Then maybe," Jacob teased.

Will laughed, muttering, "Asshole."

She listened to the brother's banter. Jacob was calling Will a cockblocker, something about Greta's first visit to the house and a tour of some kind.

Spotting her sister sitting with Harper, she pointed at them. "I'm going to say hi."

The two men paused long enough with their trash talk to nod. Making her way to the tables, she took another healthy sip of her wine. Not her smartest idea considering she'd skipped lunch, but it tasted so good.

# Chapter Twenty

Cindy woke and immediately wished herself back to sleep. It didn't work.

Her eyes, peeking open, were stabbed by the sunlight filtering through the window. She slammed them shut.

Wait. She didn't recognize the curtains.

*Where the hell am I?*

Sitting, her stomach rolled heavy like she'd eaten mud. The room had white, empty walls, an oak dresser, and the iron-framed bed she was currently in. The only adornment was simple, deep red curtains on a large window. To her left was a door.

Where it led, she had no idea.

She gripped the gray comforter, noticing she was in her panties and some man's T-shirt. It didn't smell like Will.

*Shit.*

Guilt and dread mixed with her belly of sludge. She replayed yesterday's events. They became blurrier as the day progressed. She'd chatted with her sister, with Harper, with a pretty woman with purple hair. Ate some food, drank way too much wine. Danced with someone she assumed was Will. The rest was a blank.

The knob turned. Cindy gripped the sheets, her heart pounding.

Will stepped inside, closing the door. "How you feeling?"

His voice and her momentary terror slammed against her hangover, she groaned, easing herself back into the pillow. "What happened? Where are we?"

He sat on the bed next to her. "You drank too much. We're in my old room at Jacob's." He didn't sound angry, more like resigned. Tugging at the hem of the shirt she wore, he said, "Your outfit got messed up. You're wearing one of my old shirts I found in the dresser."

Two questions answered, but she had another one. "Why didn't we go to your place? Your place isn't far."

"I finally convinced you to eat. Too bad, right after, you insisted we dance. Let me tell you," he paused, and she turned to face him. He appeared disturbed and amused. "Those two things do not mix with you. At all."

Humiliation flooded her. "Please tell me I didn't puke in front of everyone. Or, oh God, on anyone."

The first time at a gathering with his family and friends, she'd made a fool of herself. His dad probably hated her. She suspected Will didn't have nice things to say about her when they were planning the wedding party weekend together. Then she arrives as his girlfriend and gets shit-faced.

He rubbed her shoulder. "Nah. You made it to the back fence. After that, I got you inside. We spent most of the night in the bathroom."

Groaning, she rolled over, face in the pillow, wishing it would smother her. "We? Why didn't you leave me there? I'm the dumbass who drank too much and probably made a fool of myself."

"Because you were pretty torn up. I needed to make sure you were okay." There was a hollow sadness in his voice. She didn't know what it meant, but the despair tore at her heart.

He stopped rubbing her back, the bed shifted, telling her he'd left it. He'd stayed until certain she'd survived. Now he'd go.

Hell, most of the men she'd dated would've bailed sooner. They'd have left right after she lost her composure, embarrassing herself and him.

He wasn't leaving. In one hand he held a glass of something that might be seaweed, along with two pills. "Here. These will help with the hangover."

She took a hesitant sip of the gook. Not bad. She used it to swallow the medicine before laying down. "I'm so sorry. I drank too much, too fast."

"Don't worry. You weren't the only one. It was the last party for the summer. Many were stumbling, clutching the arms of their designated drivers. Hell, Lucas is here sleeping off his whiskey dreams on the couch."

"That's not the point. I came here as your girlfriend and acted like a fool."

He gave a humorless laugh. "I'm sure no one batted an eye. They're used to it with me."

Okay. Now she felt a hundred times worse. "Bullshit. Stop thinking you're still the man you were five years ago."

"Oh, I know I'm not. At least in some regards. Which is why I have to ask you something."

His tone was so serious it made her pulse jump. She took a deep breath, motioning for him to continue.

"Do you drink, get tipsy most times you go out?"

"No," she snapped.

Damn, she drank a few glasses of wine on a hot day on an empty stomach. It hit her the wrong way. It didn't make her a drunk.

He held up his hands. "No judgment. Just asking."

"Why?"

"Never mind. Forget it. You feel like shit. We're both exhausted. It's early, let's try to sleep some more." He nudged her shoulder. "Scoot over."

It sure sounded like he was judging. She should push more, find out what was bothering him. Yet every time she opened her mouth to speak, her pounding head shouted for her to keep quiet.

She made room for him. He slid in next to her, draping an arm over her waist. He slipped it under her shirt, rubbing her belly. The gentle circles he painted with his fingertips made her eyes flutter closed.

Her last thought before drifting to sleep was, she needed to continue this conversation when they woke. Something about it had the edges of unease tickling along her spine. As if something small had the power to turn big.

Will couldn't sleep, though he held Cindy a while longer before he slipped out. In the kitchen, he nursed his coffee while trying to swallow his worries. Last night, she brought back some unpleasant memories. It didn't mean they weren't good together.

They'd been dating for a few months, and most of the time she didn't drink much. A glass of wine here and there. Sure, sometimes they made her a little giggly, but this was the first time she drank in excess.

Then again, his worry wasn't really with her drinking. It was more to do with what it did to him when he was around her. Last night felt like his past was trying to escape from the dark corners of his mind, to overpower him, drag him back to places he didn't want to go.

The floorboards creaked, catching his attention. Lucas shuffled into the kitchen. He had on the clothes from yesterday, rumpled and battered as the man wearing them.

"Coffee," he croaked.

Will pointed to the counter. "The sugar's in the cupboard above."

Lucas nodded, then groaned. "Why didn't you tell me those shots were a bad idea?"

"I did. You told me to have a drink or shut up."

Sitting across from Will, Lucas laughed. "Since you don't look like a truck hit you, my guess is you didn't take my stupid advice."

Will smiled around his coffee mug. "Nope."

"Smart man."

One of the great things about Lucas was he didn't tiptoe around Will when the topic of drinking or drugs were mentioned. Or death. It was something they had in common.

Love and death. They'd both lost people they loved suddenly: Lucas, his wife, Elizabeth, and Will, his high school sweetheart, Jolene.

Lucas had initially been Jacob's friend. They met at the local college, back before he dropped out to take care of his fucked-up family. A group of them used to party together. Later, when Will moved in with Jacob, he'd see Lucas when he was visiting his brother.

Casual friends, until Elizabeth's sudden death. Then Lucas needed someone who understood the agony of losing someone they loved. Will knew it all too well.

During his darkest times, Lucas would call crying, begging to know how to survive the pain. They'd bonded over loss and anguish, causing them to set aside niceties for brutal honesty.

Therefore, Will didn't hesitate to ask the question on his mind. "Did you sleep with Harper?"

Lucas dropped his head into his hands, giving his answer without words.

"Dude," Will said, "it's been two years. It's okay to move on."

Lucas slumped in his seat, a defeated man. "I thought I was. Hell, I am. I just can't seem to say the right things when I'm with Harper."

"What happened?" Hesitation played across the other man's face, giving Will pause. "You don't have to tell me. I get it. It's not my business."

"It's more you're dating her cousin. I don't want to drag you into my shit. Although, from the way Harper froze me out yesterday, I'd say our story's finished anyway."

"I'm here if you want to unload," Will replied.

Lucas sipped on his coffee, seeming to decide if he'd share or not, then said, "Not much to tell, really. We went to her hotel after the wedding. The next morning, I screwed things up. Bad. I tried to make it right yesterday. Instead, I made it worse."

Will was going to ask how but was distracted by someone shuffling down the hallway. His guess was Cindy.

About twenty minutes ago he heard the door of the main floor bathroom lock, then the rattle of the shower's pipes. It wouldn't have been Greta or Jacob. They'd have used the one in their upstairs loft.

He was right. Cindy walked into the kitchen, fresh as a sunrise. Her hair was braided. She wore light makeup and a flirty summer dress. Where she'd found it was beyond him.

Coming into the room, she kissed his head. Damn, she even smelled good.

Making her way to the counter, she grabbed the coffeepot and a cup. Coming to the table she refilled his mug, then lifted the carafe in Lucas's direction, silently asking if he wanted a refill. He nodded, she filled his then hers, before sitting, looking ready to take on the world.

"How is it, after you took a swim in a bottle of wine you have more energy than me?" Will asked.

She smiled around her mug. "It's amazing what a shower and a little blush can do, along with the magic green drink you gave me."

"Wait. You made the Hangover drink. Why didn't you tell me?" Lucas huffed.

Will shrugged. "Sorry. I forgot. There's some left in the fridge." He focused on Cindy. "Where'd you get the clothes and makeup?"

"I always have makeup with me. As for the clothes, I asked Greta."

*Duh.* Her sister lived here, and although Cindy was taller, they had similar figures.

"Besides getting this pretty dress, I learned something new about the Grimm brothers." Cindy wiggled her brows. "Both like to sleep in the nude. *And* are in fine shape."

"I learned something about the Grimm brothers I'd rather forget," Lucas muttered, from his spot by the fridge, making her laugh.

Will smirked. "Did you learn I'm the big brother in every regard?"

"Ah, hell. There are certain things a man doesn't want to know about his friends," Lucas grumbled. He grabbed his glass of green goop, heading for the back door. "I'm going to finish my drink on the patio while trying to forget this conversation."

Cindy reached for Will's hand resting on the table. Her smile faded as she studied him. "What?"

"Are we okay?"

His worries rushed at him, but he shoved them aside. Maybe he was overreacting. All the recent changes were probably freaking him out. Opening a restaurant, along with dating Cindy were huge.

They were all good. Nevertheless, it also brought up past regrets and future worries. He wanted both, yet feared he deserved neither and he'd somehow manage to fuck up everything.

He shook his head, positive he was overthinking. Twisting his hand around, he grasped her tight. "Yeah. We're great. Ignore my babbling this morning."

She opened her mouth as if to respond, but Jacob sauntered into the room, talking. "Please tell me you guys left me some coffee."

The carafe sat at the center of the table, forgotten and cold.

Cindy stood, grabbing the pot. "Oh, crap, sorry. I forgot to put it back."

"Wow. Nice. Crash at my house, take my wife's clothes, and my thanks is cold, congealed coffee," Jacob teased, taking it from her.

"I also got to see you naked," Cindy shot back, making Jacob stop in his tracks.

He half-turned, one brow raised. "What's that now?"

She smirked, recounting her goofy story, including Will's response.

Lucas walked in the kitchen just as Jacob retorted, "I might be the little brother. However, there isn't anything *little* on me."

"Oh, hell, are you still on this freaking topic?" Lucas groused.

"What topic?" Greta asked, strolling into the kitchen.

"You don't want to know," Lucas said.

Cindy quipped, "Who has a bigger penis. Jacob or Will."

Greta blinked rapidly for a few beats, before saying, "I'm not going to touch that..."

"That's what she said—" Lucas started, then stopped. "Oh, wait..."

Everyone started laughing. He shrugged, taking a sip of his coffee.

Jacob opened the fridge. "On that odd note, who wants eggs?"

The next twenty minutes were filled with easy chatter, as everyone pitched in with breakfast. When they were sitting around the table, Cindy asked Greta if she and Jacob were going to their mom's Halloween party.

"Didn't we get tickets for that Halloween masquerade the Masonic Temple?" Jacob asked.

"Yes, but we're going the weekend before," Greta answered. Catching her husband's disappointed groan, she playfully swatted his arm. "It'll be fun. The costumes are fantastic. The people watching is great. Plus, Cindy told me yesterday Will's going with her."

Will tried to drum up some excitement, but only found sarcasm. "Yeah, look at it this way, they hate me more than you. All their scorn will be tossed at me."

"This is true," Jacob agreed.

Greta threw a piece of toast at her husband.

Cindy gave Will a gentle push, saying, "They don't hate you."

Determined not to let Sophia's shallow disdain affect him and Cindy, he shifted the topic, asking about costume ideas.

# Chapter Twenty-One

Cindy tugged at her black wig, making sure it was in place. Leaning closer to the mirror, she checked her white face paint and fire-engine red lipstick. They were perfect.

Will opened the bathroom door. Stepping behind her, he ran a hand over his slicked, gelled hair. She twisted around, straightening his bowtie then smoothing the lapels of his wide pinstriped suit.

"You make such a hot Gomez."

Running a finger along his thin mustache, he complained, "This looks ridiculous."

"It's perfect for your costume. You can shave it off tomorrow."

"Hell, I'm taking a razor to it soon as we're home from the party."

"At least wait until morning," she cooed, slipping a hand under his suit jacket, coming closer. "I have this whole Morticia and Gomez role-playing fantasy going on in my mind."

"Oh, do you now?" His gaze fell to her plunging neckline while his hands traveled down the back of her formfitting dress, cupping her bottom.

She nodded, warm tendrils of heat wrapped around her. Forget tonight. She wanted him now.

He seemed to be of the same mindset, whispering into her neck, "Why wait? Ever since you put on this dress, I've been walking around half-hard." He pressed into her. He wasn't kidding.

"Stop tempting me." She tilted her head to the side to give him more access. "My sister and your brother will be here any minute."

"We'll make it quick. An appetizer." He kissed a trail from her collar bone to the tops of her breast.

"But it will mess up my makeup. Oh—" He'd pushed aside the severe dip in her dress, using his tongue to play with her nipple.

Gripping her shoulders, he turned her. Their gazes met in the mirror. The lust pooling in his eyes matched hers. She ached for him.

"I want your lipstick smeared all over my body. For now, I won't touch your enticing mouth." He bent, gathering the hem of her long dress in his hands, sliding it up her legs until the cool air caressed her bare bottom.

"Jesus, Cindy." He hooked a finger under the string of her panties, running a knuckle along the crack of her ass.

"You see this dress. What else am I supposed to wear?"

The need stamped on his face took her breath away. She bent slightly offering herself to him.

He licked his lips, continuing to play with her thong. "Are you sure?"

"Dip your hands in my panties. You'll feel how sure I am."

Crude words, but true. And from the way his breath caught as he hastened to unzip his slacks, she'd say he didn't mind her coarse talk.

She found a condom in her make-up bag and handed it to him. After putting it on, he shoved aside her thong and gently eased inside.

She didn't have time, nor the patience for gentleness. "Harder, Will," she demanded.

His fingers dug into her hips as he pulled back, then drove into her. Within minutes, they'd become frenzied need, filling the bathroom with their moans, each racing toward their climax.

Her pleasure built rapidly. When she was on the precipice of bliss, she reached between her legs using her fingers to help take her there.

"Fuck, woman," he grated.

He was watching her hand in the mirror with rapt attention. The carnality playing over his face did it for her. She tumbled into the ecstasy of her orgasm. It would've brought her to her knees if Will didn't have such a firm grip on her.

His release chased hers. His thrust so hard, her thighs dug into the counter. She loved it. His roughness sent ripples of pleasure throughout her body.

Afterward, he brushed aside her heavy wig, kissing her neck with such tenderness it made her heart swell.

The doorbell rang. He caught her gaze in the mirror. "I'll get it."

She nodded. It was easier than talking. She needed time to find her breath, slow her heart.

He left. A few minutes later, she heard the muffled voices of her sister and Jacob. Leaning in close, she checked her makeup, straightened her wig.

Her mother was always on the search for imperfections, harping that Cindy's job made her "on-call" at all times. She had to look her best in case someone from the magazines or a fashion designer saw her.

Cindy liked to think herself strong-willed, a woman who did what she desired. Greta was supposed to be the weak sister, bending backward to please her family. The reality was the opposite.

Greta quietly did what she wanted. Moved away for college, got a degree her mother despised. Married the "wrong sort" of man and refused to return to their hometown of Petite Bois.

Meanwhile, Cindy was the loud, empty rebel. Going into the career her mother picked, attending the sanctioned parties, and dating the "right sort" of man.

Well, until Will.

And she had no illusions. Mother's Halloween treat would be to pick at the seams of her daughter's new relationship.

Cindy squared her shoulders. It wasn't going to happen. This was the first time she had someone who liked her for more than her connections or a pretty smile.

He made her body quiver in satisfaction, filled her heart with laughter, gave her the courage to share her writing and photography. Her mother wasn't going to rip apart something good because it didn't fit into her narcissistic view of perfection.

She shut off the bathroom light. Determination flooded her. Tonight, she'd show everyone the woman she'd become. To hell with those who didn't like it.

Will tried not to be impressed and failed. Cindy's family didn't just have money. They were stinking rich. Six of his childhood homes could easily fit into this freaking mansion. The Halloween decorations could have come from a Hollywood movie set. There was even a tuxedo staff with silver trays of drinks and food.

A woman walked by, looking like she'd stepped straight out of the Victorian age. Her costume appeared more real than actual ones he'd seen in museums. He tugged at the cuffs of his suit. Thank God Cindy hadn't let him wear the one he'd bought at one of those temporary Halloween stores.

In fact, she'd laughed at him. At the time he'd been mildly offended. Now he was thankful. He took a deep breath, refusing to be intimidated by meaningless trappings.

Jacob leaned in. "Do you feel like the mangy mutt tracking mud on the white carpet?"

Will let out a light snort and couldn't resist checking his shoes. No dirt.

His brother clapped him on the back as they went farther into the house with their women. They passed an opulent marble staircase with a dark wooden banister to enter a room that was a cross between a living room and the seating area for the Detroit Symphony Hall, leaning more toward ballroom.

Sure, there was an assortment of plush couches, chairs, and tables. However, most homes didn't have a baby grand on its own stage or cathedral ceilings with a chandelier dripping crystals. Oh, let's not forget an upstairs with marble alcoves and balconies, looking down on the main floor.

Cindy stopped along the way, introducing him to friends and family. To his surprise, most were friendly, even welcoming. The only odd moment was when an older woman, dressed like the Queen of England came around the corner, almost running into them. She smiled at Cindy, but it fell away when her gaze landed on Jacob.

"Perfect costume for you." She sniffed, clutching her pearls and hurrying around them.

Jacob laughed, tipping his fedora at her retreating back. "Nice to know Mrs. Turner hasn't forgotten me."

"A friend of yours?" Will asked.

"Ha. We met at a New Year's party when Greta and I were dating. She doesn't like me."

Will laughed. "Yeah. I caught that."

Greta gripped the lapels of his jacket, kissing both his cheeks. "I do agree with her this time. Your costume is perfect. You make one handsome Clyde."

"You make an exquisite Bonnie." He hugged her, not letting go.

Cindy cleared her throat. "Damn honeymooners. You two need a room? The study is off to your right."

Jacob wrapped an arm around his wife's waist. "Sorry, we couldn't fit in a quickie beforehand... like some people."

Cindy's gaze flew to Will. He held up his hands. "I didn't say anything."

His brother laughed, full of mirth and mischievousness. "No, not in words. When we arrived at your place, Greta innocently asked Will where you were. He blushed like a damn school girl, mumbling you needed to fix your dress or something."

A waiter came by with a drink tray. Will grabbed Cindy a glass of wine and himself sparkling water, muttering, "She did need to fix her dress."

Jacob handed Greta a red wine, then ordered himself a bourbon. He turned to Will, smirking. "You're blushing again."

*Asshole.* He pressed the cold glass to his cheeks, making them laugh. Though, he didn't mind the teasing.

"You are such a paradox," said Cindy, when the waiter returned with Jacob's drink.

"How so?"

"You're bossy in the bedroom. Incredibly modest outside of it."

Jacob choked on his sip of bourbon, as Will's cheeks and neck flared red hot.

Thankfully, he was saved from responding. A woman embraced Greta, then introduced herself as Lily before asking Greta about her honeymoon.

The evening passed in this fashion. Cindy introduced him to an impossible number of friends. Eventually he found his groove, enjoying the food, music, and people. Although it didn't escape his notice her parents steered clear of him, talking to Cindy when he wasn't next to her.

Not that he gave a shit. He didn't relish their company. Hell, their disapproval tried to slither and strangle him from across the room. He had no desire to deal with it up close.

Eventually his luck had run out. He'd been talking with the owner of Summer Grill when they'd been interrupted by a call from her daughter's babysitter. That had left him two choices. Stand by the hors d'oeuvre table alone or approach his girlfriend and her mother.

He was tempted to swing by the restroom instead, but it seemed like a pussy move. Plus, Cindy's deepening frown made him think she might like an interruption.

Look at him, playing the white knight, and shit. It made him chuckle. He was no one's savior.

Moving behind his girlfriend, he learned they were discussing Cindy's webpage.

"Yes, I agree Greta did a lovely job. I'm saying, why bother? You make plenty of money. Why play at this starving artist rubbish, pushing your pretty photos on to people?" Sophia took a small sip of her drink before continuing, "Harper is doing the same with her paintings and clay. It's tacky. Kindergarten is over." Sophia sighed. "At least her mother bought her a studio, stopping her daughter from selling her trinkets at crafts shows in the park."

The woman shuddered like it was equal to selling her body on the street corner. It took everything he had not to roll his eyes, to tell her she was the one who needed to grow up.

Resting a hand on the small of Cindy's back, he said, "Your daughter is a talented photographer and writer. Don't you want her to share, to grow her talent?"

Sophia's rigid gaze flicked to him. Her lips pursed, probably deciding if she'd deign to answer him. "If she's so talented, why is no one buying her work?"

It seemed spilling her displeasure all over daughter outweighed her desire to ignore him. He hurt for Cindy.

What was it like to have Sophia as a mother? His had encouraged him and Jacob with everything they tried, never forcing her agenda on them. Cindy's mom was a narcissist who wanted her daughters' pursuits to boost her snobbish image.

"It takes time," he argued, knowing he was wasting his breath. "The arts are a difficult field to break into—"

"She already has a great job. She needs to focus on maintaining, growing *that* career, and not on some frivolous hobby. She's already in her mid-twenties, the younger ones will soon be shoving her aside."

He scoffed. At ninety Cindy would still be the most attractive woman in the room.

"Mother, if I'll soon be run out by the younger, prettier girls, shouldn't I be pursuing another career?"

"You won't be if you apply yourself. Up your beauty regimen, workout more, lose excess, dead weight." Sophia's glare fell on Will, making it clear she thought he was the burden.

He stared back, refusing to let this woman make him or Cindy feel inadequate. "Your daughter is perfect, Mrs. Silverstone."

Her face twisted tight like it pained her to talk to him. "Why were you talking to Chelsea?"

He was confused. "Who?"

"Chelsea Fortes."

"Oh, Ms. Fortes. She owns Summer Grill. Where I work," he clarified.

Sophia raised one skeptical brow. "She knows you? Aren't you a dishwasher or something? What could she possibly have to say to you?"

"Mother." Cindy sighed as Will held in an incredulous laugh. "I told you he was a chef. I also told you where he worked."

Refusing to let the pretentious woman get a rise from him, he said evenly, "She was trying to talk me into staying."

"Why would you leave? I'm sure that job is the best someone like you can expect from life."

Damn the woman had a true talent for knowing the weak spots to hit.

"He, nor I, need to explain ourselves to you," Cindy said between clenched teeth and a false smile. "Now, if you'll excuse us."

She took Will's hand, leading him to the dance floor.

They swayed to the gentle melody the band was playing. "Sorry. My mom is a bit of a bitch."

He choked on a surprised chuckle. His girl didn't hold back.

"I'm getting the sense she doesn't like me," he teased.

Cindy laughed. "Sometimes I think the only person she loves is herself."

The ache for the child she had been, deepened. It must've sucked, having a mother full of vanity and conditions. Her words had stung him a time or two, but he suspected she'd repeatedly wounded her daughters.

"I think it's more she wants to live vicariously through her girls, and it pisses her off when her daughters won't play her games. Instead, you both are picking your paths."

"Why in the world would she want our lives? She seems to be doing well." Cindy took a tiny step back, spreading her arms, indicating the opulence around them.

Bringing her into his arms, he took a guess, asking, "Did your mom ever have a career? Anything of her own, like you and Greta?"

"She was a model for a short while. She met my father early in her career. They married, and shortly after, she had Greta. Since then she's joined a million committees and boards."

"None of it is her own."

She wrinkled her nose. "My mother has her hand in everything in this town. Hell, people here don't fart without asking her permission first."

He let out a bark of laughter that had a few people looking their way. Cindy waved at them before facing him.

"Okay, let me say it another way. You've taken your modeling career farther than her. She had to give up hers. She might be afraid you will do the same. Though instead of family, you'll do it for writing and photography. How people view her is very important. Unfortunately, she sees you as an extension of her. If you leave modeling to get what she deems a lesser job, people might talk. Think her daughter is getting passed over."

"Maybe the last part is why she doesn't like you." Cindy squeezed his waist. "She wants people green with envy that her daughter is dating some movie star or the son of a senator."

He gave a lopsided grin, trying to keep his voice light. "You mean, not some loser with a criminal record?"

"Damnit, Will." She smacked his arm, fire in her eyes. "Stop thinking your past mistakes are who you are now. They are part of you but don't define you."

"Fine. Fine." He brushed aside her words, not wanting to talk about him. He'd seen the stoop of her shoulders, her brittle smile when her mother berated her talent. "Don't quit before you've even started. You have talent."

"Tell that to the people who aren't interested in my work."

"It takes time."

"Says the guy who decides something, and everything falls into place," she muttered to the buttons of his shirt.

He stopped dancing, lifting her chin, he asked, "What do you mean?"

"Nothing. I'm having a pity party." She shook her head, dislodging his grip. "Oh! Kristen is here. Come on, I want you to meet her. We were in equestrian club together in high school. She is a blast."

Will didn't want to talk to some old friend. He'd rather learn what was bothering her. Instead, he was being dragged from the dance floor and the conversation.

He suspected that was the reason for the introduction. His girlfriend had a talent for avoiding subjects she found unpleasant.

Oh well. Everyone had blemishes they'd rather forget, not examine too closely. He was the same.

The rest of the evening was filled with friends, food, and light flirting. Not bad as parties went, nonetheless, relief settled over Will when they returned to Cindy's condo. She fell back onto her couch, propping her high-heeled feet on the coffee table.

"Did you have a terrible time?" she asked.

Huh. He thought he'd kept his party-pooper broody side under wraps.

"No. Why do you ask?" He removed his suit jacket. Sitting next to her, he unbuttoned his shirt, letting it fall open, exposing the white cotton T-shirt underneath, too lazy to bother taking it off.

"You were quiet, more reserved than usual." She slid sideways onto his lap. He'd have liked her to straddle him, but it was impossible with her long, tight dress.

"Was I?" The stress of opening the restaurant was getting to him. He wasn't sleeping well, second-guessing everything. However, with the way she was earlier about it, he didn't want to bring it up.

Cindy nodded. "I'm not complaining. I like the spotlight, always have. It's nice dating someone I don't have to compete with for it."

He chuckled, removing her black wig, running his fingers through her hair. "Glad you're woman enough to admit you're a total prima donna."

She melted into him, purring, "Oh, that's nice."

"Sit between my legs, resting into my chest. I can use both hands." Although, if she kept moaning and talking in that, low husky voice, she'll have to deal with his hard-on pressing against her.

She weakly protested. "You weren't supposed to take off the wig. Remember, we're supposed to have kinky times as Mr. and Mrs. Addams."

He was up for it. Literally. "You want me to stop?"

"Hell. No," she moaned, her head falling forward, giving him access to her neck and shoulders. He took the hint, moving lower.

She hummed in pleasure, before saying, "Anyway, I'm glad you didn't have a horrible time, but I do apologize for Mother and Nigel. They weren't very hospitable."

He shrugged. "I wasn't expecting a warm reception. They aren't fans of the Grimms, plus your mom knows about my past. She got her hands on both our records that time she had Jacob arrested."

"They're starting to warm to Jacob. Give them time with you."

"Um. She knows my brother's arrests were mistakes. Mine weren't." He tried shaking his despair. It had been a hectic day, and while most of it was good, he was exhausted. Tonight wasn't the time to face bleak facts. Turning away, he asked, "Ready for bed?"

She nodded. He picked her up, one arm under her legs, the other across her back. She rested on his chest as he carried her over the threshold into her bedroom like a bride. It made his heart ache to know such things weren't possible with him. Guys like him didn't make good husbands.

# Chapter Twenty-Two

Will tapped the pink razor on the side of the sink. The last remnants of the stupid mustache washed down the drain. He hoped Cindy didn't mind him using her stuff. He couldn't stand the way it tickled his upper lip.

He spent so much time at her place, he should leave one here. Along with a few other necessities. No. That was a little too cozy. Too domestic.

Having a girlfriend still gave him moments of panic. He hadn't had one since Jolene, and during his low moments it unsettled him. A lot.

Cindy reminded him of his mom, strong and independent. Bossy. Beautiful.

Yet, everyone needed someone to lean on sometimes. He wasn't good at that part. He was weak like his dad.

When Mom's cancer started eating away at her faster than the chemo could keep up, Dad fell apart. Sure, he stayed at her side, but with a bottle of whiskey in his hand.

Will hadn't been much better. He'd turned away from his family, from his mother, he should have been at her side. Instead, he was out finding oblivion. In drugs.

They'd left Jacob to pick up their broken pieces.

Will had done the same with Jolene. Pretending things were fine, that everything was under control, until, well, until it all fell apart.

"Did you fall asleep in there?"

He shook off his melancholy. "Almost done," he called.

He finished rinsing his face, then opened the bathroom door. Cindy was in bed, a few pillows propped behind her, a book on her lap.

The simple, intimate sight shot him right in the heart. It didn't matter he wasn't ready for love, it had him in its tight grasp.

He wanted a million mornings like this, her in a bed they shared, rested and content. Happy to be with him.

Setting aside her paperback, she took in his bare toes, moved to his boxer-briefs, then to his T-shirt, stopping at his face. "I see you shaved your pornstache."

"Hey! You told me you liked it." He ran a finger between his nose and upper lip.

She wiggled her brows. "Maybe I have a thing for porn stars."

"Want me to grow it back?"

"Na. You have other assets comparable to a porn star." Her gaze traveled to his boxers. "One way more important."

He coughed out a laugh. Coming to the end of the bed, he crawled up it, saying, "You are full of wit and flattery this morning."

"Just this morning?"

"Every morning, darling," he amended. "Anyway, I hope you don't mind, I borrowed your razor."

"The pink one?"

Something in her voice, gave him pause. He sat back on his haunches, her legs between his. "Um, yeah. Why?"

"It's the one I use to shave my nether regions."

He shrugged. "Oh, that's it?"

"You're supposed to be scandalized," she huffed.

He laughed, dropping forward, kissing her neck. "I love having my face between your legs, so why would I be appalled to discover I've used something that has also visited there."

"You're dirty." She reached around, managing to smack his ass. "I like it."

"I'm not surprised, given your admiration for men in adult movies." His remark earned him a tickle along the ribs, making him roll away.

She set her book on the nightstand. "Do you want to stop by your place? You can grab a few spare things to keep here."

He froze. It was like she'd crawled into his mind and found his thoughts from earlier.

"Or not," she muttered, falling back onto her pillows.

"Oh. No. I, um, that'd be great. You caught me by surprise."

Damn it. He was screwing this up. Thinking over the pounding of his heart, the racing of his pulse, was impossible.

She kept her gaze fixed on the ceiling. "I suggested you leave a few things here, not move in. So, don't wig out and run for the door."

"I'm not freaking," he lied. "Like I said, you caught me by surprise. It's a step toward, I don't know... more. I assumed you didn't do more."

"I don't. Or at least I haven't. You're different." One side of her mouth lifted into a half smile. "Does it bother you?"

His immediate response was a firm no. Her words were like a blast of sunshine in the cold corners of his heart, while at the same time, the light exposed his fears, the ones that screamed he'd never be enough. He'd eventually fail her. What gutted him was, he could see so much with her. A future. Happiness. All of which, he didn't deserve.

Unwilling to explain his fucked-up reasoning, he went with deflection. "Why me?"

"Got me. You're such an obstinate Neanderthal." Her smile faltered, and she began to pick at a loose thread on his T-shirt.

He waited her out. When she finally spoke, his world shifted.

"I care about you. A lot. I think I'm falling for you."

For a split second a lightness ricocheted through him, elation perhaps. It died before he could accurately name it. He shifted away, sitting at the edge of the bed. His back to her.

"Don't, Cindy. I'm not a good man to love."

She came around, standing in front of him. "Why? You're an easy man to love."

He heard confusion, anger, and hurt in her voice. The sound was a knife wound to his heart. Although, a little pain now was better than the avalanche of pain he'd offer in the long run.

"Do you remember the day your mom walked in on us, what she said? That I destroy everything, everyone I touch. She's right. Everything, everyone, I love..."

Cindy slammed her hands on her hips. "Stop it! You aren't the man you were five years ago. Hell, two years ago. From what I see, you've rebuilt your life and are surrounded by people who you care about. Friends, family—"

"But not love. At least not the kind involving another person to depend on me. To hand me their heart. I don't date. I don't risk it."

"We aren't dating?"

Pulling her against him, he pressed his face tight against her stomach. "What can I say? I'm a greedy bastard. I can't stay away. It goes to show you I haven't changed all that much. I still take what I want. Screw the consequences."

She gripped a handful of his hair, tugging his head back, making him look at her. "Don't be ridiculous. It isn't taking if I'm offering. I want you just as much."

*Yeah, but you have no idea the mess you jumped into, hooking up with me.*

"And what about Cora?"

The question threw him. "What about her?"

"Weren't you dating her?"

"Um. No. We're friends."

Cindy quirked a brow.

Will's lips twitched. "At the time, friends with benefits. Now only a friend. We slept together, talked shop. Feelings didn't go deeper."

"Why?"

"For the reason I just gave you. I make a terrible boyfriend. I don't want to be responsible for another person's heart. I don't have it in me."

"Okay. Fine I get it," she said.

She was backing away from him, physically and mentally. He tightened his grip around her waist. "Get what?"

She tried to shake him off. "It's fine. You don't feel the same. You don't want my heart because I don't have yours."

*Oh. Hell no.*

He stood, hugging her roughly. "No. I do. Hell, I knew back at the lake house I could easily fall for you. It's why I tried to stay away. I am shit at relationships."

She tried to push him away. He gave her a little room but didn't let go. After a second, she gave up. "Don't lie. Don't tell me you're one of those commitment phobia guys. Jacob mentioned you dated the same girl throughout high school, and after, well into your twenties. It must be me. I'm your good-time girl. The one you date, have sex with on your days off."

He was fucking up royally. Every time he opened his mouth, he made it worse. He should leave it alone, end it now before he cut her deeper.

He should, but couldn't.

"The opposite. I care too much about you. That's the problem." He cupped the sides of her face. "Yes, I was with Jolene for almost ten years. And I ruined her. I don't want to do the same to you."

"Come on, Will. I'm sure she got over her broken heart." Cindy rolled her eyes. "We've all been crappy to people we love. Said and did things we regret or ended a relationship on less than good terms."

He shook slightly and let go of her. His body was overflowing with a yearning for what he couldn't have, mixing with years of regrets.

"I wish all I'd given her were bad memories. A few tears." He ran an agitated hand up and down his face. "No, Cindy. I didn't break her heart. I took her life.."

She froze. There was an eternity in those beats of silence.

Backing away, she asked, "What do you mean? Are you violent?"

"No. God, no. But I'm destructive. Selfish." He sighed, slumping back onto the bed. "When I met Jolene, she was a straight A student, never in trouble. In the Science and Math club, running for class president. Then she made the mistake of falling in love with me. What did I give her in return? Wreckage and devastation. Death. First, I introduced her to pot, next Captain and Coke. Then Coke. Cocaine. When we couldn't afford that high, we switched to heroin. We moved in together. I destroyed her life. In the end, I took that too. She overdosed. Died in bed. Right next to me." His voice cracked. "I was too high to even notice."

Tears hit his fisted hands. It took a moment to realize they were his own.

Not wanting to see Cindy's shock, her disappointment at his failure, he kept his head down. To his shock, she brought him against her.

He pressed his head into her chest, craving her comfort even though he didn't deserve it. He noticed her heart was racing. It probably matched her thoughts.

"Will, that's awful," she whispered.

He nodded. "I am."

"No. I said that's awful, not you." She gripped his shoulders, pulling so he'd stand. When he was looking at her, she said, "You don't bear the full weight of her mistakes. Listen, in my line of work, I'm offered drugs all the time. It's my choice to say no. If I accept, the consequences are my own, not the supplier's."

He'd love to buy into her argument. It'd make the guilt easier to breathe around. However, it wasn't the same. "There's a difference when someone you care, you trust, offers it. When you hesitate, and they tell you it will be fun. That everything will be fine. Convinces you shit is gold and diamonds."

"Yes, I suppose. Then again, in the end, she chose to try. And to continue."

"Addiction isn't that simple."

"I'm sure it's not, but neither is love. I've never been in a serious relationship. I've done most things on my own, including making my day-to-day choices and mistakes. If

I consider you my boyfriend, someone I love, I don't suddenly expect you to bear the burden of my missteps."

Will swallowed the lump in his throat, meeting her gaze. She looked scared.

So was he.

"What if I'm the mistake?" he asked.

She tightened her arms around him, kissing his cheek. "Oh, Will, I've made enough mistakes in my life to know you're not one of them."

He wanted her words to be true, so damn much. His longing was nearly corporeal, twisting around his heart.

Turning, he returned her embrace. He'd try to be the man she believed him to be.

She shifted, straddling him. Kissing him with a tenderness he didn't deserve. "Are you willing to risk your heart again? With me? I need to know. I care about you too much to pretend I'm not falling for you. If you can't, I need to back away."

Since Jolene's death, he swore he'd keep things simple. Never risk hurting another person, but damn it, he couldn't let Cindy leave.

He was positive his faults would become too much for her. Until then, he wasn't letting her go.

Running a hand through her hair, he wrapped it around his fist, resting his forehead against hers. "You already have my heart. It's tarnished and imperfect, but all yours."

"I promise to handle it with care," she said against his lips.

She kissed him. He gripped her thighs, standing. Bringing her to the bed, he laid her gently down, determined to show how much he cherished her.

Will's confession and heartbreak swirled within Cindy, racing alongside fear and her building lust. Part of her did worry what she was getting into with him. His mistakes had enormous consequences that might not stay in the past.

With her job, she'd met enough people fighting addiction. She'd seen the devastation relapse caused.

He ran strong hands down her sides, kissing her with such focus and sweetness she found it impossible to picture him as the out-of-control man of his past. Maybe she was delusional to ignore his past, to see him as he was now. However, she hadn't lied; he was a gamble worth taking.

His palms skated to her nightdress, lifting it. Her concerns fell aside. Right now, all she could concentrate on was his touch. The combination of the soft silk and the rough pad of his fingertips was heaven. She raised her arms without him asking, letting him continue the path she so desired.

Instead of slipping it off, he twisted it, binding her wrists. With one hand he gripped the material, pinning her arms while moving down her body.

He took his time, exploring at leisure. His free hand brushed along the underside of her breasts before he began playing along her earlobe. Hips rocking with slow lazy thrusts, made her arch into him, needing more.

"Take them off," she begged.

"Take what off?" His smile was as languid as his movements.

She'd have smacked him for his cockiness, except at the moment she was restrained.

"My panties. Now." The last part was a whimper. She didn't care. Between his busy hands, hips, and mouth, she was losing her mind.

He didn't argue. Letting go of her wrists, he did as she demanded, leisurely sliding them along her legs.

Gripping her ankles, he brought her to the edge of the bed. He knelt between her legs, kissing along her inner thigh until reaching her center. She wriggled her hands free of her nightgown, entwining her fingers in his hair.

Oh, heaven and hell, the things he did with his tongue had her shouting his name in a matter of minutes. If she wasn't drowning in bliss, she'd be embarrassed.

He sucked, bit, and caressed every ounce of pleasure from her body. After, he kissed his way up her body, stopping to nip her hip, making her giggle. He trailed his mouth from her stomach to her breasts, giving them his full attention. Her nipples perked at his touch. The blood that had scattered during her intense orgasm was rushing south again.

She wanted more of him.

Scooting to the center of the bed, she whispered, "Come here."

He nodded before turning to the nightstand.

"Leave them," she said, her heart skipping a beat. She'd never not used protection, yet didn't regret the suggestion.

He studied her, whispering, "Are you sure?"

"Yes. I want nothing between us."

"Neither do I. Still... I've taken so many risks." He raised a hand, probably reading her spike of alarm. "I don't mean disease. I've been tested many times since my partying days. After Jolene, I've always used a condom. I'm talking about a different set of risks."

She understood what he meant. "I've never skipped the pill since I started taking it." Gripping the back of his neck, she kissed him lightly before continuing, "Of course, there is a small chance. However, with you, for some reason, it doesn't worry me. Crazy. Stupid, I know."

Her heart pounded. She was laying her soul bare before him. Would he freak, like he did earlier?

To her surprise and joy, he rested his forehead against hers. "No. I get it. It scares the hell out of me, but I get it. I feel it too." He kissed her in a way that made her believe he truly did love her.

Never removing his lips from hers, he nudged her legs apart, gently easing inside her. The warmth of him was incredible. Although what made her heart skip a beat was when he shifted to look at her. The love and trust reflected in his eyes stole her breath.

He moved, slow and easy. Her breath hitched now for an entirely different reason. Pleasure rocked through her. Words were no longer needed, as she met his pace.

Before long, her second orgasm began to build. Shifting her hips under him, she reached the needed angle. His hungry growl filled the room. He thrust harder, sending her over the edge, with him following.

His mouth met hers, his groan of satisfaction mingling with her cry of ecstasy. It was the perfect ending to their new beginning.

# Chapter Twenty-Three

"**C**ome on, put your back into it. Use those muscles you spend hours sculpting at the gym," Will called to Tim, hoisting the tree's trunk onto his shoulder and probably covering his coat with sap.

"Damnit, I'm trying. Did you have to get the biggest tree on the lot?" Tim replied, heaving the top half of the Christmas spruce up the steps of Cindy's porch. She held the door open, a smile on her face bright as the lights that'd soon be on the tree.

Most of the morning, he and Cindy, along with Emma and Max, had driven to a million craft stores, selecting decorations. The afternoon was spent at Eastern Market finding the perfect tree.

He'd never seen her this excited. She was, well, like a kid at Christmas. She'd told him she never bothered with the holiday trappings since moving to her condo. She wasn't home much and would spend Christmas Eve at some party or another, the actual holiday at her parents.

This year was Max's first Christmas. It had to be special, there'd be no holding back. She needed the biggest tree, a wreath on each door, garland across the fireplace and wrapped around every banister. Poinsettias on every tabletop.

The holiday plant sparked a heated conversation on whether or not the plant was poisonous. It turns out, it's not, but holly berries are deadly. Go figure.

Cindy confessed she was in a mood for a different sort of holiday this year. Her job would require her to go to lots of events. However, she planned on spending her Christmas Eve with him. In front of a fire, preferably naked.

Without losing too many evergreen needles, they forced the tree through the door, then Will asked her, "Did you assemble the tree stand? Where are we putting this behemoth?"

"Over here." She pointed to a corner in her living room, near the big, bay window. "What do you think, Emma? Is it a nice spot?"

"How would I know? Do I look like one of Santa's elves?" Her friend laughed.

"More like Satan," Cindy muttered.

Will and Tim brought the tree to the directed spot, wrestling it into the stand. To his amazement, the height was perfect. There was even room for the fancy star Cindy bought.

He stepped back, admiring it. The weak sunlight shone against the deep green needles. Once decorated, it would be gorgeous.

Cindy's excitement for Christmas must be catching because he hadn't cared about this crap since he was a kid. Now he was eager to dig into the decorations, to make her place into a winter wonderland.

Will turned to ask Tim if he'd help bring in the stuff from the car, paused when he found his friend checking out Emma. He wasn't very subtle, but she was too busy admiring the tree to notice someone found her way more interesting.

When Tim had arrived at Cindy's to help with the tree, Emma was in her room, putting Max down for a nap. This was his first glimpse of her. The poor man looked like someone had hit him upside the head with the damn Christmas tree.

However, from what Will knew of his friend, his fascination would end soon enough. He'd be less smitten when he learned she had a toddler.

Tim would sink all his money, credit, and good name into a business and in a city that was a risk. Or he'd spend it on crazy daredevil vacations. But, if someone wanted to truly terrify the guy, have one of his girlfriend's mention commitment.

Will bumped his friend's shoulder. "Want to help with the boxes in the car?"

"What?"

Shit. The dude was dazed. Will repeated his question. Tim nodded, following him outside.

"She has a kid."

"Who?"

"Emma. Cindy's roommate."

Tim was in the middle of reaching into the trunk and froze. It reminded Will of the Tinman from Wizard of Oz when he started crying and rusted. The image made Will laugh.

"Shut up, dude. That's not funny."

"I'm not laughing because I was joking. I'm dead serious. It's your reaction that's funny. I said she has a kid, not cancer."

"It's worse. Cancer is curable. Kids are for life."

He smacked Tim on the back of the head. "You're an asshole. You know that, right?"

"Yeah, I know." He hoisted a big box under each arm. "Listen. Back in the day, I had to play Mr. Mom to my brother and sisters when my mom walked, and Dad checked out. I have no desire to do it again. I want my freedom. That means no kids."

To Will's surprise he found himself protective of Cindy's roommate and kid. "Fine, but that means, forget Emma. Max is part of the package."

Tim shook his head. "Yeah, I know. It's too bad, something about her, I don't know, is different."

"What makes you think she'd even be interested in your ass?"

"Have you seen my dimples?" He smiled, flashing them at Will. "And earlier I remember you remarking on my gym physique."

"Dude. I was calling you a useless meathead."

"I'm pretty." Tim started for the stairs, whistling.

Will shook his head, grabbing a bunch of bags, following his friend. When he stepped inside, Cindy was asking Tim to stay, asking what he wanted on his pizza.

Watching Emma again, he backed toward the door. "No. I don't want to intrude..."

"Do you see everything we bought?" Emma said, opening one box, removing a bundle of lights. "It's going to take a week to put it all up. We could use a drudge," she winked, "I mean, a helping hand."

"Oh. Well, if you need me, I'll stay."

Emma blushed. "I better go check on Max."

She hurried from the room. When the door clicked shut, Cindy said, "Be careful, Tim. This last year has been hell for her. Don't add to it."

"Yeah, what's up with you, man?" Will was a little annoyed. "Didn't you just say a woman with a kid is worse than—"

Tim made a calming motion with hands, silencing him. "Damn. Lower your hackles. I'm not trying to add anything. She seems sweet. I want to chat with her. Maybe some light flirting. I'm not going to corrupt her."

"Um, you talking to her, might be enough," Will said, half teasing. Tim was a great friend. However, his reputation with women wasn't the best.

He covered his heart. "Ouch. That hurt."

"I didn't realize I have two guard dogs." Emma stood at the entrance of the living room, Max on the crook of her hip. "I appreciate it, but I think I can handle someone like him."

Tim blushed as her gaze zeroed in on him. "If I wanted to," she continued, "and who says I do?" Max squirmed in her arms. "Okay. Okay, give me a minute, you wiggle worm."

She set him on the rug next to his toys. He took off straight for Tim.

Will expected him to run and jump on the couch, like a skittish woman seeing a mouse. Or at least get out of the way. Instead, he picked the toddler up, lifting him above his head. Max's squeal of delight filled the room.

Tim went to set the little guy down, but his chubby hands tightened around the man's neck. "Oh, okay. Fine. Looks like I'll be your slave too." He lifted the happy little guy again, resting him on his hip as Emma had moments ago.

Will's expression must have shown his surprise. Tim laughed. "What? I might not want kids of my own, doesn't mean I don't like them. They're way more fun than adults."

*Huh. Just when you think you know someone.*

"Uh-oh, Will. You have competition for Max's love," Emma teased.

"No surprise. They have a lot in common. Their maturity is nearly at the same level," Will shot back.

Tim bounced Max, smirking at Will. "Careful, your jealousy is showing."

Cindy came around the kitchen counter, hugging him before patting his cheek. "Aw, don't worry, baby, you're my favorite."

Will pretended to sniffle. "You swear?"

"Yup. You're my favorite man-servant." She slapped his ass. "Now get to work. I need the rest of the stuff brought in from the car, the tree decorated, and the garland around the porch railing. Oh, I was thinking we should go back. I want to get two small trees to put on each side of the door."

He hung his head, slouching his shoulders exaggeratedly, shuffling to the door. "Geez, at least servants get paid."

"I'll pay with pizza and sex."

He straightened, moving quicker. "Sold."

"So, Emma, you mentioned me being your servant—" Tim began.

She cut him off. "No. I said, drudge. But I'm kind. I will give you a piece ...of pizza."

"Good thing I like pizza." He laughed, sitting cross-legged on the floor, keeping Max on his lap while pulling a shopping bag toward him.

The afternoon passed in a flash of decorations, laughter, and lots of Christmas spirit. Will didn't even mind when someone turned on carols. He hadn't gotten into the holidays like this since before his mom passed away. When everything fell apart.

Part of it was Max. Holidays and kids went together. They brought back the magic and wonder. The rest was Cindy. She made everything brighter, lighter.

She made him forget all that could go wrong and focus on everything going right. Kept him in the present, instead of lingering in the past with his mistakes. Or worse, visiting a future where his failures drown him and those he loves.

"You still with us?" she asked.

He was staring into the flames, crackling in the fireplace. He shook his head, realizing she was right next to him. "Sorry. Lost in my head."

"Glad you found your way out before Tim left." Leaning in closer, she whispered, "I think he gave Emma his number. I'm not sure how I feel about it."

This protective side of Cindy with Emma surprised him. He liked it. When they first met, he couldn't picture her caring about anyone except herself. He soon learned she was fiercely loyal to her friends, to those she cared about. He was lucky to be in that circle.

"I'm sure she'll be fine," he said. "She doesn't strike me as a woman to be charmed by a set of dimples and empty promises."

"No. Not anymore."

"What are you two whispering about?" Tim asked as he put on his coat.

Will tilted his head toward Cindy. "She's trying to tell me Santa isn't real."

Emma shushed him even though Max was curled on the couch, fast asleep. Will laughed, pointing at Cindy. "What? I believe. Talk to your roommate, the Grinch."

"Ignore him. He's a dork," she said, a lovely smile playing on her lips. "Tim, I have some coffee. Let me get you a mug for the road. It's late. You'll need something to keep you awake."

"Thanks. I could use some."

"Are you tired? You could always crash here," Cindy said.

Tim's gaze shifted from Cindy to Emma.

"On the couch," Cindy clarified.

He smirked. "No, I'm fine. I more want the coffee for the warmth than the caffeine."

Handing him a travel mug, she asked, "Are you going to Greta and Jacob's Christmas Eve party?"

"Hell, yeah. Their gatherings are the best." He looked at Will. "Are you cooking?"

"Yeah. The main dish, anyway."

"Cool. Let me know if you need help. Maybe we can make a few things we'll serve at the restaurant. Let people know." He shrugged. "Nothing wrong with a little self-promotion while celebrating."

Will nodded. That was a good idea. He told Tim they'd talk next week, plan a menu. He agreed, said his goodbyes to everyone, once again letting his gaze linger on Emma.

Damn the guy had it bad.

"This place looks great," Cindy gushed, turning in a full circle.

Will agreed. The decorations were pretty. However, if he had to pick what was beautiful in the room, it wouldn't be the Christmas decorations. It'd be his sexy girlfriend, full of smiles and delight.

"It is lovely. Thank you both so much." Emma was gazing at her sleeping son. "His first Christmas is going to be special."

Cindy glowed, reaching for Will. "Ready for bed?"

He took her hand. "Definitely. I've had my pizza. I'm ready for the other payment you promised."

"I guarantee it will be tastier than the pizza."

"I have no doubt," he growled, lining her body against his.

"Geez. Could you two save it for the bedroom?" Emma sighed.

Oops. He'd forgotten she was in the room.

"I can't even remember the last time I had sex. And tasty sex…" She exhaled.

"Wesley wasn't any good?" Cindy asked.

"You're surprised?"

"No, not really." Cindy tilted her head. "Maybe we should've asked Tim to stay. I've heard he's great in bed."

Will cocked a brow. "Who told you this? How did it even come up?"

"One of his old girlfriends. We were talking about sex."

*Hmm.*

"Really?"

She patted his chest. "Honey, women love to discuss it. In detail."

"Do you talk about us?"

She nodded as Emma said, "Don't worry, you're the envy of all her friends."

Warmth bloomed on his neck and cheeks, thinking of the things they'd done. The things he'd said to her. What exactly had she shared? Did he want to know?

*Nope.*

"Come on, love," he said, starting for the bedroom. "I'll try to live up to my reputation."

"You better, otherwise I might tell my friends." She grabbed his ass, he jumped a little, his gaze darting to Emma. She was giggling.

# Chapter Twenty-Four

Cindy took in her sister's house. One word came to mind. *Wow.*

It wasn't like Mother and Nigel's perfect Christmas splendor, where they paid someone an exorbitant amount of money to make it flawless. Her sister's place was warmer, had character. It spoke of tender memories and happy gatherings.

Large old-style multi-color bulbs lined both peaks on the roof. Multi-colored lights twinkled through the bare bushes running along the front of the house. The window box on the second level overflowed with pine and holly. At the corner of the wrap-around porch, a fully decorated Christmas tree stood. To top off this picture-perfect sight, a fresh dusting of snow covered everything.

She inhaled deeply. Winter, along with the slight scent of burning logs filled her lungs. The combination made her want to break out singing her favorite Christmas carols.

Will hugged her, resting his head on her shoulder. "Is this your first time here since they decorated?"

She nodded. With her job, December was one social event after another. Networking, being seen. It didn't leave much time for visiting the people she actually wanted to see. Over the last three weeks, she and Will had been together maybe a handful of times.

He'd skipped most of her work-related events, claiming he was either at Summer Grill or meeting someone in regards to opening his restaurant. She understood he didn't like parties. It didn't matter. Deep down, it hurt her feelings. She wanted him to be part of her life. Modeling was a big chunk of it. She'd have liked him to attend at least a few of the holiday gatherings.

She shook off her discontent. Tonight was Christmas Eve. She wasn't going to spoil it with downer thoughts. Leaning into his embrace, she said, "Yes, it is my first time seeing it. I love it."

"Yeah, it sure beats my holiday décor. It puts Mom's old ceramic tree on the kitchen table and the wreath I hung on my front door to shame."

"Don't forget you turned my condo into a winter wonderland."

He came around, taking her hand and leading her to the porch. "Maybe next year we could decorate my balcony and the inside of my apartment."

The way he casually spoke of how they'd be together next year, as if it were a given, warmed her better than a blazing fire or a mug of hot chocolate.

He opened the front door hollering, "Merry Christmas!" There was a chorus of returned greetings.

The living room was packed with people and one huge Christmas tree, beautifully decorated in reds and golds. Cindy spotted her father. He was chatting away with Will's dad like they were old friends. They waved, calling out, "Merry Christmas!"

Both men came over. Roger hugged Will, then Cindy, but before they could say more than, hello, Jacob called for his dad, waving him over. Roger excused himself, walking to his other son.

Her father turned to Will, offering his hand. "We've crossed paths briefly. However, I don't think I've ever introduced myself. I'm Cindy's father, Charles Meier."

"Nice to meet you," Will replied, appearing relaxed.

He put on a good show. Although, now she knew him better, she saw the slight tensing of his shoulders as if waiting to be hit with an insult or eyed with contempt.

Her father might have more money than Nigel and her mother combined, but he didn't have a pretentious bone in his body. When he told Will it was a pleasure to meet him, he meant it.

Father winked at her. "What is it in the Grimm men my daughters find so appealing?"

*Oh, there are many alluring things to like about this one. Not that I can mention half of them in present company.*

She bit her lip. The answer would certainly land her on the naughty list.

Father seemed to sense this or merely knew his youngest daughter. Smiling, he held up his hands. "Please. Don't answer."

Greta joined their group, telling them to get a plate of Will's delicious food before everything was gone. The two men grabbed onto the safe topic of food.

"You made everything here tonight?" her father asked. "I thought it was catered."

"Well, sort of. My friend," Will pointed to Tim sitting on the couch next to Lucas, "and I made it all. We're opening a restaurant in Detroit this spring."

"Ah, yes. I remember now, Cindy mentioned you're a chef at Summer Grill. I didn't realize you were leaving to open your own place."

Will gave her a side hug. "Your daughter convinced me the time was now."

Her dad laughed. "Yes, she is quite a persuasive woman. When you're up and running, let me know, I'm always taking clients to lunch. We'll come to your place."

Will's jaw went slack for half a second. Then he snapped it shut. "Oh, thanks."

Her father nodded like it was no big deal. Gratitude and love for him flooded Cindy.

"Come here. I want you both to meet someone." He led them further into the living room. He stopped next to an attractive woman who appeared to be around his age. She was vaguely familiar. "Do you remember Anna Kincade? She works with me."

Cindy was confused. Her father was a great boss, but he didn't invite employees to family functions.

To her surprise, he brought Anna closer, resting an arm loosely around her waist. He wore an expression of defiance and happiness. "We're dating."

"Really? An employee?" Cindy blurted. Her dad, Mr. Be-profession-al-at-work-at-all-times.

Greta's eyes brimmed with mirth. "Can you believe it?"

Their father smirked. An honest to god smirk. "I figure if my daughter could break the rules, why not me?"

"Technically, Jacob was never an employee."

"Technicalities" Father waved this away. "It caused more waves than Anna and me."

Greta scoffed, "That's because your attorney was a jealous jerk."

Jacob had joined the group and was nodding. "Yup."

Swift Financials' old counselor, and Greta's ex-fiancé, did not care for Jacob. At all.

They began talking about the whole mess, skipping the fact her sister hadn't met Jacob at work. It was a few months prior. They'd had an incredibly steamy afternoon before running into each other weeks later at Father's investment firm. Greta had shared the juicy details with Cindy—who'd been stunned, but happy her sister had finally let loose, had herself some hot fun.

As more people joined their group, her empty stomach had Cindy zoning out. She was more interested in the plates of food everyone seemed to be holding.

Will must've noticed because he asked, "Do you want to get some food? I made those sandwiches you like. The ones with egg and pesto."

Her stomach growled in approval. "Yes, please."

They broke away from the group, heading to the kitchen. Tim stopped them, asking if Emma would be coming over later. He looked heartbroken when Cindy told him she and Max were staying at her parents for a few days.

"Just when you think you know a guy," Will muttered, grabbing them each a plate from the counter.

"What do you mean?"

"Ever since Jacob introduced me to Tim, he's been the most family-phobic guy I know. Hell, if a woman even mentioned kids, the guy broke out in a cold sweat. Now he's chasing after your friend."

Cindy was surprised to find the kitchen empty of people, but thankfully, not food. The table and every inch of counter was piled with delicious holiday treats.

She inhaled deeply. It smelled like cloves and cinnamon. "If Santa was real, this is what his house would smell like." She spotted her favorite pie, pumpkin, and was tempted to take the whole damn thing but decided it was wiser to start with a soup.

Picking up a ladle, she said, "He's a good-looking guy, he's probably used to women fawning over him. Emma doesn't, maybe that's the appeal. And the fact she's hot."

"You might be right."

Cindy bumped Will with her hip. "You think Emma is hot?"

"You think Tim is hot?" he shot back, laughing, not seeming too concerned.

She was used to her dates being the jealous sort. Odd, considering most were mega-wealthy or models. Guess everyone had self-doubts. Or they were insecure jerks. Either way, it was nice to be with a man who was confident in himself, in them.

Still, she wanted to tease him, fluttering her lashes, she said, "He does have those dimples."

"What is with women and dimples?" Will huffed, taking the bowl of soup from her hands, setting it aside. "What about boring brown eyes and lips that like to kiss yours?"

"Are you nuts? Boring? Even when I thought you were a self-important asshole, I loved your eyes. They're like melted chocolate."

Laughing, he brushed his lips across hers. Her hands slid into his hair as she kissed him deeper. He responded with equal need, running his tongue along the seam of her lips. She opened, eagerly inviting him in for more than a taste.

"Hey, hey, none of that," said Lucas. "There are kids at this party."

Damn it. It had been too long since she made out with her man. She gave a forlorn sigh.

Lucas rubbed his stomach. "Sorry. Really, I just wanted you two to get the hell away from the food. I'm starving. You're between me and pie."

She picked up her bowl and plate. "Yeah, I should eat too." Looking over her shoulder, she winked at Will. "But I'm saving you for dessert."

The heat in his eyes sent a thrill of anticipation running along her spine. It was going to be a very Merry Christmas, indeed.

Will glanced at his car's dash clock, shocked to see the time was well past midnight. They shouldn't have stayed so late. They were supposed to be at Sophia's house by noon. He needed all his wits to handle her *and* Cindy's stepdad.

However, leaving the party when Tanner brought out his guitar and his girlfriend Maggie began singing Christmas carols was impossible. There was no way anyone was going home. Everyone joined in, singing every song they knew, sometimes twice.

Will shut off the car. At this time of night, the drive was less than ten minutes, yet Cindy was fast asleep in the passenger seat. Didn't even stir when he nudged her shoulder. He was tired enough to give up, lower their seats, and join her in dreamland, but not the best idea in the middle of winter. Or in Detroit.

Sighing, his warm breath puffed on the cold air as he reached to open his door. He came around to her side, bending to wake her, and he was gifted with a sleepy smile.

"Are we home?" she asked.

That simple question had warmth spreading through his chest. The way she said it, as if any place they were together, was home, settled her deeper into his heart.

Hell, he imagined this was how the Grinch felt when his heart grew three times its size.

He offered her his hand. "We're home, love."

She took it, cuddling into his arms. Pressing her cold nose against his neck. "You smell so good."

"Yeah? What do I smell like?" He wasn't one to bother with cologne. Most gave him a headache.

"I don't know. I'm too tired to find the words. You smell like Will. Like mine."

"Those are some pretty damn good words to me." He draped an arm around her waist, loving the way she tucked herself into him. "Let's get inside. We have a long day tomorrow."

"Don't even think about setting the alarm. We'll wake up whenever."

"What about brunch at your parent's house?"

Cindy rested her head on his shoulder. "We aren't the only ones attending. We'll sneak in, sit in the back. Plus, I bet Greta and Jacob will be late."

Will doubted they'd go unnoticed. Her parents were always on the lookout for slights and offenses. Using them as ammunition, their proof he was to blame for ruining their daughter.

He shoved those spiteful thoughts aside. They were annoyances, nothing more. Cindy didn't let them get to her. Why should he? Plus, the night was too damn good to spoil it with irritating, trivial scorn.

"Come on." He took her hand. "Let's get inside. It's freezing out here."

The lobby of his apartment was empty, save for the security guard behind his desk who wished them a Merry Christmas. Once in the elevator, she turned into Will's chest, head tucked under his chin. She fit like his missing puzzle piece.

Shivering against him, he slipped his gloved hands under her coat. Rubbing her back, he asked, "Better?"

She nodded. "You're always warm. I want to crawl inside your heat."

He kissed the corner of her eye, then whispered into her ear, "Now I'm picturing you naked and *me* buried in *your* heat."

His words melted away the rest of her cold. Skating a hand along his inner thigh, she cupped him. "I love your filthy mind."

"Do you now? Perfect. Because around you, my mind's always in the gutter." One of his hands roamed over her sweater dress, moving to her breasts, teasing her.

Running her palm along his now full hard-on, she asked, "Is that the only reason we're perfect?"

"No." He nuzzled her neck. "It is also because I love you."

The elevator dinged as she replied, "And I, you." She kissed him again, and this time it was more sweet than sin.

Not that it helped with his current situation. Following her to his apartment, he tightened his coat around him, thankful it was thigh length.

Soon as the door clicked shut, he pressed her against it. Taking off his gloves and shucking out of his jacket, he tossed them on the floor, desperate to feel her. She threw her coat next to his. He slid her black, form-fitting dress up her body, letting it land in their growing pile.

Her eager hands and lips were everywhere. She undid his jeans while kissing a trail along his jaw, down his neck.

He moved back, giving her more access. The pale overhead light in the kitchen let him drink in her lovely, satin skin. His gaze fell on what she wore under her pretty outfit. It damn near stopped his heart. She was all sex and lace.

Her breasts were spilling out of the small, deep red bra. She had on matching panties, along with garter stockings that hooked to a fancy lace thing around her waist.

"Fuck, Cindy," he croaked.

Taking a step back, she twirled in a slow circle. "It's Christmas. I wanted to dress up, over and under."

"You certainly are a beautiful gift." He discovered the back of her sexy undergarments was as appealing as the rest of it. The lacey design of her stockings stopped right before her plump, beautiful ass.

He admired the shape of her legs, stopping at her shiny black stilettos. They should be illegal. He'd never noticed heels until dating her. Now he damn near had a fetish.

She took his hand, leading him with a smile managing to be both coy and wicked. Once in the bedroom, he flicked on the light. He wasn't done feasting on the erotic sight of crimson and lace.

The backs of his legs were touching the bed, but when she gave him a light shove, he refused to budge. He wanted to take his time. To make love to her.

He ran a finger from her neck to her bra, tracing the fine lines leading to her peaked nipples. She gasped, watching his hand intently. He pushed the cup down, indulging on her sweet, soft skin.

She dragged a hand through his hair, her nails scratching into his flesh. The sharp pain fueled his hunger. He broke away, intent on getting her on the bed, forgetting for a brief moment she was as stubborn as him.

Shaking her head, she said, "Not yet."

She started on his shirt, one button at a time. Her pace unhurried, so fucking slow he fisted his hands because the temptation to take control and rip it off was fierce.

When she reached the part tucked into his already half open jeans, she looked into his eyes before slipping inside. She stroked him in that same maddening unhurried pace as if his blood and desire weren't racing toward her touch.

"Cindy..."

Words might fail him, but not his hands and mouth. One gripped the back of her neck, bringing her in for a rough kiss, while the other skated down her stomach and into her panties.

She rocked against his palm, a whimper on her lips. They played like this until her quick breaths, and fevered touch told him she was close.

He was more than willing to take her over the edge, plummeting her into orgasmic bliss.

However, before he could, she stepped back. Licking her lips, she appeared ready to devour him.

He hoped she would.

"Come back," he demanded.

Once again, she shook her head. His stubborn, sexy woman. "Finish undressing," she commanded. "I want to watch."

He kicked off his shoes. A smile played at the corners of his lips as he shoved his jeans and boxer-briefs to his ankles. Once those were removed, he shrugged off his dress shirt before yanking off his T-shirt.

In all his naked glory, he stood before her, spreading his hands wide, silently asking, "Now what?"

Her answer was perfect. She offered a sinful smile while unclipping her bra, letting it fall to the ground. Then she hooked her fingers at the sides of her panties, taking them off, but leaving on the garter, stocking, and heels.

She was a salacious sight. He wanted it burned into his memory. Let it become something he could reach for when the nights were long and cold.

She came closer, leisurely falling to her knees, taking him into her warm, wet mouth. Coherent thought disappeared as animal instinct seized him.

The growl that escaped from deep in his throat matched his mood. He tried not to thrust but failed.

He looked at her and nearly came. The sight of her beautiful, red lips devouring him with a hand between her legs, was hotter than hell. Her masterful licks, kisses, and strokes had his orgasm rushing at the base of his spine.

With the last sliver of his willpower, he wrapped a fist around her hair, tugging her as gently as possible. His sexy seductress stared back at him with pure blue eyes, doing things far from innocent. He stepped back before all his plans of taking his time slid down her throat.

"Stop," he grated. He wanted her receiving as much pleasure as she was giving.

To his surprise, she listened and rose. He kissed her with a violence she didn't seem to mind.

Good. He might be able to slow things down. However, gentleness was out of the question.

With her in his arms, he twisted around. Letting go, he bent slightly, grabbed the back of her legs and pulled. She fell back with a delighted shriek.

He dragged her ass to the edge of the bed, dropping to his knees. She levered herself on her elbows, watching him. Waiting.

Not wanting to disappoint, himself or his woman, he trailed kisses up her inner thigh. Reaching her center, he met her eyes. Her gaze was fastened on him, overflowing with desire.

"Put your legs on my back."

She complied. He rewarded her.

Her full body tremor and carnal moan spurred him to take more, to take everything. He did all the things she loved. It had her digging her heels into his back, calling out his name.

Yet, instead of tightening her hold, like she usually did, she pushed him away with her legs. "I want you in me when I come."

She scooted to the center the bed. He followed, crawling along her body and inside her with one thrust.

"Oh... it isn't going to take much," she moaned.

He chuckled, sweeping her hair back, away from her face. Grinding in deliberate circles, he whispered, "Good."

"Yes. Like that." Her breathing became choppy pants. She was close.

She deepened the kiss to match his rhythm, gripping him tight as her orgasm engulfed her.

*Fuck.*

They tumbled into bliss together.

# Chapter Twenty-Five

Will heard something heavy hit the floor. Cindy's book lay sprawled open next to the couch. She stood, stretching.

He smiled. She didn't return it. *Uh-oh.*

"Are you almost done?" she asked.

He shook his head.

"Can't you finish later? I'm tired of sitting around. My mind is going numb," she whined.

"I'm sorry. We have to finish this tonight." He tilted his head in Tanner's direction. "He's leaving for a show in New York in a few days. This can't wait until he gets back."

"I'm bored," she repeated.

Will tapped his laptop. "Want to use it? You could check on your website or work on one of your travel journals."

For some reason, the suggestion seemed to piss her off. He waited for fire to stream from her nose as her mouth pressed into a thin line.

"No, thanks," she practically spit. "When was the last time we went out? Hell, we didn't even spend New Year's together."

"That's because you were in Miami for a show, then decided to stay and network," he replied reasonably.

She crossed her arms under her chest, narrowing her eyes. "You could have gone with me."

Annoyance skittered, settled into his chest. He set down his pen and stared at her. When he spoke, his voice was tight. "I also have a job. My boss would have killed me if I called off during one of the busiest days of the year."

"You won't be there much longer."

"Doesn't mean I need to burn bridges."

"Whatever," she muttered. "It's a Friday night, yet I'm sitting around like some old lady. Maybe I should take up knitting." She narrowed her eyes. "And start wearing granny panties."

Tanner snorted. Will choked on his laughter and horror. "Please don't. The knitting is cool, but please, not the underwear part."

Her grin was trouble. It was beautiful.

She tapped her chin, some of her playfulness returning. "How about I knit a pair of granny panties?"

Tanner shook his head. "That doesn't even sound comfortable."

Will smiled in agreement, humor erasing the earlier annoyance. "I could work with it. Make a matching bra too. We can do some sort of role-playing sex game. Oh, I've got it." He held up a finger. "You can be one of those porcelain dolls old women collect, and you come alive."

"Dude, you're weird." Tanner laughed.

"Yeah," she agreed. "What lady would have a creepy doll in a knitted bra and panty set?"

Tanner looked at Will. "Aunt Joan," they said in unison before breaking into raucous laughter.

She put her hands on her hips, watching them with a wide, gorgeous smile. "Care to explain?"

"My mom's oldest sister. We," he pointed at Tanner, "along with Jacob and some other guys in the neighborhood, loved to go to her house in the summer because she had a huge inground pool. Well, in her basement, there was this massive doll collection. Her hobby was making them outfits. Some in rather odd clothes."

"And apparently your boyfriend used to have sexual fantasies about these dolls."

Will cocked his head to the side. "Used to?"

Tanner threw his pencil at Will. "Eew."

Cindy laughed. "Okay, weirdo, I'll get my knitting needles tomorrow, but what about tonight? When you're finished, we should go out."

"It might be a while. We have more than an hour of work here," Will hedged, the lie tasting bitter.

Tanner opened his mouth, and Will stepped on his friend's foot. He'd better keep his mouth shut.

She peered at Tanner, studying him. His eyes widened slightly before he busied himself with his computer. Will held in a thankful breath.

"Didn't you say Saul was in town visiting his mom?" he asked, hoping to distract her suspicious mind. "Why not give him a call? He's better company for the night scene, anyway."

"Oh God, 'the night scene.' What are you, ninety?"

"Further proof I'm no good at it."

"Fine," she said, apparently giving up. "Forcing you would make a disappointing time for both of us. But tomorrow we're doing something fun."

"Agreed. I have a few days off." An idea came to him. "Want to drive to Boyne Mountain? We could ski or hike."

She nodded, turning away, talking to Saul on her cell.

Less than twenty minutes later she kissed him firmly on the lips before waving bye.

When the front door clicked shut, Tanner studied Will. "What's up? Why'd you tell Cindy we had at least an hour of work left? It's closer to twenty minutes." He kicked Will's leg. "And why'd you smash my damn foot?"

"Because I didn't want you to tell her different."

"Okay. Is there a reason you don't want to spend time with your girlfriend?"

Will grabbed his glass, walking to the sink. After filling it with water and drinking some, he faced Tanner. "Today's Jolene's birthday. The last place I want to be is at some stupid bar or club."

"I'm sorry, man." Tanner's grin disappeared.

Will dumped the water down the drain. What he'd drunk was sitting like gasoline in his stomach.

"Does she know about your past, about Jolene?"

Rubbing his face, he pushed off from the counter. "Yeah."

"Then why not tell her?"

"Even if it wasn't Jolene's birthday, I don't want to spend my evening watching everyone get shit-faced. Or sneak off to dark corners and dirty bathrooms to get high."

"Again, why don't you tell her?"

"I have. I've told her being at those places fucks with me. She doesn't get it. Or doesn't care."

"I'd go with the first," Tanner said. "Your baggage isn't hers. Plus, you have to remember, what did you call it, 'the night scene,' is a big part of her life."

Will returned to his seat. "What do you mean?"

"Not only does her job sort-of require her to be seen at these places, but doesn't she like it? The dressing up, going out, and dancing?"

That bothered him. Knowing she loved it, while he hated it. There was no middle ground.

Sooner or later she'd tire of him, of his homebody ways. Tonight, she was bored. How long before *he* became boring to her?

He decided denial was the best course of action. "She likes the superficial stuff well enough, yet there is so much more to her. You should see her photos. Her writing. Why does she waste her time on the other crap?"

"I'm going to go with she likes it."

Will shrugged. There was nothing to say. She did enjoy the night life.

Tanner leaned into the back of his chair. "I could give the same advice you gave me when Maggie and I were broken up."

"Shit." He rubbed his face. "What wise counsel did I gift you with?"

"Don't fall in love. It isn't worth it."

"Wow. I was a flippant asshole."

Tanner laughed, holding his thumb and index finger an inch apart. "A little bit. And now look at you, all twisted up over *love*." He said the last word with a teasing taunt.

"Oh, please." Will snorted. "I'm not nearly the sorry sack you were that night."

"That's because you two are together. We'd broken up. Plus, you haven't had the first lover's quarrel."

"Are you kidding me? Have you met my girlfriend? She loves to argue, to get under my skin."

"Please. I don't mean the small stuff. Also, for you two, it's like a bizarre form of foreplay."

He had a point. The sex was great when they provoked each other. Or they'd end up laughing. It wasn't often the annoyance turned into actual anger.

"What I'm talking about," Tanner continued, "is the make it or break it fight. The one where you two will wonder if staying together is worth it. I'm sure couples who have decades together still deal with those moments, but that first one when you don't have years, memories, a past, only love, well, I think it's easier for it all to fall apart."

*Damn realist.*

"Aren't you a fucking bowl of sunshine."

Tanner chuckled, tapping his wireless mouse. "Sorry. Want to return to something easier, less stressful. You know, like signing away your life to your restaurant.?"

"Ha. Yeah, let's do this."

Four hours later, Will hung up his phone, catching the time on the screen. Three o'clock in the morning. Most of the bars and clubs were closed, yet he hadn't heard a thing from Cindy. He didn't know if she was still partying, went to her place, or was hurt.

He was exhausted but couldn't sleep. Not with dread prickling under his skin, pinning his eyes open while he lay in bed, imagining every horrible thing that could be happening to her.

Late nights used to be his life. He remembered what came out to play when most people were sleeping, especially in a big city. Detroit was a far cry from the college town she called home.

Giving up on sleep, he pushed off the covers and sat at the edge of his bed. As he was thinking of calling her again, his phone rang. Her number flashed on his screen. A weight the size of the fucking planet lifted from his chest.

"Where the hell are you?" he nearly shouted. "Why haven't you been answering your phone? I've been calling."

"At Blue Hearts. I didn't hear my ringer. It's loud, Dad."

Not wanting to fight, he took a deep breath. "Are you coming back afterward, or going home with Saul?"

"That's why I was calling you. We've run into a slight problem..."

His heart skipped a beat. He stood. "What's wrong?"

"Relax. It's nothing big."

"Christ. I can't. Not when it's the middle of the night, and you're at a bar saying there's a problem. Come on. Do you have any idea the shit that happens at those places?"

"Yes, Will. You may have partied harder than me in the past, but my career has me at places like this constantly. I'm not a child."

*No, you're just acting like one.*

He was smart enough to keep that thought to himself. "Okay, fair enough. What's going on?"

"Harper wanted to go. She picked us up from Saul's mom's house. She was supposed to be our designated driver. Um, she forgot. We've all been drinking. I told her we'd Uber. Get her car tomorrow. She's refusing, saying there will be nothing left except the steering wheel."

Blue Hearts wasn't in a bad area. Her car would probably be fine. Not that it mattered, she wouldn't listen. He knew how stubborn people got when drinking.

He slid into a pair of jeans. "Wait for me. I'll call an Uber. Have them drop me off there. I'll drive her car to my place."

"You don't mind them staying the night?"

"If they don't mind sharing the pull-out couch in the living room, I don't care," he half-lied.

He didn't want to spend his first morning off in weeks playing host to a bunch of hungover people. Still, it beat driving each of them home.

Hell, knowing Cindy was now safe, exhaustion was bound to slam into him any minute. He might fall asleep at the wheel if he had to drive too far.

In less than fifteen minutes, he was at the Blue Hearts. Standing outside, he tried calling Cindy.

No answer.

Fuck. He'd have to go in.

The bouncer scrutinized Will. He couldn't see the wrinkled shirt beneath his coat, although his bedhead, worn jeans, and scuffed motorcycle boots with laces hanging open didn't fit the club's image either. "I'm here to get my girlfriend. I'll be quick."

The guy shrugged, stepping aside. "We're closing soon anyway. As far as last call goes, you'll do."

Will would've been amused if he weren't walking into his personal hell. The smell hit him first. A mixture of stale, sticky booze along with the stink of late-night desperation.

Back in the day, he thought the dark corners, pulsating lights, and loud beats meant the promise of fun. Now all he saw were his mistakes in others. The glassy-eyed stare of the stoned man to his right. The drunken laughter from the group of girls to his left, checking him out. Trying to decide if he was their next good time. To the guy with an arm around a stumbling woman, leading her to the exit. Hopefully, she wanted to be led by him before she'd become too drunk to care.

The club was divided by a bar running down the middle. On one side was the dance floor, the other was a sitting area with black leather couches and chairs. That's where he spotted Cindy with her entourage.

He had to admit she looked hot. She was sitting on the arm of a couch, her legs crossed at the ankles, talking to Harper. Cindy wore a short black dress with matching high-heeled boots, ones ending just past her knees, showcasing the creamy skin of her thighs.

Some asshole came up, placing a hand on her shoulder. A dull fury oozed into Will, making him ball his fists. Her smile widened. However, when she turned, it slipped.

The smarmy fucker leaned in closer, resting his other hand on her thigh. She glanced at it, then at him before saying something. Whatever it was, he didn't like it. His face puckered like he'd bitten into a lemon or a piece of shit.

The latter worked for Will.

The fucker's response must not have been nice because her brows rose, and Saul stood, taking an aggressive step toward the guy.

Moving fast, Will stopped next to Saul. "Is there a problem?"

He was asking anyone willing to answer.

She said, "This gentleman. Okay, wait. After what he called me, gentleman is too strong of a word. Anyway, this asshole asked if I wanted to go back to his place for a drink. I refused, said I was waiting for my boyfriend." She took Will's hand and leaned her head on his shoulder. "He told me I was too gorgeous to spread my legs for one guy. Told me he'd be much more fun than you."

"That so?" He got other man's personal space. The guy's mouth kept a mulish frown. However, his gaze darted to the exit, giving away his fear.

"Oh. Now you're worried? You're lucky he arrived." Cindy taunted the guy. She pointed at Saul, then patted Will's chest. "They have way more self-control. I was going to punch you in the balls for the comment. Consider yourself lucky my ride is here."

The guy muttered something about crazy women, walking away. He was trying to play it cool, but his hasty retreat gave him away.

She smiled at Will. "My hero."

"Doesn't seem like you needed saving."

"Damn straight," she agreed. "I've been taking self-defense classes for years. I can handle a schmuck like him."

He detected a slight slur in her voice. Could she right now, with a few drinks in her? The thought made his stomach pinch. He shoved it aside, asking, "Ready? Where's the car?"

Harper stood, and Saul had to steady her. "My car is my baby. Treat her good." She handed the keys to Will.

"Does that mean I can't drop the clutch on John R.?" he joked.

She waggled a finger. "Not only would I kill you when I'm sober, but I might puke if you do it now."

Will gave an inward groan. "Let's go."

# Chapter Twenty-Six

Cindy took off her boots, tucking her legs under her. Will came around the corner carrying pillows, sheets, and a blanket. She had a soft, warm buzz, on the precipice of being drunk.

Watching her boyfriend amped up the heat in a different way, in naughtier places. He moved with a sensual grace, made sexier because he wasn't even aware of his hotness.

Saul took the pile of bedding. "Let me help."

"Thanks, man." Will bent, showcasing his fine ass, tossing the cushions from the couch.

As he pulled out the bed, his biceps flexed, begging her to bite them. Unable to resist, she got up, reaching him as he straightened. She leaned into his back, running her hands down his torso.

Before she made it to his jeans, he turned. "What are you doing?"

He sounded tired, but she knew how to wake him up. "I missed you." She kissed him.

When she tried to deepen it, he stepped from her hold, muttering, "You could've stayed home."

*What's his problem?*

"Are you too much of a prude to kiss me in front of people?"

His gaze hardened. "It's more that you smell and taste like you drank everything the bar had in stock."

"A lady spilled her drink on me," she said defensively, stalking back to her spot on the couch.

She hadn't done anything wrong. His attitude was pissing her off. It made her next sentence harsher than intended. "You should have gone with us. You need to learn to loosen up and relax."

Harper was half- dozing in an armchair while the men put together the bed. Saul studiously focused on his task.

Will asked Saul to throw the sheet to his side, then said, "Oh, yes, watching you get lit, *again*, is not what I'd call relaxing."

She heard Harper mutter, "Uh- oh."

Cindy shot angry daggers at her boyfriend's back. "Will, you look young, but you're an old man. Already dead, too afraid to live."

He whipped around, pointing at her. "And you need to grow up. Living isn't going to some fucking night club."

"No. It's spending it with friends, laughing, dancing the night away. You know, having fun. Or have you forgotten what that is?" she shot back.

"Let's not do this tonight." He returned to making the pull-out couch. "Go to bed. I'll meet you there after I have things finished in here."

"I'm going to take a shower first. I don't want my smell to offend your delicate sensibilities."

In truth, it was bothering her. She sort-of did smell like a wino. Her arm was sticky, and there was probably drink in her hair.

A part of her, embarrassed and slightly hurt by his rejection, wanted to skip washing and make him cuddle with her. On her sticky side.

He stopped her. "Are you sure it's a good idea? What if you fall?"

Christ on a cracker. "I'm not that drunk. *Dad.*"

She stormed into his bedroom, yanking off her dress, not bothering to close the door or say good night to Saul and Harper. Throwing her bra aside, she removed her panties, leaving them where they fell. She made her way to the master bathroom.

Twisting the knob all the way to hot, she stepped into the shower, letting the heat sting her skin and wash away the stink of the club. However, the longer she stayed under the clean warmth, the dirtier she felt.

She'd said some really crappy things to Will.

Between his job and opening the restaurant, the man was overworked, yet without complaint, he picked up her spoiled ass from a bar. A place he despised. And how does she thank him? Calls him names, scoffs at his worry.

It was the second part filling her with guilt. He was tight-lipped with his past. What little he'd shared painted visions of chaos and bad choices. He worked hard to escape them.

Tonight, dating her, probably felt like a terrible decision.

After rinsing, she shut off the shower, quickly drying her hair and body. She was anxious to talk to Will. Hell, to apologize to him. She skipped her regular, nightly beauty routine, only taking the time to brush her teeth.

She hoped he hadn't fallen asleep.

Opening the door, she found him in bed, waiting for her. His eye's widened slightly at her nakedness.

She waited. Curious to see what he'd say.

Was he still pissed and wanting to continue arguing? Or had he been waiting to make sure she was okay?

"Do you need something for your head?" he asked.

His voice was monotone. It was worse than anger. It sounded like he was conceding defeat. Like he'd said these words a million times and would be stuck repeating them until he died. It cut her at the knees.

She left the light on in the bathroom. Yes, she was playing unfair, using her body to distract him. Not that it seemed to be working. He kept his gaze glued to her face as she came around to his side of the bed. She pulled back the covers, pleased to see he was also naked and half-hard.

Guess he wasn't totally unaffected.

Straddling him, she cradled his face between her palms. "I'm sorry, Will."

Her eyes spoke of sincerity. Nevertheless, the dread of the evening was hard to let go. Cindy wasn't Jolene, but the way she acted tonight was all too similar. That was the part he was finding difficult to stomach.

Damn it. He'd traveled this road. He didn't want to go down it again. It led to nowhere, a dead-end filled with drunken midnight fights and tearful apologies when the sun rose.

"Hey, are you with me?" She stroked his cheek. Then as if reading his mind said, "I'm not Jolene. I like to dance, have a drink, but I don't do it every time, or in excess."

Maybe he *was* pushing his baggage onto her, wanting her to carry his mistakes.

Most people did go out, have a few drinks, even liked having a buzz. It didn't make them alcoholics or mean they'd turn to the heavier stuff.

Again, it wasn't so much he worried she'd end up like him, or worse, Jolene. Cindy didn't seem to have the same addictive tendencies as he did. No, it had more to do with *his* well-being. He wasn't sure he could stay with someone who's lifestyle threw him into his past, reminding him of the man he used to be. That man repulsed and terrified him.

Shit. He couldn't walk away, either. He loved her too fucking much.

"Will. Get out of your head. Talk to me." She ran her thumb along his bottom lip. The scent of soap and Cindy teased him as did her still warm, pink skin against his.

He focused on her lovely face. Her long hair was damp, a few droplets hit his chest. Her lips were in a slight frown. He wanted to kiss it away.

"I don't know what to say. I get it. You had everything under control tonight, but this shit makes me feel like *I'm* losing it. I can't do the drunken fights or the Friday night bar hopping." He gripped her neck, then ran a palm along her spine.

"Fair enough, but Will, I don't expect you to go to the bar with me. I get your reasons for avoiding them. Plus, I don't mind in the slightest going with my friends." She cupped his cheek. "Besides, everything can't be blamed on drinking. I was in a mood tonight, before I started drinking. I was bitchy before I went to the club."

He smirked. "You said it, not me."

She leaned in, nipping his lip. "You aren't supposed to agree."

"Oh. My bad." He kissed her.

She hovered inches from his mouth. "Before coming here, I checked my email. I had two rejection letters from magazines I admire."

His heart ached for her. Being turned down or passed over was part of the business, but that didn't mean it was easy. Taking those scary steps to share your talent with others, and having it repeatedly rejected, hurt.

He hoped she'd make it. Her talent was too strong, but her will, the desire for it needed to be stronger.

"Both magazines were polite. They told me to submit other pieces. Said my writing is good. Still, I wasn't happy." She gave a wobbly smile. "I didn't want to sit inside and sulk. I wanted to do something to make me happy."

"It bothers me, knowing I can't give you what makes you happy. I'll never be a carefree sort of guy. A man who parties to blow off steam."

Cindy brushed her lips over his. "You don't need you to be. Listen, I was being a brat earlier, but in truth, I don't mind going out with friends."

He hoped she was telling the truth.

Falling onto the mattress, he brought her on top of him. "I hope you had a nice time tonight."

"I did. However, I have to admit that when you answered my call and I heard your voice, all I wanted was to be here. With you. Like this." She rocked her hips, her heat sliding along his length.

He sucked in a breath, but teased, "What? You wanted to be with me, having sex? I feel so used."

"Well, the orgasms are nice, but I'd meant in your arms. Us talking, holding each other." Her sultry laugh caressed him. "And yes, you inside me. It doesn't get any closer than that, right?"

"Very true." He wound her damp hair around his fist, pulling. Her graceful neck offered before him, he ran his teeth along her smooth skin. She moaned while continuing to grind on him, so close, but not taking him.

It was hot as fuck. He growled, sucking, nibbling, and kissing on her. Everywhere he could reach, her breasts, shoulders, neck. She was going to have marks tomorrow. However, going by her loud moans and pleas, she didn't care.

The teasing was killing him. He let go of her hair, wanting to grip her hips, to plunge into their mutual pleasure. Before he could, she grasped his hands.

He debated overpowering her. Then she did something with her thighs that had his eyes rolling into the back of his head.

She threaded their fingers together. "Let me take over. I want to please you."

"You do," he groaned.

He wasn't lying, but damn, the determination and heat etched on her face as she shifted, wrapping a soft hand around his erection made him thank every god that had ever been worshiped she hadn't listened to him. She rose on to her knees, hovered above him, wearing a smile with the power to melt a fucking diamond.

Slowly, she lowered herself, taking his body into hers. She circled her hips a few enticing times.

He was at her mercy. She could do whatever she wanted, and he'd beg for more, plead for her never to stop. Gripping her ass, he urged her with his hands to use him, to lose control.

She didn't need much persuasion and rode him, taking all she needed. The headboard banged against the wall, competing with their sounds of pleasure. Within minutes, she was tightening around him, shouting his name as her climax slammed into her.

Holding tight to her hips, he kept her moving, letting her ride out her orgasm. His crashed through him as hers ebbed. Once again, she took control, allowing it to last, growing, practically making him blackout in pleasure.

After what might have been years, he returned to earth, sweaty and spent. Cindy lay on top of him, moving in lazy thrusts, little whimpers of satisfaction escaping between her kiss-swollen lips.

When he could talk again, he said, "Let me get something to clean you."

"No. I want to stay like this. Fall asleep, in your sweat and passion."

It worked for him. She felt great on him, and he was so damn tired it nearly hurt to move.

As his eyes fell shut, Saul shouted from the living room, "Glad you two made up!"

Cindy laughed as Will held her tighter.

"Me too," he whispered, drifting off.

# Chapter Twenty-Seven

"Are you coming or not?" Cindy asked, her displeasure loud and clear through the phone line.

There wasn't anything Will could do to help it. The bank warned him the small business loan could take up to six months for approval. That was precisely how long the process had taken. Finally, the code inspection guy was at the restaurant. Will couldn't blow it off. He needed the certificate of occupancy. This was the way to get it. Plus, Lucas, who owned an eco-consulting business, stopped by offering to look over the place, telling what they needed to do for LEED certification. Having the bistro certified as green was important, and he wanted to hear what was needed.

Sure, Tim was there, but Will wanted to stay. He had questions about the inspection and wanted to discuss a few ideas with Lucas.

"I'm stuck here. Go without me, I'll meet you at the party." He played with his black bowtie. "I'm already dressed for it."

He did want to see her. The last time they'd been together was over a week ago.

"Will, I'm already here. Remember, there is no afterparty. I'm supposed to be mingling, showing off the dresses that'll be bid on during the dinner portion of the night, not in the back calling you. I also told you, part of my pay is getting two seats at a table. You're supposed to be sitting in one of them right now."

Shit, this was a mess. He couldn't ignore things that need to be done in his restaurant, yet if he didn't, he'd be letting down his girlfriend. He had to choose between the two most important things in his life.

"Yes, I know. This is taking way longer than expected."

"Damn it, Will. I'm finally doing something local. I wanted you here for it. Is everything else in your life more important?"

He pinched the bridge of his nose. "No. I care. I made a mistake when the inspection date was set. I thought I'd have time for both."

In truth, the fundraiser had slipped his mind. He was doing too much. The stress was killing him, messing with his head, making him overlook things. He needed to get a fucking grip but didn't know how. "Listen, I'll tell them I have to leave. Tim can take over, fill me in later."

"Why couldn't he have done that in the first place?"

*Because this is my livelihood, I don't like leaving it in the hands of others.*

Ignoring her question, he asked, "Should I call you when I get there?"

"Tell them at the door you're my guest. They'll show you to your seat," she clipped, obviously not caring he was making concessions for her. "I have to go." Without saying bye, she hung up.

He groaned, slipping his phone into the pocket of his jacket.

"Uh-oh. Trouble in paradise?" Tim said from behind Will, making him jump.

He turned. "Nothing better to do than eavesdrop?"

"Please, you aren't that interesting. Lucas and the inspection guy are going on and on about the newest eco devices or something. Boring." He smirked. "Okay, fine. I admit, listening to you getting your balls twisted by your model girlfriend is way more entertaining."

"Not nearly as enjoyable as watching you pant after my girlfriend's best friend," Will shot back.

"I don't know who you mean." Always a shitty liar, Tim looked away.

"Uh-huh. Sure. Has she agreed to go out with you yet?"

Tim shrugged. "No. She keeps using her kid as an excuse."

"It's a good one. Given you're allergic to them."

"Dude. I'm not that bad. I like kids, just not taking care of them. Besides, I'm talking one date. It could be a flop, and I'll never have to worry about meeting the kid as 'the boyfriend.'" He shuddered.

Will pointed. "See, right there is why she won't say yes." He took out his keys. "Anyway, I can't deal with your phobias right now. I have a super fun, fancy party to attend."

Tim laughed. "Wow. Your excitement is almost palpable."

"Where'd you learn such fancy words?" Will teased.

"Not from you, that's for damn sure. Now go." Tim waved a hand in the direction of the door. "I got this. I'll call you later. Give you the rundown."

"Okay. Thanks." He leaned toward the backroom and shouted, "Hey, Lucas! I gotta go. Could I call you tomorrow?"

Lucas leaned around a prep table, giving a thumbs up before returning to his conversation with his new best friend, Inspection Guy.

Sliding into his car, Will rested his head on the steering wheel. Something had to give, if only he knew what.

He couldn't cut back on his hours at work. They needed him, plus he was training his replacement. It wasn't possible to back off with anything to do with his restaurant. He'd already sunk all the money he'd been saving to pay back Jacob. Then there was the collateral Tim had taken on his house for the small business loan.

The combination of the two had him going to more NA meetings. He didn't want to use, but the meetings were his safeguard. They helped keep the dark thoughts from crowding his mind. All the destructive ways he used to "relax" were whispering, suggesting they'd work again. That shit couldn't be allowed to fester.

He hated to admit, even to himself, going to these types of parties with Cindy didn't help. The rattle of the ice in cocktails, the clinks of wineglasses, the sickly-sweet smell of hops and heavy spices, all were an awful concoction of self-loathing and shame.

Yes, he should tell her this, mention he was going to the meetings more often. Admit these were some of the reasons he couldn't see her as much or why he wanted to stay home.

Every time he tried, the words wouldn't leave his mouth. He feared they were slipping away from each other. This might create a bigger gulf between their differences. Her life was fashion shows, shoots, and parties. His was work and NA meetings.

Were there two people more different than them? He doubted it.

Enough of this self-analyzing bullshit.

Starting the car, he shoved his worries aside, pulling into traffic. He was determined to have fun at the fundraiser.

Cindy caught sight of Will's tall, broad frame. He was standing beside Saul, talking with their agent, Jewels. Her stomach dipped a little. It was bratty of her, but she was happy he'd dropped everything to make it to her show.

Wearing her predatory smile, Jewels rubbed Will's bicep. The woman was great at her job. She could also be a handful.

And was a cougar. From the way she was eyeing Will, she'd found her prey.

Extricating herself from the group she was chatting with, Cindy started for him. She reached them in time to hear the tail end of the conversation. Jewels had mistaken Will for Saul's boyfriend.

Cindy stifled a smile as Will patted Saul on the back. "He's a sexy guy. However, I'm here with his friend."

"Who's that?"

Cindy slipped a hand under Will's jacket, around his waist. "Me." She looked at him. "I see you met Saul's and my agent."

Jewels nodded. "Where did you find this fine specimen of a man? At one of your shows?" She laser-focused on Will. "Are you sick of your agent? In the market for a new one?"

His brows shot up, reaching for his hairline. "Um…"

Saul laughed. "He's a chef, not a model."

Jewel's hungry gaze raked over Will. "Honey, you are much too handsome to be stuck in a kitchen. You're a bit on the older side, but I could get you some work. Let me give you one of my cards."

He waved a hand. "No. Thanks. I like my job. I'm not much of a people person either. I'd make a terrible client."

Cindy tried to swallow her resentment. Everything seemed to fall into place for him without effort. He had a job at one of the top restaurants, was getting ready to open his own. Walks into one of her work parties and offered a job by one of the top agents. Meanwhile, she was busting her butt to remain a sought-after model while her inbox is filled with rejections from travel and photography magazines.

"Models aren't supposed to eat, so how did you two meet?" Jewels joked.

He looked at Cindy and smirked. Their answer to this question was always met with teasing. "My brother is married to her sister," he said.

"Oh." Jewels placed a hand on her ample chest. "That could be messy if things go south with either of you."

He shook his head. "I don't think that's possible with our siblings."

*Ouch. Glad you're confident about us.*

Jewels must have been thinking along the same lines. She cocked her head. "But not you two?"

"We're taking it a day at a time," Cindy cut in, trying to salvage some of her pride.

She caught a flash of hurt flicker across his face before he swallowed it with a sip of his drink.

"I get it. It's all about the sex," Jewels stated in her trademark fashion. "You two are beautiful. I'd pay to watch."

Will choked on the sip he'd been taking. Saul laughed, clapping Will in the back, saying, "I take it voyeurism isn't your thing."

Cindy found it adorable how flustered he got when sex was discussed, especially if it centered around him. Most men reveled at the chance to brag, even if they weren't spectacular. He had plenty to boast about, yet he became shy. It made her want to pinch his cheeks or take him to a dark corner and coax out his demanding side.

He cleared his throat, pointing his glass at Jewels. "She'd be the voyeur. If I liked having people watching me, I'd be an exhibitionist."

The side of Saul's mouth quirked. "You sure know your kinks. So, which one's yours?"

Cindy was tempted to answer for him, but she saw the blush creeping along his neck. Instead, she rescued him. "I'm sure he'd *love* to share, but I'm going to show him to his seat. I need to make my way around the room again. The bidding starts soon, right?"

Jewels turned all business. "Good idea. Find your table for him. Though, no sitting for you. You mingle. Get your face in front of the TV and magazine people." She clapped her hands. "Come on, woman, you and your modeling career aren't getting any younger."

"Damn," Will muttered. "She doesn't hold back, does she?"

"Nope." Cindy shrugged. "It's the truth. I am on the older end for this job with new faces flooding in each day."

Still, the comment stung. More so, because it was said in front of him.

He shrugged. "Good thing you're shifting gears."

"What do you mean?"

"You're moving from a model, focusing on writing and photography."

"Let's not talk about it right now," she snapped. "I need to look happy. Play the good-time girl."

A role she was getting damn tired of playing.

"You're not happy? With modeling, or with your art?" he asked.

She waved off the question, not wanting to get into it now. "No. It's all great."

He stopped, taking her elbow gently. "Then is it me?"

She opened her mouth. No words came out. He didn't make her unhappy. However, if she were honest, his success made her a tad gloomy. But she couldn't admit such a thing to him.

His dreams were moving forward at lightning speed. Hers were crumbling. His accomplishments made her jealous.

She was such a crappy girlfriend. The shame ate at her, growing like a disease. Felt just as incurable too.

Even worse, a part of her was angry he'd introduced the idea of trying to sell her art, her writing. Bringing the dream to daylight was not nearly as fun as the fantasy.

She was supposed to be traveling the world like some vagabond, making a living off taking photos and writing stories featured in *National Geographic*. Instead, she had a website no one visited, let alone purchased items. A book she was struggling to write and articles none of the traveling journals wanted.

She was the failure her mother had predicted. She was told to stick with her looks. Use them to either find a wealthy husband or at the very least, switch to becoming an agent for models.

"Cindy?" Will prompted, bringing her back from her foul thoughts.

As she tried to think of the right response, a friend of her mother's stopped next to them, asking about the designer gown Cindy was wearing. The woman also owned Detroit's most popular magazine. Cindy switched gears, answering on autopilot, plastering on her plastic smile, playing her part.

# Chapter Twenty-Eight

The silence in the car was as heavy as Cindy's heart. The fundraiser was definitely a success. Over five hundred thousand dollars was raised for the struggling Detroit public schools, and Jewels had booked Cindy two jobs. However, the night with Will had been less than stellar.

She ran her hands down her wool slacks, fiddling with a loose thread, searching for the right words. The problem was, she didn't know what was bothering him.

It could be he was pissed with her snippy attitude on the phone earlier, or he was bored. He didn't like attending these sorts of things.

The cruelest option kept playing with her, torturing her. His boredom wasn't with the party. It was with her.

Maybe he was starting to see there was nothing special about her. Sure, she was pretty but so what? If that's all he wanted, he could buy a painting. Plus, he was the type of guy who wanted more than someone attractive on his arm.

Not to mention, he could have both. He'd caught the attention of plenty of women tonight. It also hadn't escaped her notice, the only time he'd been happy was when talking to some gorgeous woman at his table. Her mother was some famous chef, and Will started fanboying over them both. The illustrious, beautiful woman worked at her mom's restaurant. Also, she was quite the cook.

Cindy instantly hated her.

She'd spent most of the evening circling the room, showing off different auction dresses. Every damn time she passed by Will, the woman was fluttering her false lashes and touching him, resting an arm on his bicep, tapping a finger to his hand, scooting closer. Cindy was waiting for her to crawl into his lap.

The drive from the Henry Ford Estate to her home was less than an hour. They were almost to her place, and they'd barely spoken.

When the loaded quiet began to strangle her, she choked out, "Did you have a nice time tonight?"

Dumb question. She knew the answer. No.

They drove through the gate of her condo complex. "It was nice. I liked seeing you work. The food was decent."

He didn't look at her or even try to sound enthusiastic. If she weren't anxious and annoyed, she'd have laughed.

"Are you going to stay the night?"

"I better not. I have an early meeting with the bank tomorrow. It's closer to my apartment. Plus, I need to meet with Tim and Lucas before to discuss some upgrades we could do to the restaurant."

Her frustration won over her concern. "Fine. You show up late, want to leave early. Cool. I'll see you in whenever."

His jaw tightened. "It's after one in the morning. That's not exactly early. And have you forgotten I skipped half the inspection for your fundraiser?"

"Something I asked you to come to weeks ago. Yet, you blew it off, scheduling something on the same day."

"Cindy, be reasonable." Anger curled around his words. "The city picks the day. I don't get a say in the matter. I'm trying to balance it all. The old job, the career change, you. Will you cut me some slack?"

She crossed her arms, digging her long nails into her skin. "Oh, I get it. I'm a burden to be managed."

He heaved a loud sigh, nostrils flaring. He parked in her driveway. After shutting it off, he twisted to face her. He looked about as happy as she felt.

"No, you're not," he practically growled. "Honestly, I'm stressed. I don't want to mess up, to owe more people. Or have to start over at a new job. I think I've taken on too much. The pressure is getting to me. I'm sorry if I seemed off today. Yes, I wanted to spend time with you. With *you*. With what little downtime I have, I want to relax with my girlfriend, not go to some party."

"And all I wanted to do tonight was show my boyfriend a piece of my life. My career." She grabbed the door handle, disappointment clenching her heart. "My mistake. I remember now. We're dating, but you don't want my burdens. They're too much for you. I forgot, we don't share the important stuff."

He slammed a palm on the steering wheel, his patience seeming to snap. "Are you fucking kidding me? I'm trying to share with you now. Telling you how I feel, what I'm going through. Or are you too self-absorbed to see it?"

She gasped, swallowing her hurt.

He reached for her. "I'm sorry. I didn't mean it."

"Yes, you did." She opened her car door. "Go home. You have big important things to do. I need to get some sleep. I'm leaving for Spain tomorrow afternoon."

His grip tightened around her arm, stopping her. She yanked free. "What?"

"You're leaving the freaking country. Tomorrow."

She swallowed, nodding. *Shit.* Had she forgotten to mention it to Will? She wasn't used to telling the men in her life her plans, and the getaway was a last-minute idea, Harper had insistent on, nearly begging Cindy to take the trip.

"For how long?" he asked.

"A week or so."

"For work? I thought you'd told me you had some time off?"

"I do. It's not for work. Harper and I are going. February is the worst. I've had enough of this cold."

They'd planned on only staying for a week. Although, with his attitude, she wasn't in a hurry to rush home. Plus, it's not like he had any time for her anyway. Maybe she'd spend the rest of her time off in the south of France. There was a cousin on her mom's side who lived there. They could meet up.

"Wait." He shook his head in short jerky jabs as if trying to shake loose something unpleasant. "You're leaving the country for a little vacation and didn't bother to mention it to me? You accuse me of not sharing shit. Seriously."

*Okay. He did have a point.*

She backtracked. "It was all last minute and slipped my mind. Besides, you said it yourself, you're overwhelmed and don't have time for me. Do your thing. I'll do mine. We'll see each other when I get back. I'm tired of this weather."

"The point is you made plans to leave the country and never thought to tell me." He gritted through clenched teeth. "When did you and Harper come up with this idea?"

Looking at her hands resting on her lap, Cindy considered lying but couldn't. Not to Will. "We've been throwing around the idea since New Year's. She called me last week, asking if I wanted to go. I said yes."

"A week. You planned this seven days ago. You didn't think it worth mentioning to me?" He faced the windshield, putting more distance between them. "When were you going to tell me? When the plane was taxiing down the runway?"

"Come on, Will. It slipped my mind. We hadn't talked much this week. When we did, our phone calls lasted maybe ten minutes."

"Planning a vacation overseas slipped your mind?"

"Yeah, believe it or not, it did. It isn't a big deal. I have a passport. I do this all the time."

"Fine. Whatever. No big deal." He pecked her on the lips. It felt cold and impersonal. "You should get inside. It's late, we both have busy days tomorrow."

Wow. She was being dismissed.

Fine. Message received.

Opening the door, she got out and refused to look back.

Will hung up his phone, smothering the urge to slam it down on the Formica table. Cindy wasn't answering his calls. It was past ten. She had to be awake, but not yet at the airport.

He shouldn't have left last night. His mom had always said never leave or go to bed angry. That was good advice when you're not dead tired. If he'd stayed around, they'd have ended up in a full-scale fight. Though now she was ghosting him. It seemed, either way, he couldn't win with her.

Freaking stubborn woman.

Or maybe not.

Maybe their relationship had run its course. Perhaps neither of them was able to love deeply.

He rubbed his sternum. Then, why did the idea of losing her hurt him physically? It made his heart ache, bleed.

Tim slid into the booth across from Will. "You know, I'm surprised at how simple and cost-effective Lucas's suggestions were to make our place eco-friendlier."

He rattled off some of them, low-flow faucets, lightbulbs, something about reclaimed or bamboo wood. Will nodded but was only half listening. He was trying to decide if he should send Cindy another text.

Tim tapped the table, snagging Will's attention. "You with me? Thinking deep thoughts, Jack Handy?"

Setting his cell face up, he eyed his friend. "Jesus, SNL stopped showing those over twenty years ago. Get new material."

"Those are classic. They never go out of style."

"Let's agree to disagree." Will took a sip of his coffee. "Anyway, what the hell took you so long? Did you fall in the toilet?"

Tim quirked a brow. "Really? You want details?"

Will laughed. "Nope."

"I'm kidding." Tim smirked. "I wanted to stay away until the bill arrived. And you paid for it."

"You're such a gentleman. A great friend."

"Hey! My company is payment enough."

"If you say so…"

The waiter returned to the table with Will's credit card, asking if they were leaving or wanted more coffee. Tim said he was game.

Will checked his phone. No missed calls or texts. "Nope. No plans."

"You aren't going to see Cindy before she leaves for Spain?"

"No. I don't think so— Wait. How'd you know she was going?"

Tim leaned back in the booth, a self-satisfied smile spread over him. It wasn't just his mouth, his whole freaking body glowed. "I went out with Emma the other day. She mentioned it."

*Nice. Everyone except me knew Cindy was leaving the damn country.*

Will flipped his phone, no longer caring if his maybe-girlfriend returned his call. Wanting to shift the focus off himself, he said, "Wow, she finally agreed. I'd say she was probably bored or wanted a free dinner. Wait. Did you hide in the bathroom until the bill was paid then, too?"

"Nah. I only bless you with that move."

Will shook his head. "How'd it go?"

"Good. Too good?"

"What the hell does that even mean?"

"I like her. She's fun and smart. And her smile, those lips." Tim's eyes clouded as if caught in a daydream about the woman. Seeing him enamored was odd. He met Will's gaze. "But, damn, I'm no good at being a kid's step-in dad."

"Is she pushing you to see Max? For the three of you to hang out together."

"No. The opposite. She doesn't want to confuse him or have him getting attached to me."

"That's smart."

"Yeah. Don't get me wrong, I'm relieved." He ran his hand through his hair, yanking at the ends. "Okay, fine. I'm annoyed too."

Will tried to hide his shock. "You? Why?"

"Got me." Tim was silent for a few beats, then said, "It's because she's writing me off as a fail, after one date. So positive we aren't going anywhere."

Will furrowed his brows. "You want more?

"Hell if I know." He clapped his hands together. "Anyway, enough about me. Why are you here? Shouldn't you be heading for the sunny beaches of Spain?"

*Because I wasn't invited.*

"It's a girl's week. And I don't know if you got the memo, but you and I are opening a restaurant. It isn't the best time to take my first international vacation."

Tim slapped his cheeks. His mouth fell open in mock surprise. "Wow. You and I." His hands dropped to the table. "Seriously. You've never been outside the US?"

"Does Windsor count? Drinking age is nineteen. Back in high school, we used to go to the bars every weekend."

"Doesn't count."

"Then guess not." He gave a one shoulder shrug. "And I don't care to. Right now, my focus is on getting our restaurant open. I don't have the time or money to jet off and lie on some beach."

Even if he'd been asked to go.

"'All work and no play makes Jack a dull boy,'" Tim quoted.

"'All play and no work makes Jack a mere toy,'" Will shot back.

"Did you make that up? I don't remember hearing that part in *The Shining*?"

Will scoffed. "Turn off the TV. Open a damn book. The two, together, is a proverb. From the sixteen hundreds."

"Whatever." Tim took a sip of his coffee, obviously not offended or the least bit interested in a history lesson. "Now, are we done? Anything else you want to know about yesterday's inspection?"

More than happy to get lost in work, to forget his personal life sucked, Will leaned forward. "No, we aren't, I have a few more questions."

"Of course you do." Tim caught the waiter's attention, holding up his mug. "Hit me with it."

# Chapter Twenty-Nine

"What do you want to do?"

Cindy turned from the Alboran Sea, focusing on Harper. "I'm good doing this." She spread her arms wide, indicating the ocean and beach of Playe de la Malagueta. "I'd like to stay for the sunset."

"Okay. Then?"

"Get something to eat."

"After that..."

Cindy knew her cousin wanted to go dancing. It made sense. Malaga had some famous nightclubs, and clubbing was their thing.

The problem was, she wasn't feeling it. At first, Will had pissed her off so much her first instinct was to leave him behind, jump back into her old life. To partake in her three favorite hobbies: traveling, dancing, and men.

However, she found her old ways didn't fit anymore. It was like trying on her favorite shirt from high school—pretty but no longer her style. And if she were being honest, somewhat restrictive.

"I was thinking of taking a day trip to Granada. We'd need to get to bed early."

Harper stared at Cindy. "Are you okay?"

"I'm fine," she lied. "What's the big deal? You act like I never visit touristy or historic sites."

"No. I know you do, but Granada is, what, two hours away. It's not something requiring us to be out the door at five in the morning." She fanned herself with a magazine, the pages fluttering. "Hell, it's when we normally go to bed. Yet, we've been in Spain for two days and every night has been an early one. What gives? Don't you want to dance at Pache Costa or Silk? Both are supposed to be amazing."

*No.*

"Sure."

"Wow. Your enthusiasm is off the charts."

Cindy laughed. "Sorry I'm in a mellow mood. I'm sure once I get on my favorite club wear and have the bass thrumming through me, I'll feel different."

Tossing aside *ARTnews*, Harper crooked her knees, resting her chin on them. "Is it Will?"

"He has nothing to do with it." Cindy studied her toes, digging them into the warm sand. "I think we might be over."

*Damn, that hurt to say out loud.*

"And even if we weren't, he was never bothered by me going out. He'd never told me not to."

"I can't imagine a guy ever telling you to do something." Harper snorted. "Never mind. I can picture the full-on massacre, blood and guts. His."

"You speak the truth." Cindy smiled, and it felt good. There weren't many since her fight with Will.

"Anyway, I'm referring to what you'd told me on the plane. You said you might be done with him. I don't understand it. You two are perfect together. I've never seen you like this with a guy." Harper inhaled sharply. "Wait. Did he dump you?"

"Pssh, now that's crazy talk." Although in her heart, she'd known it was only a matter of time. "Okay, first, I don't know what the hell you're talking about. We don't balance each other. We're total opposites, not even on the same scale. Second, I'm not upset."

Damn, she nearly choked on her false and bitter words. She now realized why she'd stayed away from love.

It sucked.

She had to move on. He was growing irritated, bored with her. Pride demanded she left before being dumped.

"You are so full of it," Harper said, echoing Cindy's thoughts. "He's a nice guy and hot as sin. Plus, you smiled around him, laughed more than I'd ever seen. Have you, um, considered trying to fix things?"

"There's nothing to fix. Sure, we cared, fine, loved each other, but deep down, we understood we were temporary. We're too different. Neither of us wanted anything serious."

"Are you trying to convince yourself or me? Either way, it doesn't matter. From what I saw, it seemed to have happened anyway."

Harper's hope and positivity cut Cindy's fragile heart. She couldn't keep talking about Will, or she'd do something embarrassing, like cry.

She changed the subject to one she was positive would throw Harper. "Enough about me. Why don't you tell me the story of you and Lucas?"

A smile tugged at the corner of the other woman's mouth. "Well played. What club did you say you wanted to go to tonight?"

"I didn't." Cindy debated. The curiosity was killing her, she wanted to pry. In the end, she let it go. Neither of them wanted to dive into relationship disappointments. "Let's try Silk. They have live music."

They arrived at the club around midnight. The band was fabulous. She wore her favorite blush wrap skirt and cream blouse with the dangerous dip in the back. The man dancing with her was the epitome of Spanish hotness—dark, bedroom eyes, heavy brows, a sinful smile, and clothes hinting at a killer body.

The combination should be the trifecta for a perfect night, yet she wasn't feeling it.

She kept comparing every man in the room to Will. They all fell short.

Or her mind would wander, wondering what he was doing. If he was missing her.

It wasn't like she'd never had white-hot flings with men before Will. However, this was the first time she couldn't let go. All because she had gone and fallen in love with the most unlikely man.

Jacob's older super-serious brother. The workaholic homebody. The guy with so much baggage it'd be denied at the airport for its weight.

The man who made her body melt and shudder in ecstasy. The one who lightened her heart with laughter and kindness.

Didn't make sense, not that her heart seemed to care.

"Want to get a drink?" asked the Spanish hottie.

She debated. His lips weren't as sexy as Will's. Although, damn, his accent was like champagne and strawberries.

"Yes." She was thirsty, and perhaps a taste of this stranger would help clear her palate of Will.

After ordering, they found two empty barstools, far enough from the stage they wouldn't have to shout to be heard. There she learned her Spanish hottie's name was Santiago. He'd grown up in Malaga, left to attend a university in England before returning home.

He had style to go along with his good looks. He wasn't heavy with his flirting or his hands. A finger resting for a second on her knee while asking where she was from, leaning in to ask what brought her to Spain. His gaze traveling over her body, never lingering too long on her breasts or legs, when he'd invited her to dinner with him the next day.

"Thank you, but I'm here with my cousin. I can't bail on her." Cindy searched the dance floor, spotting Harper.

*Hmm. I might be the one getting ditched.*

The way she was dancing with her partner was one move away from illegal. It was hot.

Returning to Santiago, she found him checking out her legs. He grinned. "Your cousin could come with us. I'll bring a friend."

She took a sip of her Kalimotxo, stalling, trying to decide if she should accept.

Resting an elbow on the bar, he asked, "Be honest, is it me or your cousin? Don't worry. My ego can handle it."

She didn't doubt it. The way other women were eyeing him, she'd be easily replaced. "Truthfully? Neither."

"Then what is it?" He held up a hand. "Let me guess. You're a beautiful, interesting woman. I'm guessing a man's the problem."

She laughed. "Aren't you guys always the problem?"

"Some are worth it," he countered.

"I'm not so sure..." She waved a hand. "Anyway, yes, you're right, it's a man. We're finished, but I'm having a hard time forgetting him."

Another light touch on her bare knee, lingering longer this time. "I could be the man who helps you forget him."

"I can't decide if I want to forget."

He leaned back, reaching for his drink. "Well, if he has your heart, I can't compete."

They finished their drinks. He was a gentleman, asking if she wanted to dance. Being a lady, she declined. She was sure he wanted to move on, find a woman looking for the possibility of love, or more likely, a night of fun. That person wasn't her.

She was on the other side of the world from Will. He hadn't called since the morning she left. It didn't seem to matter. He might be done with her, but he'd crawled into her heart and was with her no matter how far she traveled.

# Chapter Thirty

"You know, I'm the guy who tells you how to make your business greener, not the one implementing those changes."

"The soft opening is in two weeks. I'm calling in all my favors. It needs to be perfect." Will tossed the old lightbulb in the box. "Besides, what have you got going on today? Thinking of calling Greta's cousin for a date?"

Okay, that was a low blow and none of his business. His crankiness leaked out sometimes.

Lucas stopped working on the faucet, giving Will his full attention. "You mean, Cindy's cousin? How's she doing?"

*Asshole.*

Will shrugged. "I have no idea."

Jacob came into the kitchen, wiping his hands on a rag. "How in the hell did I get stuck installing the water-saving toilets?"

"With Will's shitty mood, he should be doing it," Lucas groused.

"I don't know what you mean. I'm fine," Will lied, grabbing another LED bulb

The two men laughed. Jacob said to Lucas, "So, I'm not the one only who's noticed he's even more grouchy than usual?"

Lucas nodded. "He's worse than my sister's teenage daughter." He shivered like the thought of her was downright terrifying.

"Damn, guys. I'm opening a business, aren't I allowed to be stressed?"

"Yes, it's allowed, but I'm thinking it's something else," Jacob replied.

"Nope. Just have a lot on my mind," Will lied again.

He struggled not to fidget under his brother's perceptive gaze. He always saw too much. Shaking his head, Jacob said, "Bull."

No shit. The woman he'd fallen for didn't want anything to do with him, and he couldn't blame her. They were a bad match.

"Did you invite Cindy to the opening?" Jacob asked.

He was fishing. Will refused to bite. "Nah. She's probably busy. Traveling for work or something."

"From what Greta tells me, Cindy isn't taking many jobs. Their mom is pissed. Says Cindy is getting old and needs to take them while they're being offered. Or at least start managing some fundraisers or other socialite crap."

Once again, Will was left wondering how in the hell Greta and Cindy didn't end up being shallow, narcissistic women, like their mother. He wanted to push aside his sympathy for them, but his curiosity found it impossible. "What's she doing instead?"

"Taking online classes. Photography and writing, I think. Greta's helping her build an online platform."

It still stung at the way Cindy had brushed him off as if he was nothing more than a pleasant diversion. However, he was proud of her, genuinely happy she was pursuing something she loved.

The selfish side of him wished it was him she loved. Not that he deserved it.

Sure, he no longer believed he was unfit for love, but still thought she was better off with someone who had less baggage, a lighter heart.

"Will you ask her?" Jacob insisted.

"I sent out the invites weeks ago. It's probably too late to mail her one."

"Are you kidding me? She isn't some acquaintance. You've seen her naked."

"Oh, if you're naked with someone, it means you're close?"

"Nope. Not even if you'd like it to be different," Lucas muttered.

Will's gaze jumped to his friend than back to Jacob. He opened his mouth then closed it, looking at their friend.

Lucas reached for a wrench, waving them off. "Don't mind me. I'm talking out of my ass. Though, he's right. You should call her."

"Why? We haven't talked in over a month. I'm sure the last thing she wants to do is spend an evening at her ex-boyfriend's restaurant."

"She's more than an ex," Jacob said. "Remember this was one of the reasons Greta didn't want you two hooking up. It's impossible for you not to run into her."

"No big deal. I can handle seeing Cindy." He'd faked being fine for years when using; he could pretend around Cindy. "But there's no reason for her to come to this. We aren't together anymore. Why would she be interested?"

"Greta will be there, her father, and many of her friends. Plus, she's the one who convinced you to get off your butt, to take the risk. Don't you think she might want to see the final result?"

Will studied the bulb he'd been holding since Jacob mentioned Cindy. "Maybe. I'll think about it."

"Stop being stubborn. Call her."

"Fine. Fine. I will. Now shut the hell up and get back to those toilets."

Jacob threw the dirty rag he was holding. Will batted it aside. "You know, big brother, if we weren't related, I'd dump a box of tampons down every toilet on opening night."

His brows rose. "You have a stash of them?"

"I'm married. I know where to get them," Jacob said with a shrug.

"I'm keeping an eye on you opening night. I remember the pranks you pulled on me when we were kids. Our parents should've named us after the Norse gods, not the Grimm brothers. You'd be Loki." Will pointed at himself. "I'd be Thor."

"More like Hod," Jacob said, and laughed.

"Wasn't he blind?"

"Yes, he was." Jacob started in the direction of the restroom. "Call Cindy."

Cindy hung up the phone, staring at her laptop, not seeing it. Butterflies were twirling in her chest, light and airy.

"Was that Will?" Greta asked.

"Yes. He invited me to the opening of his restaurant."

"Will you go?"

She nodded, her heart racing at seeing him again. "I'd like to talk. I hate the way things ended."

Sliding her hand from the mouse, Greta said, "I don't think the stress-filled night of his soft opening is the time."

"No shit, Sherlock."

Greta gave Cindy a death glare. She ignored it. "But if I blew off his offer and didn't go, I'm sure he wouldn't want to talk later. Plus, I'm excited for him and Tim. I want to support them."

Wow. Look at her, excited for someone else's successes. Maybe she wasn't just like her mother after all.

Greta smiled as if agreeing, before turning to her laptop. They were updating Cindy's photography website.

"We need to make it easier for people to sign up for your newsletter," her sister continued, though Cindy listened with one ear.

Her thoughts drifted to Will. She missed him terribly, knew without a doubt she loved him.

The time apart had also opened her eyes. She'd always considered herself a bit of a daredevil, doing as she wished. She'd discovered it was with things that didn't matter.

Travel the world. Yup. Fast cars and reckless driving. Sure, fun times. Date and sleep with whoever caught her attention. Check. Speak her mind with a sharp tongue. She loved the cut.

However, most of the time, what she said was a whole lot of nothing. When it came to actual risks, she was as timid as a rabbit, running from real vulnerability.

She was hand-led into modeling by her mother. With her influence, Cindy didn't have to take the crappy jobs or worry about being taken advantage of by the millions of shady workers in the industry. She never struggled for her career, merely maintained it.

When she offered a small piece of her pride, submitting to a few travel journals, she nearly quit after a few rejections. She was weak.

Then there was Will. He seemed to adore all of her, the pretty and ugly. She'd fallen in love with him, but ran at the first sign of difficulty. Instead of asking if he was tired of her and was thinking of leaving, she left.

That had been her motto. Disappear before the good times end. Leave before they left.

She shook her head. "I'm so dumb."

A line formed between Greta's brows. "It's not a big deal. Most people find widgets confusing."

Cindy chuckled, resting her head on the edge of the desk.

"Oh. You weren't talking about the webpage. Let me guess," Greta said. "You weren't listening."

Twisting her neck, Cindy rolled her head to look at her sister. "I am. Sort of. Widgets are good for, um, something."

"Are you bored?" Greta pushed back her chair, stretching her long legs. "Want to stop?"

"Sorry, Will's call has me losing what little focus I have for this stuff."

Greta rubbed Cindy's back, using her nails, like when they were kids. She used to do it when their mom had upset her. Though this time, Cindy's unhappiness was her own fault.

"Listen, I know I haven't asked what happened with you and Will. I apologize. I'm sure you want to vent, but he's Jacob's brother, and I like Will. I don't want to take sides. However, you're my sister. I'll always have your back. Spill, if you'd like to get it off your chest."

"There isn't much to say. I messed up. Will was always busy with work, opening the restaurant, and other things. Maybe NA stuff. I don't know. He hated talking about his past. I didn't offer to help, never asked if he was tired in general, or of me. I was too afraid to know the answer. Instead, I whined, rebelled, walked away." She sat straight, running her fingers through her hair. "Now I want to ask him, but I'm even more scared. What if he's only inviting me out of obligation?

Greta gave an unladylike snort. "Oh, please, the Grimm men don't do anything out of obligation. If he asked, he wants you there."

"Maybe as a friend. I don't want to be his buddy. If I go and he's not affected by our split, it'll kill me. Or worse, what if he's moved on?" That last bit hurt like a knock-out punch to the stomach. "Maybe his feelings for me were never deep. Hell, he tried to call me for one day, then gave up. Doesn't sound like a man in love to me."

That still pissed her off. She wanted someone who'd fight for them, for her.

"Jacob would've told me if Will was seeing someone."

"Oh, really?" Cindy crossed her arms. "Did you know he was sleeping with his boss, your friend, Cora?"

Greta's mouth fell open. Cindy swallowed a giggle. It felt nice.

"Okay. I didn't know about that. I never saw them together. Nor had either mentioned they were a thing. However, there's the difference. You were his girlfriend. For Will that's huge. You meant something to him. According to Jacob, that hasn't happened since Jolene. We're talking more than five years ago. Jacob used to joke he was waiting for Will to take vows as a monk." Greta smirked. "Although now learning about Cora, that wouldn't have worked. Anyway, you are important to him. He isn't going to get over you in less than a month."

"Maybe, but it doesn't mean he wants to give me another chance."

"You won't know until you try. Believe me, it's better to know than wonder."

Cindy was willing to bet Greta was remembering her breakup with Jacob before he proposed.

It wasn't the same.

"Easy for you to say. When you two split, Jacob would've done anything and everything to convince you to come back to him."

Happiness lit her sister from within, making Cindy a little jealous. She wanted a man to love her, as Jacob did her sister.

"True," Greta agreed. "That was nice. However, when I saw Macy hanging on him like a cheap suit, that was pretty awful. At the same time, it gave me closure. Gave me motivation to move on."

Cindy quirked a brow. "Oh, really? You'd moved on?"

Greta gave a wry smile. "I said it gave me motivation, not that it was working."

"I don't need an incentive to let go. It's been weeks. Him not calling is it. To me, it seems going would be inviting needless pain." Cindy sighed. "My cup's already full, thank you very much."

Greta's eyes filled with sympathy. "From what I know about Will, he doesn't want to be a burden to anyone. Including you. If he thinks he's dragging you down, making you the slightest bit unhappy, he'll let you go."

"Hell, what if he always believes this? Every time we have a problem, he'll give up. I'll think he doesn't want me anymore, and I'll run." She laughed sadly. "It's not the best combination."

"The other option is worse, don't you think? Not even trying..."

Cindy wasn't sure. Each one hurt like hell.

# Chapter Thirty-One

Cindy's heart hammered, and her hands shook as she opened the glass door to Will's restaurant. Once inside, she gripped the countertop running along the floor-to-ceiling windows, waiting for her heart to slow. It wasn't happening, and after a minute she gave up.

She'd been too nervous to eat much during the day. The tantalizing smells of roasted garlic, bacon, and bread made love to her senses. She breathed it in, her stomach rumbling in protest at its empty state. It didn't care about her stress and broken heart.

"Cindy! So glad you could make it." Tim came toward her, arms open.

Hugging him, she said, "It smells like a dream in here."

His smile widened. "Thank you. Do you want to sit with your sister?"

Nodding, she followed him, halting when her gaze snagged on seven framed photos along the brick wall opposite the ordering counter. They were different shots of Detroit.

They were hers.

She'd sold them less than a month ago. She'd known the person who bought them was local, but not who.

Her pulse spiked as embarrassment and delight exploded in her. Did everyone know they were hers? Did they hate them?

She tapped Tim's shoulder, pointing at her beautifully framed pictures. "Why are those here?"

He studied her for half a second, seeming confused. "Will came in with them some time awhile back. We both agreed they're perfect for the restaurant. We were right. People have been commenting on them all evening. Why?"

Tim didn't know she was the photographer. For some reason, this made her happy.

No, she knew why. It was knowing he liked them because they were good. His opinion wasn't clouded by him knowing the person who'd taken them.

She shook her head. "No reason. The place looks great. You and Will did a fine job."

They stopped at the biggest table, where Greta and Jacob sat with Father and Anna, Lucas, Harper, Tanner and Maggie, along with Will's dad and Tanner's mom. The way she was leaning on him, Cindy wondered if they were dating. She'd thought Carleen only went for musicians. Roger was a retired police officer.

Shrugging off her curiosity, Cindy said to Tim, "I know you're busy. Thanks for taking the time to bring me to my table."

*Since Will's nowhere to be seen.*

Was his absence on purpose?

"No worries," Tim said. "It's great seeing you again, though I better get back in the kitchen. Make sure Will is okay. I haven't seen him in close to two hours."

So maybe Tim had heard the silent question and was trying to reassure her. It did help. Somewhat. Every time his name was spoken, or the door to the kitchen swung open, was a defibrillator to her heart.

She pretended otherwise. Taking her seat next to Greta, she hugged her, asking what was new.

Her sister ignored the question, leaning in close with a knowing smile. "You look pretty."

"Really?" Cindy ran her palms over her new, fitted pale pink slacks. "I grabbed whatever was closest in my closet."

Okay, that was a half-truth. The white, Victorian blouse she'd bought in Paris last year was unbuttoned enough to be sexy but stay classy. However, the slacks and highlights in her hair were new.

Sure, Will had been attracted to her personality. Although, it didn't mean she didn't want to knock him on his ass when he saw her again.

She suspected Greta knew this but was kind enough not to tease. Instead, she asked if the website improvements had brought in any new traffic.

They fell into a discussion about social media platforms, which Cindy was surprised to discover she found interesting. As a model, she had a PA handle that end of things, but she was doing it all with her writing and photography. She found experimenting and playing around to discover what works was fun at times.

She was laughing, telling Jacob about a few crazy DM's when the kitchen doors swung open. Will exited with a curvy blonde. Cindy's breath caught. He looked a little tired, a lot stressed, and beyond handsome. He had on black slacks that accentuated the muscles in his thighs, and a slim-fitting gray dress shirt with micro white dots. The finishing touch was the wide leather belt.

She was positive it was the same one he'd used one time to bind her wrists. Memories of that night flashed through her mind, warming her cheeks and between her thighs.

He was deep in conversation with the blonde, who was staring at him with way too much admiration. So enamored, she damn near ran into a patron's chair as they walked and talked.

Seeing the oncoming disaster, he reached for the girl. At the same time, his gaze locked on Cindy's. He paused mid-step, his hand falling to his side.

She waved, offering a weak, nervous smile.

When he returned it, joy sprang to his eyes, chasing away her shadows. She nearly sprang from her seat to run to him, wanting to jump into his arms.

The woman next to him tapped his shoulder, bringing his attention back to her. She pointed at some paper in her hand, then to a man sitting at a table off to the left. Will said something before giving Cindy the universal "give me a minute" gesture.

She nodded, thankful for the time to gather her racing heart and building hopes. They needed to be set aside for now.

The soft opening was important for him. The focus needed to be on the food and classiness of the place. There should be no mention of some crazy woman declaring her love to one of the owners.

However, when everyone left and the doors locked, it would be about them.

Will was frozen to the floor. He was being torn in half. He *needed* to meet with the man sitting at table three. He wrote a popular restaurant blog. Will *wanted* to talk to Cindy.

The phone call to invite her to tonight's soft opening had been awkward and brief. They'd spoken like strangers, not even acquaintances. Yet here she was, smiling at him like he meant something to her.

"Will? Hello?" Another tap on the arm from Lisa, Tim's sister, the new head waitress. "Mr. Waltz told me he needed to leave soon but wanted to talk to you first."

He nodded, making his way to the blogger. Half his mind was on the interview, the rest on Cindy.

He wanted to know if she'd thought of him at all in the weeks they'd been apart. If her empty moments were filled with the ghost of his laughter and touch. Or was that just him?

Life had become too crowded, he'd feared buckling under the pressure, believing simplifying it would ease the strain. So, he'd let her walk away. Didn't fight for her, for them.

He'd gotten what he wanted. Sort of.

His life was empty. However, without Cindy, it felt incredibly hollow.

Waltz rapped on the table. *Shit*, another question missed.

Will focused on him. "Sorry, I'm not normally this scattered."

"I get it. Opening night is a crazy time. Lots to think about. I'll keep it simple, enough for a quick overview to post online tonight. If you're interested, I'll leave my contact information. When things settle down, we can do a longer interview."

"Thanks. That would be great."

Waltz seemed like a patient man, nevertheless Will didn't want to come off as rude. The rest of the time they talked, he didn't let his mind drift. When it tried, he gave a mental slap. Thankfully, after another five minutes, and a few simple questions regarding the menu, they were finished.

After shaking his hand, Will started for Cindy's table, having no idea what he'd do when he got there.

Kiss her? Shake her hand? Wave like an idiot?

He soon discovered, getting to her was as difficult as deciding what to do once he stood in front of her. He'd spent most of the evening in the kitchen, helping the new head chef, while Tim handled the dining area. Now that Will was out, everyone wanted to talk or congratulate him. Every few steps, he was stopped by a friend, family member, or guest.

It took him nearly twenty minutes to make it across the room to her table. Once there, he didn't have to decide what to do. She did it for him. He wasn't sure he liked it.

Everyone at her table stood, hugging him, and praising the success of the opening. She was one of the last people to reach him. She embraced and kissed him, but it held as much passion as the peck on the cheek from Tanner's mom.

The smile Cindy gifted him with when he first spotted her was now guarded. Leaving him to wonder what she was trying to protect. Her heart, or his feelings?

He wouldn't push now, though he wasn't letting her leave tonight until he had answers to all his questions.

Hours later, he wiped his hands, tossing the towel on the counter. He was exhausted, but mostly content. If the official opening was as successful as this one, he'd be a happy man.

There had been hiccups. He'd spent most of his time in the kitchen, putting out metaphorical fires and a small real one, due to unattended hot grease left on the stove.

Thankfully, Tim handled the dining room like a star. Will, along with the head chef, had the guests raving about the food.

They made one hell of a team. The night had been damn near perfect. He should be drowning in relief and satisfaction. Instead, he peered between the swinging door leading to the main dining area, like all his disappointments were out there sitting at the tables, lingering around for last call.

In a way, they were. In the form of a woman *not* waiting for him.

After their stiff greeting, he was called back into the kitchen. He didn't know if Cindy was still here or went home hours ago. Or what to do with either outcome.

He'd physically let go. However, extricating her from his mind was impossible.

There was no doubt he loved her, but it didn't mean she felt the same. It had been pure arrogance to believe if another person cared for him, he'd be wholly responsible for her well-being, mistakes, her everything.

Jolene had made her choices. As had he, and they'd both suffered the consequences. For too many years, he'd let his fears rule his life, but wouldn't any longer. If Cindy had left, he'd go after her.

She was almost a decade younger yet had far better judgment and had way more maturity than he'd ever shown at her age. Hell, he barely had it now. She was a strong woman who knew what she wanted. She'd never bend and contort herself to please him.

The door swung inward, making his pulse jump before crashing to the ground when he saw Lisa.

Will peered past her, into the dining room. It was almost empty, only a few stragglers.

"Do you mind if I go out back for a smoke?" she asked.

"No, just prop the door, or it'll lock."

She nodded, and he watched her go. Grabbing a stray knife, he tapped the handle on the palm of his opposite hand. Should he follow her to make sure she didn't get locked out or chat with whoever was left in the dining room?

"Do you like what you see?" came a smooth, familiar voice.

He sucked in a startled breath and whipped around, dropping the knife. It clattered to the floor, resting between them. She was so close her warmth caressed him. Longing crashed through him.

He cleared his throat. "Damn, woman, I think my heart jumped into my throat."

There was less than a foot of space between them. He could smell her scent of vanilla and lavender. He didn't step back. Neither did she.

He ate up the sight of her like a starving man. He wanted more than a taste.

She bent, her head nearly brushing along the front of his slacks. He closed his eyes, trying to remember to breathe.

Straightening, she held the knife. "Why didn't you call me?"

# Chapter Thirty-Three

Cindy waited. There was no sense messing around with small talk. She needed answers.

He'd never tried to contact her in Spain or when she returned. Tonight, besides the stiff greeting, he stayed in the kitchen. She wasn't sure if it was avoidance, work, or indifference.

She could deal with all except the last one. If she meant little or nothing to him, they were done.

Yes, she loved him but refused to fight for a man who wouldn't do the same for her. Or worse, never truly loved her.

Everything about him shouted exhaustion, from his stooped shoulders to the shadows under his eyes. Maybe he was stressed from the opening of his restaurant. She wanted to believe it was because he missed her. That like her, he felt empty, hollowed out.

Each beat of her heart was painful as she waited for him to heal it or break it. When she couldn't take it any longer, she tilted her head to the side and asked. "Well, are you going to answer me?"

He licked his lips. "Want to set the knife on the counter first?"

"Is it so bad you don't want me holding sharp objects?" she teased, though dread coated her heart.

His gaze traveled down her body, stopping at her favorite stilettos. She swore there was hunger in his perusal. Her need for him responded, and warmth thrummed through her.

"It's more that you're wearing those. Aren't they the ones you were wearing the day we arrived at the lake house? I don't want to chance you falling again."

The fact he remembered such a small detail thrilled her all the way to her sexy peep-toe heels. An uninterested man wouldn't recall such things.

She tossed the knife onto a nearby counter. "Oh, you remember the shoes I wore almost a year ago, yet you managed to forget I'm your girlfriend."

His eyes turned cold. "Don't play that game. I was giving you what you wanted. A guy can take a hint. You planned a vacation, didn't mention it to me, didn't answer my calls before you left. Didn't try to call me the whole time you were gone, or when you got back." Will crossed his arms over his chest. Sometime during the evening, he'd rolled his sleeves. His corded muscles were on full display. She tried not to ogle and failed.

"Tell me, why would I call?" he asked.

That hurt. A lot.

She loved him, but maybe he didn't feel the same. Wouldn't a man in love take an extra step for his heart?

"Aren't I worth the effort?" She hated the weakness in her voice.

"Your reason for ending it with me is because *I* didn't call you first? I didn't because I thought you were done with me. Am I a toy, a game to play until you're bored with me?" Anger flashed in his eyes. His lip curled. "I know you're younger. I didn't realize you were immature."

He was being unfair. Fire lit her gut. She rushed forward, pointing a finger roughly against his chest. "No. Asshole. It isn't a game, and my age has nothing to do with it. If you don't want me around, I'll leave." She let her hands drop in defeat. "I'm gone. I might love you, but I have my self-respect."

"You still love me?" he whispered.

She nodded. There was no sense denying it. However, coming here, to him, was a bad idea. He no longer felt the same. She started toward the door.

He stopped her, threading his fingers with hers. "I love you too."

At his words, an explosion burst through her chest, light and airy. It was a ray of warm sun at the beginning of spring.

She smothered it. His love wasn't worth much if he let it go easily. "Yet you let me walk out of your life without a fight. Hell, not even a whispered demand for me to stay."

"Because I love you too much to drag you down. I was offering you a clean break."

"A clean break," she repeated under her breath.

What was he talking about? Wasn't it the other way around?

"I'm not the type of man you need," he finished.

Annoyance heated her blood. "Christ. This. Still. Oh, pray tell, what type of man do I need? If you use your past as an excuse again, I'm going to scream." Her gaze flicked to the discarded knife. "Maybe I will cut you after all."

A flash of a smile tugged at the corner of his mouth, only to disappear an instant later. "It's not an excuse, although it does matter." She opened her mouth, fully intending to screech in frustration. He quickly held up a hand. "But not in the way I'd originally thought."

That stopped her. She waited for him to continue.

He ran a hand through his hair, gripping the back of his neck. "From the start, I knew you called to my damaged heart."

"Damn it. It isn't damaged! You. Are. Not. Damaged."

"Wait. Let me finish."

She motioned for him to continue.

"I *will* be fighting certain demons all my life, but I get what you're saying. I have changed, healed. I'm stronger than I was."

He came closer. The plea reflected in his eyes made her heart weep. She needed to know if he was begging for her to understand or let him go.

"At first," he continued. "I was terrified I'd fall in love with you and end up destroying you like I did Jolene. I couldn't see past my weaknesses to realize your strength. Once I saw it, I understood you'd want more than I had to offer. I told myself when you wanted to leave, I wouldn't stop you."

Confusion clouded her anger. "Um. What can't you offer? All I want from you is your love. Can you give me that?"

He answered without hesitation, "Yes, but I keep wondering if you deserve so much more. What we want from life is completely different. You're young. Go, have fun. Dance, travel, party. I can't do any of those things, and I'll be damned if I'll hold you back."

"Did it ever occur to you to ask me what I wanted?"

The look on his face told her the answer. Her stubborn, hard-headed man.

"Listen, the things you've named are fun. That's all they are. Fun. I'd put too much importance on them, never realizing what it was costing you."

"But, it's also part of your job," he argued.

"I don't care anymore. You're more important. Plus, for ninety-nine percent of those events, boyfriends aren't invited. And when I do go out for fun, I don't require a man on my arm to enjoy myself. Two, I'm twenty-five. I'm at the end of my modeling career." She smirked. "I know in your mind I'm a toddler, but in the modeling world, I'm an old lady. I have no interest in becoming an agent or manager. Nor do I want to become a socialite like my mother, flitting from one fundraiser dinner to the next. What I do want in my life is *you*. It's why I'm here tonight."

"Then why did you leave? Why didn't you call when you got home?"

Guilt made his gaze too heavy to hold. She looked at her pretty painted toes, peeking from her shoes instead. "For the same reasons you've given. I thought we were too different, that our love was burning out. After we split, I learned something..."

His fingertips brushed against her chin, pushing gently. The hope swirling in his chocolate eyes awoke hers.

Maybe they did stand a chance.

"What did you discover?"

"We are complementary colors."

A smile twitched on his beautiful lips. She wanted to kiss it, make it grow.

"Care to explain?" he asked.

"Side-by-side, we are a strong contrast. When combined, these differences mix, they blend, creating a new beautiful color." She ran her thumb over his lips. He inhaled sharply, desire on his exhale. "My lightness for your dark. I'm impulsive. Your cautiousness grounds me."

"I take life too seriously. You show me the light, the fun," he added.

She smiled. "I'm immature. You act like a geriatric. Together we're just the right mental age."

Will laughed, bringing her into his warm, strong arms. He kissed her. She tasted his love and longing. It mixed with hers.

"I've missed you so much," he whispered against her mouth, pressing in closer, tightening his hold, running his tongue along the seam of her lips.

She could have responded with words. Instead, she showed him. Opening, she deepened the kiss.

He groaned, taking control, conquering her lips with his skill and growing need. It set her body on fire. Heat rushed through her veins as he lifted her onto the counter. She opened her legs. He moved between them, not allowing a sliver of space.

Someone cleared their throat. Over Will's shoulder, Cindy saw the woman who asked to go outside to smoke. She was watching them with a mixture of embarrassment and amusement.

She popped out a hip, resting a hand. "You and Tim told me to make the guests feel welcome. Good to know the bosses take it seriously."

He shook his head, chuckling. "Lisa, I'd like you to meet my girlfriend." He paused, looking at Cindy as if asking if he was telling the truth. She kissed his cheek, threading her fingers with his.

*Most definitely.*

Lisa offered her hand to Cindy while saying to Will, "Tim told me you'd broke up with some hot girl. It's why you're such a grump." She studied Cindy. "Guess he was right about her being hot, wrong about the other part. How's your roommate?"

"Um..." Cindy was somewhat unsettled. Earlier, she'd seen Lisa's admiration toward Will. She also seemed to know a lot about his personal life.

"Leave her alone, Lisa," he warned, then explained to Cindy. "Lisa's Tim's sister. He's mentioned Emma a few times."

Nodding in understanding, Cindy answered, "She's good. Although, not too sure of what to make of your brother."

"Tell her good luck. He has pretty much raised me, and I don't understand him at all." Lisa laughed, moving past them. "Anyway, sorry I interrupted your scorching make-out session, but my friend texted me. He's waiting outside. I wanted to let you know, so you didn't freak when I'm no longer out back or in the restaurant." With a quick wave, she shot between the swinging doors.

Cindy leaned into Will. He kissed her ear, asking, "Now what?"

"You tell me. I came here to lay myself bare before you. Risk having you crush my heart because I love you too much to simply walk away. However, I need to know, am I worth it to you? Do you want to try again?"

"Cindy." He gently gripped the side of her face. "There is no trying. You have me. My heart is forever yours."

She blinked, fighting the tears trying to spill. "No more assuming, okay? We talk, never walk."

"Yes, my sexy," he kissed her chin, then her lips, "smart and beautiful girlfriend."

Hugging him tight, she said, "Good. To answer your earlier question of what happens now, you take me home. I want you to show me how much you've missed me."

"Good call." He pointed toward the door with his head. "Come on, let's go."

Not wanting to let go completely, she wrapped an arm around his waist. Stepping into the dining room, they found Tim and Will's family, along with Lucas, Harper, Tanner, and Maggie.

Jacob leaned on the wall near the kitchen doors, smirking. "We wanted to have a small congratulatory afterparty, but it looks like you two have other plans." His smile was warm. "It's nice to see you've worked things out."

"I'm just glad they decided not to have make-up sex in the kitchen," Tim piped. "Lisa said they were pretty hot and heavy in there."

Roger groaned like he was in pain. "There are some things I'd rather not hear about."

Cindy laughed, wanting to sink into the floor. She hid her face in Will's shoulder, while he grabbed a plastic salt shaker and threw it at his friend.

She heard laughter, then Tanner's amused voice, "Yeah, it's right up there with stopping by your mom's place and seeing your best friend's dad in nothing except old boxers."

*What*?

Cindy's gaze whipped between Tanner and Jacob's dad. Roger's face was as bright as an overripe tomato. Carleen was laughing, not showing any discomfort. Tanner's mom was the coolest.

"She'd forgotten you planned on stopping by," Roger muttered to the table.

"Stop giving him a hard time. You know you love him," Carleen said.

Tanner shrugged. "Still, Mom, warn me next time."

"Knock next time."

"Oh, believe me, I will."

"As fascinating and awful as all of this is," Will cut in. "Do you mind if we head out? I'm, um, tired. It's been a crazy day."

"Is that what they're calling it nowadays?" Tim's mom teased.

Cindy ignored the heat blooming on her cheeks, letting go of Will to hug her sister, Jacob, and Roger. Will said a hasty goodbye. They were outside in less than ten minutes.

The cool night air erased some of the heat from her cheeks, but none of her desire. There was no chance of that happening. Not when very soon Will would be naked before her, so many wonderful inches of firm muscle and beautiful man to savor like her own personal dessert.

Sometimes life was pretty damn sweet.

# Epilogue



Will grabbed the throw from the couch, taking the few steps to the patio door. Crossing the patio, he jumped the stairs landing in sand still a little warm from the hot rays of the sun.

Digging his toes in, he took in his beautiful surroundings. The houses were dark, and the sky was putting on a spectacular show. The only sound was the swell and crash of waves from Lake Michigan, along with the swish of the beach grass.

"Will?" Cindy's voice drifted, mixing with the night sounds. "Is that you?"

"No. It's a wolverine," he teased.

When he reached the edge of their blanket, she propped herself on one elbow. "There aren't any in the wild, smart ass."

He shook open the large throw. "Loch Ness monster, then?"

"Wrong country."

He could almost hear her roll her eyes. He swallowed his chuckle.

"Good thing I'm writing the travel blog and not you. Now get under this blanket. I need your body heat," she demanded.

"Yes, ma'am." He sat next to her, snapped the blanket, letting it cover them.

Laying back, he shifted to his side, bringing her into his arms. She sighed, nuzzling into his neck. He opened his legs. She snuggled between his.

"I adore it here. When we are old and retired, we need to buy a house like this one. Spend every evening watching the sunset from our back porch."

He loved how she spoke of their future together with such certainty. It'd been a year since they'd gotten back together after their brief split, and while it was filled with highs and lows, they tackled them together.

She pulled back from modeling to focus on her writing and photography. She was building a strong online platform with stories of her travels, even thinking of self-publishing a travel book of Europe at the end of the year. If it went well, she wanted to do one about the hidden gems in Michigan. With her insight and humor, the book was bound to make it big.

Plus, she was selling her photography online, in his restaurant, and Harper's art studio. They were beginning to produce a steady income.

His hours at the restaurant were brutal, but they were creative in finding time together, happily barricading themselves in the bedroom when they both had a free day, catching up on rest and pleasure.

When Will had to work long hours, Cindy would bring her laptop to the restaurant and visit with him during his slow time. Also, to her mother's complete horror, Cindy was helping at his restaurant. She was an excellent hostess, making the rounds, talking with the customers, handling the difficult ones with ease.

Still, he missed having uninterrupted days with her. He'd convinced Tim and Lisa to manage the place for a week, surprising Cindy with a mini-getaway.

He loved his job, but damn this week was heaven. They'd slept in, made love throughout the day and well into the nights, went for lazy swims and meandering walks. Or like, now, gazed at the stars.

"I don't want to go home," he groaned. "Forget waiting until we're gray. I should open a restaurant here now."

She kissed his neck, grazing her teeth along his Adam's apple. "Who's the impulsive one now?"

Grabbing her ass, he fell onto his back, bringing her on top of him. "Guess you're rubbing off on me."

"Rubbing on you, huh?" She wiggled, making everything in him tighten and thrum with need.

He kissed her hard. She responded in kind, her hips shifting from playful to carnal in a matter of seconds. Reaching to her waist, he tugged at the string of her bikini bottoms.

She stilled, whispering against his lips. "Here? On the beach?"

"Do you want me to stop?"

"No. I never want you to stop. However, it would be embarrassing to end our last night here in jail for indecent exposure."

"I do remember a certain incredibly sexy woman doing some rather naughty things to me a few summers back in the woods near here."

He felt her smile more than saw it. "Yes, in my defense, I thought that was my last chance with you. Desperate times, desperate measures. Plus, we were in the forest, hidden, now we're lying on the wide-open beach. For all to see."

"It's past midnight. We, with maybe a few wolverines, are the only ones out here. But," he rolled on top of her, kissing along her collarbone to her thinly covered breasts. "I'll stop. If it's what you want."

He pushed aside her small bikini top, teasing her in a way that never failed to drive her crazy. Her whimpers and the way she gripped the back of his head, bringing him closer, screamed keep going.

When he scooted up to find her lips, she tugged at his shorts. "Take them off."

"Here? On the beach?" he asked with mock-scandal.

She slapped his ass, then kneaded it. "At this point, I wouldn't care if it was two in the afternoon and we had an audience. The only thing that matters is the sweet relief you will give me."

Every fiber of his body called to hers, begging for the same thing. He tugged his shorts to his knees and kissed her, before sliding inside with one deep thrust. He groaned with hunger and the promise of satisfaction.

Moving his hips in a smooth, slow motion, he rested his forearms at her sides. He could see the barest outline of her form. She was breathtaking. Light, or dark, Cindy was beautiful.

And his because there was no way he'd ever let her walk away again. Not without fighting for her with everything he had. There was no other option because she owned his heart.

He wouldn't have it any other way.

As if reading his mind, she said, "I love you. Today, until my last day, and every single one in between." Kissing, she stopped before the heat engulfed them. "I never knew what I wanted out of life, hell, I still don't. However, one thing I am sure of is you. I want you."

He shifted, swallowing past the now pounding in his pulse, that was no longer only from the carnal heat. Brushing a stray lock of hair from her cheeks, he whispered, "Forever?"

She nodded, no longer rocking her hips.

He'd wanted to wait for the perfect moment, maybe more romance, less erotic. Yet, unconventional had always worked for them. "Marry me, Cindy."

"Yes," she whispered without hesitation.

She kissed him. It spoke of forevers before morphing into searing passion.

One simple word meant the world to him.

"Yes," he repeated, loving her with his body, his soul, his future.

Her breath caught as he began to move faster, taking them both to the edge of bliss, and falling together. As one. Forever.

# Bonus Story

Welcome to the end of Maggies and Tanner's journey—not really. Not only will they be in the other stories of the *Opposites Attract* series as secondary characters, but unable to let these two go, I've written a bonus short story.

You don't need to read this to enjoy the other books, and there aren't any big reveals in *Lust and Love*. This is just a little fun story that takes place in the future shortly after this book. It's a weekend getaway for Jacob (Tanner's good friend) and Greta—right before everyone arrives for their weekend bachelor/bachelorette party (as experienced in *Taste of Passion*).

Visit DKMARIE.COM and sign up for the newsletter, and the FREE short story below will be delivered to your inbox.

# Dear Reader,

Thank you so much for reading this book. This is my first book; however, even if it was my tenth or twentieth story, I will appreciate the time you give to my books. I sincerely hope you enjoy reading this as much as I enjoyed writing their story.

If you're not ready to let go of Cindy and Will, talk to others about them —by leaving a review on Goodreads or whatever site you love.

Even a simple sentence would mean the world to me (the author) and will keep their passion in others' minds and hearts.

Last, you can visit them as secondary characters in the other Opposites Attract books.

Keep reading for an excerpt of Fairy Tale Lies

Thank you!

DK Marie

Greta Meier dashed down the carpeted hallway of Swift Financial, ignoring the agony of power walking in three-inch heels. That pain was minuscule compared to the dread pooling in her stomach. She'd lost track of time. Again.

Sure, she'd managed to fix the in-house software issue but, meanwhile, had forgotten the new client meeting. Glancing at her tiny gold Rolex, she groaned. Less than five minutes to make it to the other end of the building.

She could picture her boss's disappointed face, made all the more stressful because it was her father. The image had Greta quickening her pace to a near sprint.

Rounding the final corner, she sighed. The large glass doors were propped open. Relief calmed some of her anxiety. She wasn't late.

Inside the conference room, her assistant Rae motioned to the empty seat next to her. Greta nodded and skated alongside the outermost edges of the table, wishing she were smaller, invisible. She hoped no one would notice her near tardy arrival. The last thing she wanted was to come across as the empty-headed daughter of the boss. Someone who'd gotten the internship through nepotism. Therefore, any misstep ate at her confidence like termites to wood.

She took her seat next to Rae and tried to squash her rampant doubts. Running a shaky hand over her chignon, she made sure every hair was in place.

"Where's Allen?" Greta glanced around the table while needlessly straightening the collar of her pale, pink blouse. Realizing she was fidgeting, putting her anxiety on full display, she stilled and met Rae's gaze.

She handed the client folder Greta hadn't had time to open and sighed. "Another virus was detected on Blake's computer. He demanded we fix it, like yesterday. Allen's working on it."

Greta accepted the portfolio, her worry shifting to annoyance. She didn't want to talk about her ex-fiancé, much less be reminded he was in-house counsel. Before their breakup, they hardly ran into each other at work. Now Blake kept inventing problems with his PC and contacting the IT department. Rae and Allen found it hilarious, but Greta despised the drama. It made her and Blake appear unprofessional.

Refusing to meet Rae's playful smile, Greta peered down the table at her father. His back was to a large window with its blinds pulled. The leaves from the giant elm and oak trees swayed in a lazy breeze, helping to block Michigan's hot summer sun from the room. She'd love to be out there, relaxing in the shade, enjoying her summer and free of stress.

Her gaze zeroed back in on her father, and the usual mixture of pride and discontent filled her. She understood he only wanted the best for her, but sometimes his rigidness was stifling. Carrying her father's expectations, and his disappointment of her, was a heavy burden to shoulder.

Thankfully, he hadn't noticed her near-late arrival time. There'd be no displeased glances, no lectures concerning punctuality. He appeared distracted, deep in conversation with a man she assumed was a new client.

She gave an inward sigh of relief, allowing some of her distress to dissolve. Father's career talks turned back the clock, and suddenly she was closer to seven than twenty-seven. Enjoying the reprieve, she relaxed into her seat and studied the client. He sat sideways, elbow propped on the table, large hand covering most of his face as he talked with her father. There was something familiar in the set of the client's broad shoulders and his inky black hair.

Inexplicably, her heart began to race. Watching him filled her with trepidation and an unexpected yearning.

Her father faced the room, pulling her gaze from the stranger to the wall clock. Yup, ten on the dot. A meeting never started late.

She glanced back at the client and choked on an exhale, her heart plummeting. He'd dropped his hand and was facing forward.

*It can't be him.*

Her heart skipped with joy. Then promptly flooded with dread.

"You okay?" Rae whispered. Her voice sounded far away, wrapped in fog.

Greta couldn't answer because the client's familiar icy-blue gaze had locked on hers. His eyes widened in recognition.

He was clean-shaven, and today his hair was neat and combed back, but there was no mistaking him. *Jacob*. He had one of those striking faces, impossible to forget. The memories of the way those bedroom eyes had heated as he'd taken in her naked body, or how those full lips had ravished her, made him unforgettable.

However, she wished he'd slip from her memory and the conference room. Whatever his reason for being here wouldn't be good for her.

"Good morning. Let me introduce Mr. Jacob Grimm."

Hearing his name, he turned toward her father, allowing her to breathe.

Rae nudged Greta, probably waiting for an answer. Too bad. She was admitting nothing.

"He runs Rework, a business repairing and refurbishing antiques. We're taking it to the next level," continued her father. "He plans on opening a brick-and-mortar shop in Detroit and developing a better online presence."

*Business owner? No, no, no.*

There had been some mistake. He wasn't supposed to be sitting at her father's conference table. Jacob was a deliveryman. He worked for his uncle. It's what he told her at her mother and stepfather's home. So, why wasn't he lifting heavy things and breaking promises?

Greta flipped through the file Rae had given her. Successful was an understatement. His client base was impressive, as were the big names in the dossier. Stapled to the back of the folder was a copy of Jacob's license.

Foolish woman. Hadn't her father always told her to come to a meeting prepared? Had she even glanced at the file, she'd have recognized Jacob in an instant. Weeks had passed, but that foolish, impulsive afternoon was far from forgotten.

As her father addressed the room, Greta focused on Jacob's picture. She found it safer than facing the actual man.

They'd only spent a couple of hours together, but his wicked full mouth and penetrating gaze had been impossible to forget. Along with his magical ability to destroy all her restraints. Greta still couldn't quite believe how easily her inhibitions had fled in the company of a perfect stranger.

She closed the folder and rubbed her sweaty palms on her pleated linen skirt. She stared at her father and tried to concentrate on his words, though he could've been speaking another language and she wouldn't have noticed.

There was no way she could swallow her embarrassment and work with Jacob. Not even for a day, let alone a week or more.

Her pulse thudded in her ears. What if he bragged about his one-night-stand with the boss's daughter? Father would kill her. Not literally, but professionally. He wouldn't want the family name smeared with tawdry office gossip.

He'd promised, after she graduated with her Master's in Web Development, she'd take over Swift's websites and handle the clients needing web development help. Would the offer still stand if he learned of her history with Jacob?

So much for proving herself with a summer internship. Greta wanted to weep at the disappearance of her imagined stellar portfolio. Swift Financial would have been wonderful on her resume.

*Focus. I need to focus and get control of the situation.*

Leaning in, she whispered to Rae, "I need to go. Would you and Allen mind handling this account? I'll owe you one."

"What's wrong?" Rae's forehead furrowed in concern.

That question was too big to answer now. Later. "Will you do this for me?"

Rae bit her lip. "I'll try, but you know your father wants you in charge of web designing."

*Yes, I know. Hopefully I'll come up with a stellar excuse to wiggle out of the Rework contract.*

She'd worry about it later and mouthed a thank you and gathered her papers. When there was a pause in the main conversation, she addressed the room. "I'm sorry. There's been a mistake. Allen Carnaby will handle this account with Mrs. Caitlin." She stood. "I'll find him."

Her father's stern voice stopped her. "No, Ms. Meier, the account is yours and Mrs. Caitlin's. I have another project in mind for Mr. Carnaby." His tone brooked no argument.

*Darn it.* There went her quick and painless getaway.

She nodded. To argue was pointless and would only anger her father. Returning to her seat, she glanced covertly at Jacob. He'd lost most of his color and looked like he'd been poked with a cattle prod.

Replaying the exchange, she realized she'd been addressed by her last name. Jacob must have caught it, grasped its significance. He appeared rattled.

*Good.*

Maybe he didn't want to share their secret any more than she did. Thank goodness. It would save her from her father's wrath.

Next challenge—squashing her lingering thrill at seeing Jacob again.

## Chapter Two

Her, of all people!

Jacob blinked. Nope, she hadn't disappeared back into his fantasies. Her!

He tried not to stare but found it difficult to accept the rapid-fire shocks. The most nerve-racking item of the day was supposed to be signing his financial dream on the dotted line. Instead, he sat face to face with the woman who haunted an entirely different set of dreams.

He'd strived to banish the memory of their spring afternoon together. He wanted to forget the way her laughter had made him lighter, more alive. He'd tried to forget those soulful hazel eyes and sexy, full lips. Lips made for kissing.

He sure as hell hadn't forgotten the way she'd barely given him time to dress before shoving him out the back door. Confused and insulted, he'd returned to the grand salon, or whatever rich people called those extra useless rooms, to help his uncle finish the job. She'd disappeared, obviously embarrassed by him and what they'd done.

Going by her current reaction, things hadn't changed. She still saw him as a weed in her impeccably manicured life.

Not that he wanted to make their past known. A Meier, not a Silverstone!

The delivery order had clearly stated the items were for a Silverstone residence. Hadn't she made the comment the home was her parents'?

*Shit.* Was she Charles Meier's niece, daughter, or young wife? Each one of those options landed like a brick in his gut.

Seriously, of all the women in the world, why did it have to be her? Here? Now?

His life revolved around building Rework. His focus so complete, he couldn't remember the last time he'd been on a date or even noticed a pretty woman.

Then two months ago, his uncle Marty called, asking if he'd help deliver and install an antique chandelier. Jacob agreed, expecting nothing more than a little extra cash.

Instead, he'd been knocked on his ass at the mere sight of the woman who answered the door. Her jewel-like amber eyes, accented with those full lips, was captivating. What's more, after they'd left for lunch and talked, her confident reserve and quiet ferocity seduced him. To his surprise, she was as drawn to him as he to her. Watching her struggle between virtue and wickedness, and letting her wild side win, had been the hottest thing he'd ever experienced.

"Mr. Grimm?"

He gave a mental shake and focused on Charles. Freaking Charles *Meier*. "Sorry, what did you say?" Jacob was proud at how calm he sounded.

*A Meier, not a Silverstone...*

"Would you please accompany Mrs. Caitlin and Ms. Meier to their office," her father or uncle or husband repeated.

Jacob suspected Charles made this request a few times.

"They'll need your insight for the new webpage and additional information to upgrade your accounts."

"Okay. No problem," Jacob replied.

The two men stood and shook hands. Jacob's was trembling, but at least he'd been able to talk past the anxiety trying to claw its way out of his throat.

He followed the two women from the conference room, wondering if he'd jeopardized years of hard work with one impulsive and incredibly hot afternoon. He couldn't lose his contract with Swift Financial. Every bank had turned him down, said his company was 'too niche', this was his last chance.

What was she to Charles Meier? Would she tell him how'd they met and what they'd done?

Sleeping with his wife or daughter might be enough to have the man searching for loopholes in the contract and dumping Rework.

Once in the corridor, Jacob moved next to the women. His focus shifted from the woman who used and dumped him, to the pretty African-American. She was watching him with open curiosity.

He didn't want to have this conversation with an audience. "Greta, can we talk... alone?"

She didn't even bother looking in his direction, answering in an imperious tone and sounding like the princess she thought she was. "No. There's no need, and please address me as Ms. Meier."

The other woman gasped, her gaze jumping between him and Greta. "You two know each other?"

"Yes," Jacob replied.

Greta spoke over him. "Not really."

The hell she didn't. Was she going to pretend they were complete strangers?

"Mr. Grimm," came a man's voice from the conference room.

All three swung around at the unexpected interruption.

The guy stumbled back. Jacob could only imagine the expressions on their faces.

"We forgot to have you sign a couple of things. Will you please come back? I'll show you to the IT office after."

Jacob ran a hand down his face, peering at Greta. From the hard set of her jaw and defensive posture, her talking probably wasn't going to happen. He nodded to the man, moving away from the two women.

Before returning to the conference room, he stopped and faced Greta. "We aren't finished. We have to talk."

The prospect didn't seem to please her but screw it, he needed answers. And to set things straight. There was no way she was going to ruin this for him. After years at a standstill, his business was moving forward.

Want to keep reading? Get more information at DKMARIE.COM

AN OPPOSITES ATTRACT NOVEL
Fairy Tale Lies
She's sweet. He's sexy. Together they
might be a new kind of fairy tale love...
DK MARIE

# Also By DK Marie

**Love Songs**

*She sings to the wild side of his heart, strumming his needs against his desires, disrupting his harmony.*

## Colors of the Heart

*His life has become gray and drab. Her vibrancy paints the dark shadows of his heart, turning them into shades of love.*

*New series-* Lake House Love

Romances with Heart, Heat, and a Splash of Humor.

DKMARIE.COM

# About Author

DK Marie loves to indulge in all things hot. Men, writing, reading, and coffee. The order of importance depends on the day.

Like characters in her books, she lives in Michigan, enjoying her happily-ever-after with her husband and kids. When not writing, she loves the heater, concerts, and to travel.

DK loves to hear from readers. You can find and connect with her at the links below.

Website: https://dkmarie.com

# Acknowledgments

First, my family, who've supported and understood my need to disappear into my stories for weeks on end.

Also Shanna, for always supporting me during this journey. My wonderful writer friends on social media.

I have to give a shout-out to Rowena and Inappropriate Acres—you ladies keep me going on those hard days, and make me laugh every day. You all are the best!

Avery Kingston, for these awesome new covers—you're an awesome designer, writer, and friend!